CW00520400

MUAY THAI, LOVE
AFFAIR

Copyright © 2023 Elsa Sparks
All Rights Reserved.

No parts of this book may be reproduced without the written permission of the publisher. For more information, contact the publisher at elsasparkspublishing@gmail.com.

Cover illustration by enortondesign.

With never ending thanks to Helena, Charlotte, Vicky, Liz, Loula, Kev, Blu, Ju, John, Anthony, Henderson, Gavola, Beow, Uncle Lung-Lung, and a myriad of others on journeys short and long.

"I sleep in the road," he said,
"You sleep in the sea."

1. The End

All year Hannah had felt a feeling of foreboding, as if everything had…*stopped*. Glasses broke in her hands; lights went off when she walked into rooms and her passion for kickboxing had transgressed into a feeling of inevitable surrender. It was partly her job; the daily grind, the axe that yields - answering to 600 people daily with a forced grin, whilst suffering at the hands of a cut-throat management takeover was taking its toll.

Not only was she a slave to the desk, but a slave to the word. As a six-year-old child, her teacher (Miss Williams from Wales) had let her write stories in class time and nothing else. Her masterpieces were stuck all over the classroom walls, complete with pictures of crocodiles. At spelling-time there would be two queues – one for her and one for the teacher.

"You're like a breath of fresh air," the set-permed teacher would say, before teaching them a Beatles song on the piano. Alas, those days didn't last – she got pulled up a year because she was bright, and then all she found were numbers that she didn't understand.

She made it through her shortened school years, deciding against dance school and its grim prospects, and instead completing her arty A-levels and Film degree with glowing colours and relative lack of effort, but then – inevitability - to the slurry heap with everyone else, stopping off for an incidental career between travelling spouts which had led her to this current role – PA to the MD of a Housing Charity.

Mostly her writing had fallen by the wayside, but when she was drunk or high she'd sit in corners at parties scribbling on cigarette papers and she kept them all - poems of love and pain, the beginnings of songs - most of them staying on scraps of paper in the bottom of her bedraggled party handbag.

That was at least until a couple of years ago, when a fresh stint in London had succeeded in reigniting some forgotten flame, keeping it alight long enough to pour out her secrets in coffee shops onto an oversized, whirring laptop. She posted her musings onto a blog, published weekly on a Friday: *Godiva's Escapades*. It was a real hit: '*Sex & the City meets The League of Gentleman*', wrote one reviewer (with whom she subsequently had an affair).

In recent months the blog had dried up, and her day job was draining the life out of her. Without words life was reduced to a dull ache, and without passion her soul was dripping away. How she wished she'd chance upon change or that it would just turn up to sweep her off her feet.

She looked around her lifeless flat. wondering what she was supposed to be doing there. She was stuck; the mortgage, bills, dodgy pipework and the squirrel invasion. The furry vermin awoke her every sunrise – scuttling into her eaves, scratching and thudding around to their little hearts' content. A repulsive man named John came to set traps in the hide-out cupboard. On his last visit she sent him into the cupboard, and after a two-minute silence she finally heard something - a physical retching.

"WHAT HAVE YOU DONE TO ME??!...HANNAH! WHAT HAVE YOU DONE?

ERR….ERR!! THIS ONE'S PREGNANT! EURGH, IT'S DISGUSTING! WHAT HAVE YOU DONE?!!"

It wasn't *her*, it was the squirrels, and she didn't care much for John after the time he asked if the guitars belonged to 'her boyfriend'. Hannah was blessed with natural good-looks, and passed for quite a well-to-do, almost glamorous blonde at times, earning her favoured attention on a weekend, but unwanted leering most everywhere else. She kept her cool with John the Squirrelman, giving him his fee and sending him on his way for the very last time. Now the squirrels had gone she was alone, and somehow amongst her endless procrastinating she allowed herself to dream - and finally, as she reached breaking point in the half-light of her lonely room, it came to her: Thailand.

Escape from the humdrum, the uncouthly lit office, the empty love affairs and daily inevitabilities and the deep sense of loneliness that swaddled her, shivering, when winter crept rudely in.

2. Moving on Up

Three statuesque men entered Hannah's petite lounge, ready to stash her belongings in a loft somewhere. With the few things remaining, she jumped into the van with them and they drove to her new lodgings - she still had three months until she flew away and needed somewhere to crash.

Her parents' place wasn't an option – lovely people, but she'd never last that long in the countryside with those incongruent to her state of transition: within hours she'd be scowling at the poor people who brought her into this world.

She'd made a desperate plea on Facebook for somewhere to stay, with no success, until one day she received a phone call on her landline from an obscure friend of days gone by to whom she affectionately referred as Nostrovsky. It felt strange turning up at Number 14 with the blue door after months of little contact, its peculiar dolls and bric-a-brac wedged in the bushes out front. Yet, gushing and smiling, Nostrovsky opened wide her door and deftly scooped up several boxes, whisking them inside and up the stairs into the single room which Hannah should call her own.

The meagre duo saved up for the electric, popping pound coins in an old coffee jar when they could, and did not *dare* put the heating on for the fear of gas prices in November. So, Hannah froze day and night, her S.A.D. kicking in big-time, and further she withdrew from the world. Yet somehow – *somehow* – the day of departure arrived.

* * *

At 4.30am her father came to take her to the airport. The roads were dark and frosty and cloaked in early-morning fog, emanating a timeless atmosphere for their journey - all washed down with hot coffee from a thermos. They listened to rousing classical music, not feeling the need to speak as the landscape filled time and space - an understated yet dramatic backdrop for her leaving.

At the airport they said a tearless goodbye for the sake of appearance and Hannah strode into Departures with a sudden pang of nerves and uncertainty: *What was in store for her?* She had been to Thailand before - instantly falling in love the moment her feet touched the ground from the heaving coach at the service station. Back then she had been unprepared for such a revelation and had ever since felt an incessant need to return; in fact, she *had* already gone back – in 2004, when the devastating Tsunami hit. Though safe on the other side of the peninsula, her family couldn't be so sure as they sat anxiously around the Boxing Day breakfast table waiting for her call. *She* was sitting obliviously sipping cocktails, completely unaware of the tragedy, until casualties started to wash up on the beach. This

---

[1] S.A.D.: Seasonal affective disorder, a type of depression that has a seasonal pattern, usually occurring during winter.

time she would be away from family and friends at Christmas again, but fear of catastrophic disasters aside, she set her eyes forward to an unknown future.

    * * *

Aboard the low-cost, rammed flight, she forced her thoughts to gather. She'd only gone and done it: waved goodbye to her job, flat and financial ties in Blighty with nothing but an empty page ahead of her - an empty book, in fact. She couldn't wait to shake off her winter shivers and unleash a creative stream which would *of course* lead to an ocean of words.

At Abu-Dhabi she changed planes and her body clock shut itself down as she shuffled through to the next gate where more Thai passengers were gathering, getting her excited.

Aboard the aircraft, she was sandwiched between two ageing sex-tourists: neither of them could figure out the in-flight entertainment and one frantically popped pills while the other looked dead already.

In the final thirty minutes of the flight the inevitable happened: the one from Iran started talking to her - and wouldn't stop. As he offered delightful ruminations on congestion zones in Iran, expressing intrigue with London having 'four rings around it' she winced, trying to avert her eyes from the black-and-white hairs sprouting from his nose. She agreed to help him fill out his landing card: his name was Mohammed Ali and he was going to Pattaya. The shameless influx of toupee-clad Germans, and a man in a wheelchair covered in boils, disembarked.

At Bangkok, tired but 'nearly there', she got to her gate for the final flight to Krabi in the South. A Buddhist monk sat opposite her on the transit bus, chubby with nipples like Oreos, making a video on his mobile phone.

* * *

Hannah anxiously rushed between the exits of Krabi airport until finally she spotted a man walking quickly in the heat towards her. Efficiently he ushered her into a clapped-out minivan and tossed her and her bags into the sweaty backseat as she tumbled in beside them. Suddenly the long journey, her out-of-kilter body clock and the terrible heat combined, yielding a sickening inertia. As it became clear that the driver didn't understand English or have a clue where any of them were going, she became incensed and, like a panicking matron, grabbed a *Lonely Planet* from an unsuspecting Italian and deliriously started trying to direct the driver. The driver - largely numb to this highly-strung Westernism - nodded at Hannah before continuing on his mission to deliver mysterious piles of paper to 7-11. After two baking hours and a car ferry across the small inlet that divided Koh Talay from the mainland, they finally reached the port and the driver magically found his way down to the dirt track that led to her lodgings, imaginatively named 'Relax Don't Do It!'

She had arranged her accommodation through Noi - a Thai guy she had met at a rainy rock concert in Hyde Park - who now happened to own a backpacker's paradise here on Koh Talay. It was Noi who had arranged the sketchy minivan and would be there to help her settle in. She looked around somehow expecting him to bound up to her, but he was nowhere to be seen - in fact there was no-one in sight - so with difficulty she picked her way through the overgrown path that led to Relax Don't Do It!

A makeshift wooden sign pointed to reception, so she turned the corner with expectation but still found no sign of life. She peered about the backpacker's 'paradise' – her hell –which was filled with dusty tree limbs and mosquitoes. In the corner she could make out two lanky figures through a smoky haze, lounging on cushions. She picked her way through to them, the smoke obscuring their faces, and as she stepped ever closer towards them - finally stopping right in front of them - still they made no sound.

Finally, the stringier of the two spoke, "Hallo," he said, quietly.

"YES! I'm looking for Noi!" she barked briskly.

"Oh, he's not here," came the dopey reply.

"Well, when will he be back?" she gasped, exasperated, "He's reserved me a room!"

The two lanky Finns continued to lounge, unmoved by her alarm, "Uuuum, I saw him vis morning, 'e was drunk. Er, I fink he's gone to Bangkok."

"WHEN WILL HE BE BACK?" she demanded, at odds with the purple haze of the dusty tree house.

"Don't know…erm, maybe Monday, yeah, Monday I fink."

Unsure of how to help this agitated sweaty apparition, the meek-mannered Yerry got up sleepily and trotted up a wonky wooden staircase, limply ushering for her to follow. She opened the door of the 'room' she was being semi-shown. The walls didn't meet, and the limp partition curtain revealed a questionable mattress tentatively lying on slats on the floor. She hadn't travelled 10,000 kilometres to stay in a feral pit! Her face gave her away and Yerry and Yonny suggested enquiring next door with Noi's brother – Nok.

Feeling the pangs of panic, she reassured herself that she would find a room – there *must* be a plethora of options - but this was taking too long and beginning to feel like a warped nativity. As she turned to continue her hunt a small Thai man shuffled in, bare-chested and naked save for what looked like a swaddling cloth covering his modesty, "Helloooooooooooo...*Helloooooooooo*!" he whined oddly at her, "That you, Hannah?"

"Yes, yes!!" she hurriedly responded in relief.

The small man showed no sign of emotion, "I have room for you. Come!"

The petite, muttering Thai man shunted her along to a little bungalow built from the fruits of the jungle: here was to be her home.

3. Here Comes the Bride

With relief, she set down her luggage as Nok trotted up to the other end of the path to mend his remote-control car. Her dainty bungalow was made of stone with shell wind-chimes hanging from the porch and an over-sized Manchester United cushion propped up on the chair outside. There were hooks for her to hang up her things and a decent mosquito net covering the generously sized bed. The bathroom came complete with a bucket shower, frogs, lizards and a spider as big as her hand. She had an electric fan and - most importantly - miraculous, miraculous broadband; for what jungle is complete without it?

She resisted collapsing in a fit of exhaustion on the bed and instead ventured outside to explore the little village. As she passed Nok he gesticulated urgently at her, thrusting a decrepit mobile phone into her hand. It was Noi, drunk in Bangkok.

"Hannah! You OK? I in Bangkok! I know you not like Relax so you find bungalow yeah?"

"Yes, yes!" concurred Hannah. Noi was horribly drunk and after some muffled sounds and squawking he rang off. She handed Nok the phone and continued on her jaunt. She turned the corner and Salee Mart presented itself appealingly to her and opposite a small bar where she could get some food. Inside a larger-than-life character in sarong and bandana chirpily minced about. He was more than hospitable and grinned goofily at Hannah with a pot belly looming over the top of his eccentric attire.

She ordered a pancake and a coffee and as she expected the coffee resembled gravy, the pancake not the beautifully hand-whisked delight of days gone by; instead, a spongy, gooey mixture - raw in the middle, yellow egg seeping onto the plate. With a sigh, she realised that Thailand must have discovered packet cake mix and abandoned fresh eggs - oh the sorry progress of tourism!

"Arooooooooooooi?!" the plump man asked: *Delicious?*

She feigned her best grimace and wondered how long it would take for salmonella to kick in.

"Aroi!" she confirmed politely. He invited himself to sit with her and so she put on a smile and answered questions about where she was from and what she was doing before excusing herself – she was tired from the road. He looked harmless, but the more he talked the more leery he became - perhaps he hadn't seen a tourist for a while?

"My sister," he grinned lustfully, "She get married next month – you come!"

"No thanks," she rebuked brightly.

"Yes, yes, Thai wedding, very nice! Many people!"

Yes mate, very nice trapped with you trying to touch me up every five seconds, she thought.

"You marry me maybe?" he chuckled creepily.

"No!" Hannah scowled.

"Maybe in a year?"

To try and appease him she said that when she was sixty, and if her eyesight had failed, she *might* consider marrying him. She'd only just arrived, and a good reputation was paramount - she didn't want this freakshow on her case every time she popped into the minimart for rehydration salts. In her head she nicknamed him 'Pom-pooey' – an endearing Thai jibe meaning 'chubby'. He lamented that he liked Thailand but not Thai people – they were always drunk - and she recalled that rumour had it you could buy amphetamine whisky. At her request he turned off the tinny pop and put on Pink Floyd, then flounced back into the kitchen. Hannah started to relax - but he returned all too soon.

"Where you stay?" She gestured around the corner with her hands. "You stay with me! Have room!"

"No!"

"Why?"

"I don't want to!! Sorry!"

Pom-pooey started to hum '*Here Comes the Bride*' whilst playing with the towel around his groin.

"NOOOOO!" she shouted finally and made a quick exit - where to next?

She'd seen that there was a boxing stadium at the end of the road. She was a keen kickboxer back in the UK but wasn't sure if she was prepared to delve into a new world of bruised shins and cut eyebrows – after all she was here to write a book – but there was no harm in looking, so she picked her way carefully to the top of the long track where the Muay Thai stadium loomed conspicuously. There was no-one to ask about classes, but next door she found an ugly concrete building - The Fitness Centre – that seemed to be less abandoned. She peered through the window into the office and eventually a small, smiling Thai man appeared.

"Yes? Can I help?"

"Er… I was just wondering about Muay Thai training…"

He led her into the gym where two cheeky girls stood gossiping and powdering their faces behind the counter. He gave Hannah a timetable and explained that the training gym was two kilometres away up in the hills, but that he could arrange a lift for her if she told him when she wanted to train. She wasn't sure when - and certainly didn't want to start making arrangements in her delirious, overtired state - so she took the info, thanked the man, and trotted back to her hut.

4. Where Have all the Good Times Gone?

Acclimatisation, it would seem, was nothing short of boring. It still wasn't busy in the backpacker's village - just the two stringy Finns, Nok, his wife and his remote-control cars, and a young American who relentlessly banged a young girl from Laos as if she was the bedpost herself. Hannah asked the locals and the kind lady in the shop why it wasn't busy despite being 'high season', and they all reassured her that it was coming – just wait until the week before Christmas. Christmas – she was dreading that.

Swimming in the sea was satisfying enough, but if she got caught in the wrong current, swarms of sea-lice would get caught in her bathing suit, nipping her agonisingly and scarring red her breasts and hips with their painful bites.

One afternoon there was a knock at her hut door: it was Noi returned from Bangkok, minus his Western girlfriend and baby, and he wasn't sure if they were ever coming back. Together, they went to an organic farm hideout that he'd built, and for the best part of an afternoon they lay about in hammocks drinking tea and smoking. It transpired that Noi had recently sold Relax Don't Do It! to the mild and vacant Yerry - who was only 21 - for an extortionate fee. After the long, pleasant afternoon swinging and talking, Hannah was walking back through Relax to her bungalow when Yerry stopped her on her way.

"Noi says you do tarot, right?"

"Erm...yes, why?"

Yerry was looking pale-faced indeed, "I would like to have it." And so it was that she collected her cards and, in exchange for shots of whisky, laid out a spread.

"Now," she pre-warned him, "This won't be all love, light and laughter. I only do hardcore tarot - it will only tell you what you already know yourself – and probably what you don't want to face, so brace yourself!"

The tarot told of difficulties in partnerships and agony in making hard decisions. Things, it would seem, were not looking up for poor Yerry. With Noi still obliviously tucked away at the farm Yerry unfurled his situation. As Noi wanted to focus on the organic farm and Yerry had loved staying at Relax, he had agreed to take over the place in the hope of making some money. Yet a few months in, there had been a few too many teenage kicks in the early hours and, one particularly raucous Scandinavian night, some locals had got annoyed with the noise and set the place on fire – this a place made entirely from combustible wood.

Not too much damage had been done to the structure itself, but now poor Yerry was on constant high alert should something else happen – just last night somebody had run their dog over on a motorbike, right outside the front entrance. An accident, a co-incidence, or a dark, Thai foreboding? Though Yerry wanted out, Noi had sucked all the cash out of him, leaving him with a miserable *nothing* were he to walk away - but at least he'd be able to sleep at night.

In Thailand reputation was everything – as a foreigner yearning for approval from the locals you should lay low, not cause havoc at night and demonstrate respect. Therefore, Hannah wanted no affiliation with a shady underworld, where dogs got run over and things were set on fire.

On the way back to her hut, she spotted a guitar propped up against a wall. Yerry said that it was Noi's but that she could probably borrow it. She took it with her to her hut. Across the way, the American was banging the Laos girl noisily again. He finished and angrily stomped outside.

"Hi neighbour!" Hannah hollered.

"Hiya!" he responded, red-faced from the fornicating.

"I never had neighbours before!"

This beginner's gang would have to do: a sex tourist, a drunken Thai guy, two Finns and a guitar.

How she enjoyed the first evening with her new-found musical friend. She tried out a few Christmas songs – perhaps there would be more people to play for soon. And then another sleepy night crept in with the fan on full blast, the mozzies kept out but buzzing around the net and the froggies croaking in the bathroom.

* * *

The next morning it took her a while to come to in the heat, and then followed a slow realisation that she was in a happy place. The morning chorus resounded through the thin wooden walls, and bathing in it she lay there for some moments, squinting about her.

She had tied up yesterday's soy milk in a carrier bag next to the door – the place she figured it would keep the coolest - only now the bag didn't seem to be there! She sat bolt-upright – had a sneaky gangster been in the night to steal her things? Where were her traveller's cheques, the guitar, her passport – her laptop?! *Noooooooooooo*!!

In fact, the answer *was* no - everything of value was still in its rightful place: there was just the mystery of the missing milk to unravel…

Lazily she flung off the mosquito net, swung her legs off the bed and visited the bathroom for her morning release. Sitting on the khazi she noticed a curious scene: to her left, the carrier bag containing the soy milk now lay ripped open on the floor. Soy milk curdled in a pool around it – and in the centre one single pellet of poo. Something had been in the night - and whatever it was didn't like soy milk enough to finish it.

The morning, as usual, passed without dramatic incident. At lunchtime the American sex tourist took Hannah to eat up on the road at a bamboo chicken shack, where they feasted on barbecued chicken and *som tam* – a sour, spicy and sweet green papaya salad, and she left contented.

In the afternoon she wandered through to Relax, where the lanky Finns sat smoking, and Noi sat holding court at a high table drinking whisky. Without much thought she accepted a glass from him, and not too much later the talk had become loose. Even though Noi was a useful person to know, Hannah hadn't grown too close to him – it was hard to with his drunken, manic behaviour. But he did make her laugh, and so today when night fell - just after 6pm - she found herself still there. Suddenly Noi stood up, swaying with drunkenness and grabbed Hannah in a sloppy embrace - his arms wide and open like a chimpanzee - and announced, "Guitar! NOT YOURS!! You borrow, but not keep. Understand?! Mine! Mine! This is *my* place, not yours!...I give you coffee yes! Cheap price! I buy you soup! But guitar is MINE, cannot take to your bungalow!!"

She gulped back her surprise, as he added insult to injury, "One day we have sex, yes?"

"Erm, no," she said, quietly.

"Why not? *IIIIIIII* would like to!" he said, swaying with drunkenness before her.

She returned to her hut to iron out the slight pain she felt from the confrontation, then dashed back briefly to return Noi his instrument. She knew it was fair enough, but she had just wanted some time alone with a guitar.

And just when it seemed as her already-limited friends were decreasing in number, a truckload of new arrivals parked up outside Salee Mart. They tumbled off in various directions – *some* in the direction of her bungalow. It was the week before Christmas and arrivals were becoming more frequent.

She settled down outside her hut with her laptop - still ideologically constipated - as a few backpackers arranged keys and moved in around her: to the left, a sweating, crazy-eyed South African, to the right two Canadian lesbians and up the way a pair of cheeky young German boys. Tourist season had begun - at last, she was not alone!

Now sober after the brief whisky incident, she decided to take action: in the morning she would start Muay Thai training.

19

5. To Boxing She Shall Go

She awoke, groggy, at 8am and wandered into Relax in search of sustenance. A bright-faced Slovenian sent her back to her bungalow – it was all taken care of - and briskly whisked together a mound of muesli, fruit and yoghurt together with filter coffee and delivered it to her very door! *This is the life*, she thought.

She rummaged through a pile of clothes for something suitable to wear to training, and unconvincingly cobbled together a costume: black jersey shorts, a sports bra with its wires poking out and a gnarly but tight old vest - it would have to do. In the already scorching heat she trotted up the uneven dirt-track to the road, past Salee Mart and the pervert's reggae shack, and tentatively approached the fitness centre.

She always felt anxious entering gyms – there was something unnerving about aloof receptionists staring at the clientele from behind their counters – and she smiled semi-confidently then asked the two girls behind the desk about getting a ride to the Muay Thai gym. They looked at each other in confusion but with indifference - they hadn't a clue what she was on about. As one hurried off to fetch the smiley man that could speak English, the other stood awkwardly grinning. When the former returned it became clear that no lift had been officially arranged, and all was uncomfortable indeed, until eventually (and reluctantly) one of the girls grabbed her handbag and keys, smiled for formality's sake, and took Hannah out of the full-blown aircon back into the burning sun.

They hopped on her scooter and were gone with the wind - throwing caution to it without helmets - Hannah unaccustomed to the speed at which they rode with her feet skimming the ground before she quickly picked them up to wedge them back onto the footrests.

It was exhilarating – she'd only ridden up back a few times in her life - and this journey was long and scenic. Food stalls and the occasional 7-11 marked the way with the national forest that ran through the middle of Koh Talay running alongside them - thick, lush and green - omitting sumptuous wafts of eucalyptus. After three kilometres or so the small girl that drove so masterfully turned a corner up a sandy track, then continued along into the hills before a curving steeply downwards as the sounds of bags being kicked and Thai boxers grunting loudly filled the immediate air. Here she was – Talay Boxing Gym.

She'd seen pictures of the owner on the website, but they were clearly dated - as the old man who approached her was now far from photogenic. In baggy shorts, with a nose so punched-up it seemed to have grown back into his face, he welcomed her with a leery smile - the faint whiff of cheap whisky and cigarettes lingering in the air around him.

Hannah thanked the small girl – Faa – for the ride, took off her battered trainers and walked quickly into the gym. It wasn't busy. She looked at the people about her: the old man, a young string-bean of a trainer and a short instructor called Man who was holding pads for a Westerner in the ring. Excitement started to build inside of her – kick-boxing training back home was relentless and productive - but nothing could compare to a one-on-one with a Thai boy from the jungle.

A trainer showed her to a row of rubber tyres and told her to bounce on them to warm up her legs. She climbed aboard – praying all the while not to lose her balance or grip or twist her ankles, and after ten minutes of vigorous bouncing and switching it was time to start training for real. A young, thin, limby guy approached her and they began padwork on the floor-mats. Though physically fit and able to keep up, her low-weighted kickboxing stance had to be constantly corrected, and her trainer reassured her that standing up straight with her arms relaxed but still guarding her body and head was now the right way to fight.

She loved it – kicks came easy, knees and elbows were harder to grasp, but her punches were strong and flying. After some basic technique on the mats, it was time to put on a pair of 10oz gloves and climb into the ring. The padwork started: off they went, no holds barred, the trainer shouting, "Knee! Knee! Ewaboooooow!" at regular intervals. Though his English was basic it didn't matter; Muay Thai was the language of a sharp mind and agile body. Between rounds she gulped water from a cooler and walked outside into the aggressive heat to slosh some over her head and chest which were already swamped in sweat.

He worked her hard and at the end of her session the older trainer came over to her and pointed in her face, "You fight? You fight Sunday?"

What? A few punches and kicks and it was time for the ring already? She laughed it off, saying she wasn't ready, and packed up her things to go. The gym was quiet, and still she had no way of getting home.

"Mai mee motorsai," she told them: *I don't have a motorbike*. The Thai trainers nodded around at each other and the guy who'd been training her sprinted off to fetch some keys. Through the sweltering heat of the day, they rode back to the fitness centre and, slightly broken, she dismounted.

He turned and smiled at her, "You come see me fight on Sunday? I fighting!"

"Maybe," she smiled, and hobbled off back down the track to her little village home - the bungalow with the fussy rats and the frogs in the bathroom - feeling good.

6. Uncle Lung-Lung's Chicken Shack

Life started to flow quite beautifully without effort nor mishap. Every morning the sweet Slovenian girl would bring her a wholesome breakfast to the table on her porch and, if diarrhoea and hangovers were at bay, she would wander up the dusty track to hitch a ride to the gym in the jungle where she'd get her fight on.

Her legs were permanently covered in a thick dusting of purple bruises from kicking the mashed-up pads – sometimes with Old Squishy-Nose and sometimes with the lithe and nimble Kam - who would proudly ride her home when he could, mildly perving at her all the way. Though she had found him attractive at first his face now warped into a mutated 1980s Michael Jackson - not a look she went for these days.

The American Sex Tourist had introduced her to Uncle Lung-Lung – a smiling, whistling old man from the Esarn region in the far stretches of the North-East - who had helped out his girlfriend in times of trouble. He owned a small grilled chicken and som tam shack on the roadside – popular with locals and tourists alike. Whenever she approached, he would punch the air, exalting *Muay Thai! Muay Thai!* with delight, and though he couldn't speak English he was fast becoming her favourite character: always fun, always singing or whistling a melodic Thai tune as he set her down a glass of water with ice and took care of her by way of chicken.

She felt loved, and she now had foreign friends too – Bobbo the manic South African, the Baby Germans and the Canadian Lesbians - who took her on jaunts in a beaten-up tuk-tuk to the Old Town where decrepit, ancient women bathed in sarongs whilst chewing their gums in betel-nut highs. Wooden shacks advertised their Facebook sites in paint, '*Hammocks for Sale*'.

Happy was Hannah, but somewhere in the neglected recesses of her brain the true aim of her stay loitered with intent: the book, the book - when would she start writing? She hadn't given up her entire life in England *just* to eat chicken and ride in tuk-tuks - no matter how fine - nor had she come here just to batter her shins on broken boxing shields.

The girls next door in her small, imperfect neighbourhood would ask her what the story was about, and '*Dunno,*' would come her reply, '*I just want it to be deep, prolific, mysterious, inspiring and magical!*' They would nod and get back to sewing up bags that the rats had chewed through.

One afternoon at the boxing gym, she went into the office to pay for her sessions, and next to the woman who was always there – an obese Thai with a haughty manner - was a girl Hannah hadn't seen before: a Westerner with beady-eyes and mumsy, curly hair who sat glaring at Hannah, her face cast in steel, not saying a word.

Hannah escaped back into the gym and bounced on a tyre until sweat flowed off her.

Kam, the Michael Jackson lookalike, was off training someone else and Old Squishy-Nose sat uselessly by a rowing machine with an injured leg.

So it was that a new face approached to train her, and a different kind of face to that which she had become accustomed. Spiky, thick black hair jutted unattractively out of his head, but *my*, the muscles on him: a semi-naked fallen Adonis before her, complete with carved-out chest and stomach, with elegant yet masculine tattoos on one side of his chest, strong legs and a cocky attitude to boot.

"My name Tee!"

"I'm Hannah."

It was he who was to train her - and train they did, good and hard, with nothing of the lame smiles and fake praise of Kam nor the jibing sneers and broken pads of Squishy-Nose. With quick, deft and exacting technique he instructed her with intensity.

When they had finished, no-one materialised to take her home: Kam was skulking about moodily, Squishy-Nose sat fundamentally defeated and the amazing guy she'd just been training with shrugged his shoulders with a '*mai mee motorsai*'.

She loitered outside awkwardly, looking for signs of a Westerner who might offer her a lift, but all she saw was a cloudy sky threatening rain. Gingerly she trotted back through the gym and knocked on the office door. Through the glass both women – the large, scary Thai woman and sour-faced Brit - stared back at her icily.

"Excuse me," she began, "Normally someone gives me a lift home but there's no-one around today - I live at the other end of Yao Beach and I don't drive."

The colossal Thai woman, 'Lek', disappeared out the back whilst the mumsy white girl stared at her unflinchingly.

After a long and ungratifying pause Lek re-emerged, "No, sorry."

"Sorry!" parroted the white girl.

The sky had now broken, and heavy rain poured onto the dust track in front of her, turning into slippery clay. With no other choice, she started the three kilometres home on foot. The road was long and wet and she clumsily staggered, her flip-flops sliding in the red mud, Thai people gawping in wonder at this creature covered in sweat, dirt and bruises, meandering unconvincingly up the road. With her blood sugar plummeting and eyes wide with adrenalin, she picked her way up the path.

She was strangely enjoying this mini-adventure - even the curious attention it commanded – and no sooner than forty-five minutes later she was nearing her little village. She noticed things along the way that she had never seen while flying along on a bike: closed-down bars - previous owner unknown, food stalls, jungle clearings, small family-owned shops and old men selling bootleg petrol in bottles by the side of the road.

And up ahead now, just before the corner onto the home straight, was a rather cosy-looking coffee shop. How she loved fresh coffee - a taste hard to satiate on this little island - Salee Mart only offered a 'pour it yourself' nescafé at the break of day.

Yet here was *good*, real coffee - and here was Hannah in a vest and shorts drenched in sweat and rain and muck, with the compulsion to explore. As she slid up to the wooden counter another glory presented itself: a cake counter, complete with cinnamon rolls, banana cake and chocolate croissants! She gasped loudly towards the owner - a tomboy Thai, who sat languid and skinny in an oversized tee-shirt and combat shorts.

"Wow! Cake!"

The owner laughed and Hannah ordered a chocolate croissant and coffee to take away, which came in a flimsy paper cup with soggy handles. The woman behind the counter smiled lazily then rested her head back down onto her folded arms.

"Rain makes me sleepy!" she explained, her laptop blinking away at an unfinished game of *Diamond Dash*.

The rain drizzled on into the afternoon. She had lunch at Uncle Lung-Lung's Chicken Shack with the American, who turned out to be a decent, entrepreneurial kind of guy. Hannah had the opportunity to write a travel article for a contact in Bali and wanted to run some ideas past his shrewd and calculating mind. The brief was '*anything interesting and local – you'd be surprised how hard that is.*'

They considered an interview with the Sea Gypsies of the Old Town, whose land was slowly being taken from them, forcing them to discard their traditional way of living and instead adopt more contemporary lifestyles - but they were hard-to-reach and couldn't speak a word of English.

Hannah's only other idea was to cover an event but not much went on in Koh Talay. A few days ago however, she had spotted a poster advertising '*The Miss Talay Ladyboy Pageant'*.

She ran it past the American.

"Hmmmmm," he nodded in contemplation, "Could be interesting."

There was a large 'ladyboy' community on Koh Talay and Hannah was already friendly with a few of them so maybe she could get an 'inside angle', as it were: the real cultural story - why most homosexuals here were labelled '*katoey*' - ladyboy - despite their gender preference. Why were there hundreds of thousands of transgender people in Thailand? Did they *truly* feel like women, or had society dictated that it was the only acceptable way for them to live? Was there anything in the rumour that families sometimes sent *katoey* teenagers to the big cities or tourist hotspots to make money?

"Yes," Captain America agreed, "I think you should definitely do it."

He was smart.

"You should see if Faa, the ladyboy from the fitness centre, would do an interview," he suggested. That was confusing - there weren't any ladyboys at the gym!

"But there aren't any ladyboys - hang on - Faa?!"

"Yeah - you know, the best looking ladyboy on the island. She's really beautiful."

They sat in silence as Uncle Lung-Lung brought over his spicy delights and they tucked in. Hannah's mind wandered to the faces she knew at the fitness centre; there was nobody 'obviously transgender' there, but wasn't her regular ride to the gym called

Faa? The beautiful petite girl who sped her expertly round corners and up into the jungle?

7. So this is Christmas

Christmas - the endless eating, the glum cheer, the family spats. In Thailand no-one seemed to care: the Muslim locals didn't celebrate it nor the Buddhists, and the travellers were taking it as an excuse to rebel in bikinis and santa hats, a cocktail in hand.

Still, here it was, so how should she spend the day? In the morning she Skyped her parents and the American provided entertainment by joining her in a pair of his girlfriend's hotpants. At noon she received a surprise message - a Dutch air-crew couple she knew from Australia would be beaming in for the day and arriving on her beach! She couldn't remember that much about them, except that the girl was very beautiful and the man had tried to kiss her once in a bunk bed.

In the meantime, they had finally got together, and now they had a few days sojourn on Koh Talay – saving Hannah from an empty day. At around 2pm when she found them, they were gleaming and gorgeous, and couldn't give a hoot about any Christmas tattle. They walked together to a beach further north where the pair were staying and cracked open some duty-free wine and snacks from 7-11 as the sun went down and the aircon unit growled and shuddered and spat out filthy, warm air. They laughed and looned as if time had never passed between them.

After several cocktails on the beach to a backdrop of fire-dancers they dined by the ocean on barbecued tuna until the waves caught up with their feet and it was time to move on. Romantic in the moonlight, their beautiful smiles warmed the occasion and the fair silence and love in the air made for magic in the midst.

They wandered up the sand bank to a clearing and from the darkness came an unsubtle clang of Thai music - they moved instinctively towards it. In the clearing a large gathering of fat women were dancing to boisterous noise made by their men. They wore unflattering, mis-shapen white tee-shirts and ballooning bright orange skirts, and their feet followed a ritualistic, repetitive pattern as they danced in the round. Though not remarkable, with the live drums and the atmosphere it was mesmeric. Hannah managed to find someone who could speak a little English to ask what it was all about – it didn't feel very Christmassy – and a kind man explained that it was 10 years since the devastating Tsunami had ripped right through Koh Talay, and they were marking the anniversary in this way. Without hesitation Hannah whisked the Dutch girl into the throng and started on the one-two-three, filmed all the while by their male companion. Before long some straggly local men joined the girls dancing and it was bright smiles all round before a swift escape back to the hotel room.

At 11pm Hannah said goodbye and treated herself to a tuk-tuk home in the dark. A young Muslim couple sat on the motorbike whilst she hopped in the sidecar. The young girl clung onto her beau all the way with the stars bright above and the forest wind hurling by as Hannah smiled in the Christmas night.

8. Moving On Up

On alternate days she walked up to the Fitness Centre from where Faa would drive her to the Muay Thai gym in the jungle on her speedy motorbike. Sucked in by the alluring strength that Muay Thai had given her, she was moving more and more into a world full of semi-naked North-Eastern Thai boys and further away from her true goal – to write. Though physically strong, training drained her of mental or creative energy, save for staring vacantly into the void for 24 hours after each session - yet the adrenalin high was a buzz that no banana milkshake could match. Over breakfast she would read a manual she had found online – *The Ancient Art of Muay Thai* - a publication from the 1970s detailing its long history with rudimentary diagrams of elbows, knees, kicks and jabs.

On Friday morning she awoke amidst the cocoon of her mosquito net to find only one earplug still in place. The orange rubber bungs handed out on the plane had been put to good use - blocking out the Thursday-night techno parties on the beach - but why now was there only one? Lazily she turned over and cast the net aside to peer about her dank old hut. Curtly propped against the corner was a haphazard pile containing an empty packet of peanuts, a pair of dirty knickers…and a half chewed-up orange earplug. Her face turned to horror: This could only mean only one thing, THE RETURN OF THE RATS!

Oh, this was too much - *yes*, natural living was a beautiful ideal - but she had stopped visiting the powder-white beach quite as often, preferring to hang out with Uncle Lung-Lung and the Thai boxers at the Chicken Shack, sitting behind the counter with Jeab, the owner of Salee Mart, watching the backpackers go by as they joked about starting up a disco night out back or a women's rights group for the prostitutes - who were far more interested in bleaching their already washed-out faces in attempts to look 'western'.

In the midst of this mini soap-opera lay a question – what next? What about the rats? Was it time for change? Didn't she need a place where she could truly attempt to write a book without several backpackers staggering into her path offering up drams of Thai whisky? Somewhere slightly more 'adult'?

It was time to hunt around for a monthly rental: it had to be right and it had to be cheap. Some locals pointed her in the direction of the road that swept around the island, and she checked out a few rooms above restaurants and computer shops where geeky teenage Thai boys sat around tables eating rice.

Slightly nearer the beach was a sign: *Grand Palace Hotel*. She had never ventured down that track before, and it led her past some chicken coops to a shiny large building, its steps immaculately polished by staff wearing matching polo shirts. Surely it was too plush for her, but it had to be worth a try. Behind her trotted up the husky from Relax – he had been following her and was bound to make mischief. An old, lean man sprinted out of the front doors, grabbed a hose and sprayed the dog until finally he retreated. He switched off the water and stood in front of Hannah, staring.

"This dog with you?" he enquired - not angrily but somewhat cold.

"Yes, erm, sorry - he's mad!"

"CANNOT COME HERE!" he said, then exited back up the polished steps from whence he had sprung.

Great - a chance for a fresh start and the dog had ruined it for her. Still, in her best pertinent fashion she slipped off her flip-flops and walked on inside the hotel. Behind the grandiose desk sat an older Thai woman, her hair bouffanted in an efficient manner. She wore a conservative flowery dress and a wide sneer upon her lips – scrutinising whomever entered and judging whether or not they would pass the mark.

"Yessssssssssss?" she eventually sneered, not breaking into a smile no matter how hard Hannah grinned at her, yet suddenly releasing a manga-style cackle.

"Er...I want to know the price of a room? Long term? One month?"

"800 for one night," she said sharply, and grimaced.

Bad news - Hannah had been paying just 200 baht per night, and that was really as far as her budget could stretch.

"Erm, possible for one month?"

"One month 9000 baht!" The old woman swung her legs around from the chair they were resting on and grabbed some keys from an old mahogany drawer. Hannah quivered with anticipation, gazing up the stairs to rooms with balconies, air and light, but the old woman didn't take her up any stairs...

"Upstairs possible?" Hannah enquired politely.

"No! Long term downstairs - can make money upstairs!" They entered a room at the back of the building, which stank of damp. The gloomy balcony looked out onto a cement wall and some untidy shrubs.

"Other side maybe?" she tried. Finally, they went to Room 3 – it was still downstairs and slightly damp, but had a bright, front-facing balcony, clean tiled floors, a desk to write on and a sparkling bathroom with cold shower. They went back to the reception desk where the woman showed her a calendar.

"Cannot now! Have group of Romanians staying! After New Year okay?"

"Okay!"

It was a step up from her current arrangement, and the stern yet kind owners could guard her against danger - albeit with an eager eye - with Jeab around the corner and Uncle Lung-Lung up the road.

9. Welcome to 2558

New Year did not seem a big event on Koh Talay – just a 'do as you wish' affair. The American and his girlfriend, Yerry and Yonny invited Hannah along to a little beach bar not far from their shambolic huts. Together they trudged towards the ocean and found a bamboo booth on the sand, removed their shoes and sat together on the floor around a table. Cocktails flowed and fireworks exploded, music playing as Blu, another dog from Relax, cowered beneath their table for protection – at regular points tipping over their drinks and snacks.

It was nice to be part of something - Hannah wouldn't have hoped for more - and at midnight they dispersed and straggled home, bumping into backpackers letting off lanterns on the beach and wishing one another a Happy New Year in good cheer.

Back at the bungalows Hannah jumped on her laptop to say Happy New Year to her friends and family, still ahead of time. As she glanced at the corner of the screen, she saw that the digits had changed to read '2558': The Buddhist calendar – of course!

* * *

On New Year's Day she awoke to a gloomy sky, heavy and dark with clouds blown in from the mainland that gathered into heavy clumps over Koh Talay and would break only when their burden weighed too heavy to hold.

Hannah was British - she was not only used to rain, but actually *liked* it. She wouldn't let it ruin her

New Year's Day and besides, she was hungry. Outside everything felt quiet and calm, as if the rain was washing away the ills from last year, peacefully making everything anew.

She didn't have an umbrella, but she did have a pashmina-style affair, which she threw over her shoulders and head, then made her way up the treacherous, sludgy clay path to the road. She was building up an insatiable hunger, and in the rain Uncle Lung-Lung and his chickens were nowhere to be found - nor was anywhere else open. The downpour had carved trenches down either side of the road where the water flowed south. Hannah followed its path, but after a good ten minutes was getting nowhere and, now drenched, decided to head down the first track she saw leading to the beach - where hopefully she could find somewhere to dine.

To the right arose a five-star resort - Royal Talay - and though she looked like a washed-up sea gypsy, she fancied the trespass. She crossed to the entrance and took the most discreet path through for fear of interception, all the while glancing about her with a foreboding feeling that she would be reprimanded and whisked back up to the road. Yet no-one seemed to mind her crossing their path; in fact, a beaming older gentleman in full service-dress approached her with an oversized umbrella and escorted her through - whistling a happy tune all the way.

Hannah smiled at him and the other staff, who were hanging out at the back of the kitchen laughing and joking, and continued through to a clearing. Before her stretched the formidable ocean, the beach deserted in the rain. She stepped out onto the sand

and intuitively walked in the opposite direction to her abode, relishing the momentary tranquillity. The waves rose rough and wild and the sky shone white with rain not yet fallen.

As she gazed at the horizon a voice came from across the breeze - soft yet deliberate. "Hello! Hello! Thai boxer! Hello!!" It was a small Rasta guy who worked at a nearby bar, softly spoken and sweet – and monged-out on weed most of the time.

Hannah smiled then went to sit with him on a small wooden platform. He passed her an earphone and together they listened to an odd array of Thai folk music, as they sat with their legs dangling looking out to sea and nodding away at the new day - the new year - under the shelter of his umbrella.

When enough time had passed, and the music had turned decidedly rock, she bid her leave with a nod and breezed back off in the direction of the village, her heart now full and vibrant and ready to finally eat.

Sitting alone eating fried eggs, she started to think about what this year could mean: would it mean no more struggle? She hoped for that – and no more concrete office blocks. Peace was what she needed, and she was near right now: the only mosquito left buzzing in her mind was her novel - or the lack of it. Tomorrow she would move to Grand Palace Hotel – and then she would start to write.

10. Fight Night

And so she moved to Royal Palace Hotel, and she started:

'Once upon a time there was not much time. All of the animals from the mainland had been shipped over to an island to escape the uncertain weather - rather like Noah's Ark – but actually it was a cunning government conspiracy to extradite them.

They quite liked the island and they built shacks out of dirt and mud, and they all got on - and got it on - and they mated, and they interbred, and they did it so well that they all became random creatures with no pedigree or breed and no 'pure' species to cut them down.

Funny looking things, some of 'em: There were furry things with bird's heads, jaguar-like creatures, and some that couldn't do anything except dance really well.

There was also rumoured to be a 'third sex', yet nobody had genitals that could be easily distinguished – just brains inside skin and feathers, hairy bits and proboscis, webbed feet and slime.

There was only one human, Mr. Pee, who made pizzas and everyone wanted to hump him because he was such a beautiful specimen - but Mr. Pee didn't know that humans usually rank above animals and just wished he had more fur instead.

He was a shining beauty god, and there really WAS a god - a small, brown, dog-like thing.

The whole year built to a climax in the form of an event named 'mataday', when all of the animals congregated in a Muay Thai boxing ring and had a dancing competition – the prize a year's worth of self-esteem - before it was time to get ready for the famous mating ceremony.'

It wasn't bad - not exactly a masterpiece, but she had to start somewhere.

It was very *nice* at Mama and Papa's Palace, but she was bored, and right now she could hear loud techno music being pumped out from the Muay Thai Stadium up the road. Every Sunday night it became a hub of activity when the rich but ineffectual owner shipped in paupers from the mainland to fight the boys at his gym - with a few foreigners thrown in for good measure.

Hannah hadn't been to a fight yet - it all sounded rather…*loud* - and she'd holed herself up at her new room with minimal social contact, save for Jeab and Uncle Lung-Lung. She felt slightly uncomfortable about the prospect of such a new experience, yet she knew the only thing keeping her away was fear.

She wandered into the reception area where Mama sat grinning behind the desk with her feet up, blissfully making her way through a playlist of *Country Classics,* and Papa pottered about clearing up empty beer bottles left by the Romanian package tourists.

"Helllooooooooo!" said Mama, "How ARE you?"

"Erm, okay - na beua nit noi!" – *I'm a bit bored!* "I want to go to the Muay Thai fight but it sounds loud - maybe too much noise?"

"Don't think so!" commented Mama, "Think goooooood! Think good for YOU!!"

So tentatively Hannah returned to her room and shoved on her jean shorts and a vest: she could make her way up the track, have a look and *then* decide what to do.

As she neared the stadium, the noise sounded far less threatening and more exciting; the bright lights, music and crowd of spectators gathering in anticipation on high benches.

She carried on walking past, not 100% convinced that she wanted to go in, but as she passed a dark but familiar figure arose from the shadows where he had been leaning up against a four-by-four, smoking: it was Tee, the good-looking trainer with the strange spiky hair and Chinese eyes, "You come?" he barked at her from the shadows.

"Erm, not sure - mai mee dang mahk!" - *I don't have much money.* He grabbed her, ushering her strongly towards the stadium entrance where Lek, the scary Thai woman from the gym, sat gleefully raking in the 1000 baht-note entrance fees. She glowered mildly at Hannah as she approached.

"Yeeeeesssssssss?! You want ticket?"

The trainer who had pushed her in, dark and calm with his irresistible, drunken swagger, swiftly stepped in to haggle for her.

"500 baht: Okay?" spat Lek.

"Okay!" Hannah agreed, and with that she was in. Steps led her to a bar area, at the back of which Thai boxers limbered up and locals hung about chatting. The bar itself was awkwardly positioned on a raised platform and to reach it you could easily lose your step.

She ordered a whisky to calm her slight jitters. Faa, her transexual ride from the Fitness Centre, served her with flirtatious grace - bumping and grinding with her fellow bargirls to Beyoncé: this could be fun.

Hannah turned her focus towards the giant boxing ring, which rose up formidably from the darkness. She only had a ticket for the backbenches, which were filling up by the minute with Scandinavians slurping beers, and she didn't fancy joining them so instead she slipped down from the bar and rested her whisky on a nearby makeshift table, purveying the scene.

Old Squishy Nose approached her, gregariously sinister and sleazily rubbed her shoulder - his deformed face peering too closely into hers. She edged away and nodded in acknowledgement and dismissal, and as she turned her face away, she noticed a familiar face behind her – Uncle Lung-Lung the chicken man! Rejoicing, she sped to him and they punched the air in triumph.

Peering behind her she could see other trainers from the gym milling around preparing for the fights. Kam fluttered about busily, but Tee stood alone at the bar; sturdy and firm, swigging on a beer. Hannah joined him and quietly and deliberately they swigged until the first fight, when instinctively they moved in closer to the ring.

Two lithe Thai boys, who looked about 12 but were probably nearer 17, were quickly walked through the auditorium by their trainers, before hopping over the ropes and taking their places at opposing corners. Lean and gristly and shining with oil and vaseline they prepared to fight. Excitement within Hannah built as the bagpipes started their mighty wail and the boys circled the ring, tracing the ropes with the top of their gloves before bowing their heads in respect to each corner.

The entrancing music continued as the boys knelt facing opposite directions to perform the *wai kru* – a ritualistic fighting dance showing respect to their masters – in anticipation of the real 'dance' which was about to begin. Arm movements swooped low, then rose up for the Swan, and then with deliberate ease the fighters stepped and bounced, raising their knees in a steady pattern – *1, 2, 3 knee* - bouncing, side-stepping to the right with rolling arms before a daring turn and heavy stamp for The Archer, pulling back and shooting imaginary arrows at their opponent: *Look what I'm going to do to you...*

When the spectacular display had ended each fighter returned to his corner where his trainer removed his *mongkon* - a headpiece weaved from intertwined rope - signalling time to turn and do some quick stretches or bounce off the ropes for bravado, fitness and focus. Tee slipped down even closer to the ring and with a subtle but intentional jerk of his head, Hannah followed.

Round One! *Bleeeeh-la-laaaah, blee-blee-la-laaaaaaah*! went the strangely hypnotic bagpipes, as the boys eyed and squared each other up, tentatively looking for weaknesses and where to hit hardest. There was no rushing in like some burly heavyweight from the West, the movement was considered and slow, almost stepping in time, until they saw an opportunity to go in and - *Bleeeeh-la-laaaah, blee-blee-la-laaaaaaah* - around they danced, every so often one of them suddenly going in for a round-kick, the noise thwacking through the auditorium but if no pain shown, no points were gained.

The boys took their time – there were five rounds to get through - a punch, an elbow, a twisted clinch wedging one fighter between the ropes until the ref released him.

Mesmerising and skilled, Hannah was unable to take her eyes off them. Tee felt it too, and in Round Three he handed Hannah his beer to leap over to the corner with one knee in the ring, hollering advice like a crazed Muay Thai madman.

"Kick, kick, kneeeeeeeeeeee!" What a round! Red marks started to appear around the boys' kidneys, a cut above the left eye for the blue corner but still the fighter continued on. With two more rounds to go the boys must have been exhausted, but neither showed the faintest sign of tiredness.

Round Five: *punch, punch kick! KNEE! KNEE!!* Then the bell rang for the last time, it was over. The ref collected the scorecards from each judge and the fighters stood with their chests heaving in and out with exhausted breaths, awaiting the result...and up went the hand!

"RED IS THE WINNERRRRRRR!"

The champion ran up to the ropes, climbing to stand on them with his arms stretched wide above his head in victory, Blue bowed around before swiftly disappearing and Red continued on with his proud parade.

As Red stepped out of the ring and passed her, Hannah's face fell open in amazement - a new virginity lost and Garden of Eden found, accompanied irresistibly by the smell of adrenalin mixed with boxing liniment and fresh sweat.

Tee now led her like an obedient puppy back to the bar, bought her a beer without asking first, took a large gulp then put it in her hand. He leant alluringly against the bar where Faa and her friend were still bumping and grinding the night away in their corset-tops and puffball skirts.

The champion passed her again and happily posed for a photo. As she brought her phone back to check the picture, she glanced up at the commentating corner, where a happy toothless Thai man rumbled out various incomprehensible exclamations. To the left of him a familiar face stared stonily back at her - it was the cold Western girl from the office at the gym – glowering and glaring with narrowed eyes: was it jealousy because Hannah, the new girl on the block, was stealing the limelight?

She checked the photo again and noticed this time that the jealous girl could be seen in the background peering over her nose with disdain and envy. Hannah passed it off and, slightly merry from whisky and beer, flounced back to Tee. Though an obvious animal attraction buzzed between them like a magnetic field they remained calm, measured and controlled – Thai-style. Hannah wasn't about to blow the good reputation she'd built – not *just* yet, anyway.

Tee disappeared to help prepare some fighters and Hannah loitered around the local people who stood up against the ring, shouting and cheering - Tuk-tuk drivers and Muslim women alike, hungry for the fight with fists full of baht to gamble. She felt oddly at home here, despite being a foreigner amongst the common-folk, enjoying the sensations of being caught up in a lucid dream.

A little giddy now from excitement (and booze on an empty stomach) she felt a hand on her shoulder and turned to see Kam, who took both of her arms in his and stroked them, peering lovingly into her face. Although taken aback she was also taken in – but surely these boys from the villages didn't fancy Westerners.

"I like your eyes," he said, smiling adoringly then squinting dramatically at her. Hannah *did* have small, almond-shape eyes but wasn't convinced by his mating talk, and no sooner had he delivered his golden line than he had run back off to the boxers' quarters. What a turn up for the books! Not a sniff from the male species for months, and here she was being wooed by two Thai boxers at the same time! She couldn't complain!

Blaring dance music announced the headline fight and anticipation built and bubbled in the stadium. Here they were: a Thai tough guy and a large oaf from Sweden (whom she had seen smashing bags into oblivion at the gym). She was surprised that foreigners would *want* to fight Thai guys – surely their lifetimes of training would make them near-invincible? She secured a spot close to the bar, surrounded by lank-haired blonde Scandinavians with beer bellies.

Mesmerised and drunk she stood anchored to her spot with a straw sticking out of her mouth, her eyes wide and fixed on the ring, ready.

The Thai fighter stepped steadily around the ring looking for opportunities to strike, staring at the

Swedish beast's legs and unable to meet his eyes, but no such measuredness from the Swede, who came flying in with punches and knees, crouching down by the ropes then launching his heavy body at the poor Thai - who was much slighter and no way in the same weight category. The crowd whooped and the Thais hollered.

In the short breaks between rounds the trainers rushed into each fighter's corner, deftly slipping a metal tray into the ring and plonking on it a plastic chair for the fighter to sit on as they were vigorously rubbed with boxing oil and sploshed with water, small boys helping and trainers shouting instruction in their adrenalin-struck faces.

In no time at all the Jeab sounded for the next round: up rose the bagpipes, round paced the men, panting but with no sign of ever giving up – and in swoops the Swede with an overhand which strikes the Thai guy's skull, and he's down, and he's out – a clean KO! A humongous whooping from the Scandinavians in the crowd and a rush in to revive the poor Thai guy who is laying flat-out at the side of the ring. A victory parade from the monkey-like Swede and the fight is over. Around Hannah the people rejoiced – she had been standing with the winner's family all the while!

Together they clinked glasses and without warning the entire stadium started to swarm out past her – fight night was over and it was time to move on. She moved out the way of the flowing human traffic and tucked herself at the side of the bar where Faa and her bargirl friends were packing up with urgency. She looked around to say goodbye to anyone she knew and, as she looked, she felt a firm, reassuring hand on her arm - it was Tee.

"Where you go now? You come party?" he asked.

"Oh no - I have to go home, I'm a good girl! Have to sleep, have to write!"

She still didn't feel quite ready for what might follow – the afterparty at a cement monstrosity known as Charlie Chang's where foreigners and Thais gathered after the fights, and prostitutes danced around the bar with drunken clients. Her night felt complete enough already; she had thoroughly enjoyed the fights, the attention from Tee and had even managed to retain her composure.

Smiling sweetly, she calmly walked out of the stadium, past the hordes of motorbikes about to zoom off with wobbling drunken tourists, past the tuk-tuk drivers now away from the ringside and touting for business, and back down the little dark track that led to her door.

With her ears ringing from the booming bass and her eyes wide from the excitement she now realised something: she was hooked and why should she hide it? She was venturing into the Muay Thai world, and she had never felt more alive.

11. Sleazin' at the Chicken Shack

The excitement and adrenalin made for an unsettled night's sleep, and when she awoke it was past nine which didn't leave her enough time to leg it up the path and steal a lift from Faa to go boxing. Deflated, she slipped out of the side door so Mama and Papa wouldn't see her and waddled, barefoot and bedraggled, in swamp-pants and a vest, to the shop to purchase yoghurt and bananas.

Jeab was stoic and chirpy as usual, now accustomed to Hannah in her bleary-eyed state of semi-consciousness. They exchanged a few words about fight-night, Hannah's voice belching forth in a low growl to Jeab's delight, and Jeab handed her three shining, round oranges to take home with her.

"I bought them in Krabi!" she said, "They're organic!"

With this delightful addition to her morning feed, she set up breakfast on her balcony and read her 1970s Muay Thai manual, as a herd of Romanian tourists piled out of a minivan. She looked down at her toothpaste-stained vest and pants, which were losing their elastic, and decided that it might be time for a personal groom. She looked down at her legs, which were rather 'boiled-chicken' in colour – should she attempt a tan? Her fair skin usually turned the colour of barbecued pork within minutes, but wouldn't brown legs be nice? A tan might even cover up some of the bruises from boxing.

After procrastinating over her book, but still not writing, she sploshed herself with cold water, stuck on a skirt and trotted to the beach. It was sweltering and there was no shade, so she covered her head with a light shawl and exposed her trotters for a blast of sun.

Hot, hot, hot! After only half an hour she checked the time in disbelief – if she could just manage another half an hour she would be on the road to beautiful brown pins! Sunbathing was an arduous task that other people made look easy, but not Hannah, who sat panting with a shawl over her head, her shins blistering to red in the sweltering heat.

After *nearly* another thirty minutes, she was in need of fast relief and replenishment - to Uncle Lung-Lung's Chicken Shack she would go! In the relentless midday sun, she hobbled – Uncle Lung-Lung would furnish her with endless water in an icy glass and at Uncle Lung-Lung's she could rest.

She approached the row of bamboo stands. At one end stood Aunty - Uncle Lung-Lung's wife - in the modest kitchen making the som tam, and nearby Uncle Lung-Lung on the grill, posing coolly barbecuing his chicken, liver, giant river fish and anything else he had found at the market that morning.

Hannah grinned on sight of her favourite man on the island.

"Chok chok!" he cried, punching the air - *Punch, punch*!

He carried on whistling his happy tune with resonance a canary would envy. She ordered her som tam, *ped ped, mai wan* – spicy not sweet - and a succulent chicken leg freshly grilled and bursting with juices, and went to find a seat.

Although the eatery wasn't full there was nowhere obvious to sit, and the other customers didn't look willing to share. Yet who was that over there, yabbering away boisterously in colloquial Thai? Kam and Squishy Nose from the gym!

She opened her mouth to greet them but was stopped in her tracks as they grabbed and pulled her into their booth. Kam started to rub her back vigorously.

"Farang[2] ron! Farang hon!" looking perplexed – *You are so hot and sweaty! Why?!*

Hannah reddened further – Thai people preferred to stay out of the sun, not only for the danger aspect but due to white skin being a sign of higher class, and she felt unable to explain her sunbathing antics. Instead, she grimaced out a smile and Kam fanned her with his hand, before pouring strong beer into her glass without asking. She took a sip, not quite comfortable with the situation, and the men continued yabbering forcefully about fighting or some-such - a discussion that could easily be mistaken for an argument.

Hannah sat sweating, occasionally dipping her spoon into the spicy Esarn soup that the men weren't touching – beer seemed to be their food of choice. Kam slung his arm around her, slipping it down at one point to squeeze her bum. She flinched but remained still, as he reached down to brush the dust from her feet. This action surprised her – Thai culture

---

[2] Farang: Mildly derogatory, but widely accepted, term for 'white foreigner'.

saw feet as dirty and 'low', so to touch them...a romantic gesture? A possessive thing?

She wished she had sat somewhere else – she was really hungry and wanted to enjoy her meal in full, but when her food finally came it was put in the centre with the other bowls, and she was forced to take polite miniature forkfuls in accordance with the two men. Suddenly Kam exclaimed.

"FARANG HON!" - *hot sweaty farang!* - and moved her over to sit with the old, salacious Squishy, who immediately remarked '*sow souay*' – *beautiful girl* - to Uncle Lung-Lung, chortling and clamping a toad-like hand on her shoulder.

This time she wriggled away, shaking her head and asserting loudly "No! No!" At least Kam had muscles and talent, but Squishy Nose was twice her age with a broken body, tobacco-breath and skin like waxed leather - no thank you! A moment later he suddenly got up and whizzed off on his motorbike, leaving Hannah and Kam alone together. Kam winced at her - it was likely supposed to be a smile, but without warmth.

"You beautiful, you beautiful! Your eyes!" He pointed to his own eyes and once again squinted cruelly. Hannah let out a half-laugh - though not fully attracted to him, his courting style was intriguing. As she sat there looking at him with circles of sweat ever increasing around her armpits, Kam's face suddenly went grey and he hopped up in panic.

"Aah! Hong nam! Hong nam!" he quickly breathed, looking about him - where the hell was the toilet? Uncle Lung-Lung motioned to a small tin-shed contraption on the grassy verge near some trees and off hopped Kam. A charming lunch-date, Hannah chuckled to herself – she wasn't interested in his advances, but it was intriguing so she stayed out of curiosity. What other lines was Kam hiding under his belt? She didn't notice him return, but was suddenly aware of someone else stepping quickly towards their table – a smiling but weary looking Thai girl.

"Hi there! How are youuuu? Do you train Muay Thai?" she mewed in a perfect English accent of sorts. It took Hannah a while to adjust her ears from the prior growling.

"Yes! Yes!"

"You like Muay Thai?"

"I love it!"

Kam stood on the other side of this chirpy Thai girl and wrapped his stringy arms around her.

"She girlfriend! She girlfriend me!" He urged, pointing incessantly at his chest.

"Oh!" said Hannah brightly, not bothering to veil a heavy whiff of sarcasm.

"Nice to meet you!" She gathered her things to leave.

"Not staying?" purred the lovely Thai girl politely.

"No, no, must get home, *dong kian*!" she said: *I need to write*. Training was her excuse not to write, and writing not to train.

She bolted out of there feeling slightly nauseous: not from the spicy raw papaya, which played havoc with her guts, but the leering: She wouldn't say she'd never experienced casual sexual harassment before, but these were her *trainers* – teachers - she showed *them* respect so the least they could do was feign a little back in return, surely?

Their behaviour didn't sit well with the sacred image of Muay Thai she held - the King's favourite sport and the nation's pride, a majestic art – yet she supposed these dirty dogs had grown up with no support, having to break their bodies to survive, then spending their jackpots on whisky. Abusing themselves in differing ways, the brief golden glory days subsiding into injury and subsequently retirement to a Muay Thai gym to teach huffing, sweaty, overweight foreigners whose primary aim was to show off their gold-embroidered shorts and knock someone out regardless of skill.

Hannah was a believer in *dhamma* – of living through your actions – and by that measure the scene at the chicken stand had not sat well with her. She scuttled off to Mama and Papa's for a gratefully received ice-cold shower and a sit down: What should she do now?

It was early afternoon – the hot, no-man's-land of the day - and she had nothing to do. The audio on her laptop was terrible so streaming movies with Mama's unpredictable wifi wasn't an option either. She sighed loudly, and lowered herself heavily onto the bed…

Wait a minute - wasn't there a training session in the afternoon at around 4pm? Yes, yes, there *was*, said the screwed-up leaflet she found under the table, blown there by the ceiling fan: To Muay Thai she would go!

She headed to the fitness centre for a ride but Faa and her friend weren't able to leave so there was no lift – only one thing for it, she would have to walk. With the sun beating down on her she started on the long road that curved around the island, which was built for two wheels. It was a boring and exhausting trudge but she was determined to train; yet halfway along she was struggling. Bikes zoomed past her in their dozens, wondering why anyone would care to walk anywhere in this heat and it was taking much too long. Just as she wondered if she'd *ever* get there, *and* that she'd be in no fit state for fighting, a quirky '*beep*' alerted her. It was Faa, who smiled and beckoned her over to sit on the back.

"Hiiiiiiiiii," she said sweetly, "My boss come and say okay to go home. I live at the gym, the owner Don is my uncle!"

Hannah happily jumped on to enjoy the ride, freewheeling in the breeze to the gym in the jungle. They drew up to the entrance sharply and with precision where Hannah jumped off and Faa continued to her room.

Hannah strode in, pleased to have made it, with Kam and Squishy Nose surprised to see her. She was straight onto the tyre with no messing for a warm-up and chance to focus - whilst slyly perusing the gym's goings-ons. The stony-faced Western girl from the office approached her.

"Hi," she said in a high-pitched mumsy voice.

"Hullo," Hannah grunted flatly: this girl had not impressed her much so far, with her lack of help and wicked scowls at the fight on Sunday.

"Are you traiiining?" she enquired further.

"Yep!"

"I am too! We can spar together!"

"Um…yeah, okay." Hannah continued with her routine, nonplussed by the appearance of the curt-lipped office girl, oversized in her shorts with her doughy white legs looking more suited to riding cattle than fighting. As Hannah punched the bags yet again the girl approached her.

"So, what's your name?"

"Hannah."

"How long are you here for?" The girl's eyes were piercing as she demanded more information, which Hannah felt reluctant to give.

"I'm here for three months and got here early December…" Hannah deliberately used few words – this was a Muay Thai gym and she was here to train, not to be interrogated. She tried to throw her off by striding off to the ring to see who was about to train her, but the girl followed her persistently like a puppy. Hannah turned in a second attempt to shake her off but was interrupted.

"My name's Melanie – people call me Mel! I work in the office - I didn't realise you were a long-timer, and a Brit too! If I had I'd *definitely* have spoken to you sooner!"

Oh, you would, would you now? Whoop-de-do, she thought, *Instead of refusing me a lift in the torrential rain whilst you sat on your laurels staring at me with your shark's eyes?*

"Let's spar!" insisted Mel. They moved into the space together and began to move around.

Mel was no agile boxer and she didn't seem to understand that sparring was a playfight of testing things out: attack, defence, blocks, easy does it all the while. Her demeanour was menacing as she tried to catch Hannah out but luckily Hannah was able to block her heavy advances. Kam passed closely behind

60

the two of them, as Hannah grew increasingly frustrated with Mel's clumsy flailings.

Suddenly, Mel hissed at her, "Has my mascara run?"

"What?"

"My mascara - has it run?" She peered closely into Hannah's face.

"No." Hannah took a step back - mascara and boxing weren't exactly a match made in heaven, and good luck to the woman who tries to look attractive whilst thrashing around a ring. Come to think of it, Mel wasn't really thrashing at all – she was hardly moving and certainly not sweating, so what was she actually here for? Hannah was starting to get visibly annoyed: she was pumped, ready and eager to train and this office girl seemed nothing but a timewaster. As she desperately sought a way out, Mel lifted a cumbersome knee, catching the top of Hannah's foot awkwardly sending a sharp pain through the bone.

"THAT'S NOT A BLOCK!" Hannah spat through gritted teeth, unable to suppress a verbal outcry. Her foot was floppy and felt broken, and she pressed her lips together and looked down to ensure she didn't meet Mel's gaze. She mumbled a faux apology for her exclamation, then hobbled over to sit next to Squishy Nose, who also forlornly sat nursing an injury.

"Hurt?" he asked her.

"Yes...Mel!" Squishy Nose nodded in understanding and the pair sat in silent pain together. A few moments later Tee approached her.

"You want to do padwork with me?" *Hell, yeah* - but overtaking on the inside lane was a boisterous Kam.

"With me! You come train with me!"

Gosh - a battle! Hannah hesitated and let the boys decide who ranked higher – it was Kam. So, she forgot about the foot, and set to leaping about the mats with him.

"Gooooood! Goooooooooood!" he jeered in rehearsed monotony every time she moved. *What's good?* she thought, *Leering at my chest every time I lunge at you?* Adrenalin loosened her tongue, and she barked back at him when she knew she hadn't twisted enough or kicked with enough power.

"NO good! NO good!"

After three rounds in quick succession, they were done. She was hyped and had forgotten all about her painful foot and no sooner had Kam gone for a break than Tee was directly in front of her with his pads at the ready. Hannah had more to give, and her stamina and power was amplified with his intense stare and masterful instruction, as he manoeuvred her about the space one-on-one - their attention deeply anchored in each other's psyches.

When it was over and she had warmed down she looked for Kam to get a lift, but he shook his head and looked down somewhat bashfully. Confused, she stood, dripping with sweat, wondering how to get home. At that moment Mel popped out of the office, lathered, waxed and polished like a clapped-out volvo, a big and triumphant grin on her face.

"Need a ride home?"

Chapter 12: Her Milkshake Brings All the Boys to the Yard

"WHERE DO YOU LIVE?" Mel yelled over her shoulder in the wind.

"Yao Beach! The other end!" she replied. Hannah didn't like other people knowing where she lived – there was little privacy in such a small place, unlike the big cities where she loved to dwell. *Where you stay?* was often the first question Thai people asked, quickly followed by *How much you pay?* Mama and Papa's was her only sanctuary, and she couldn't bear the thought of visitors turning up unannounced.

Although Hannah couldn't drive, she was an experienced passenger and Mel wasn't rating high on her list of motorbike rides. Hannah was covered in sweat from training and it was nearing mosquito hour when they would feast upon her juicy flesh, but as they turned onto the main road, Mel suddenly stopped, "Fancy a shake?'" she asked with incredible intensity.

"Well, I usually go home and wash first but…okay!"

They stopped at the first place they found, a modest roadside stand with a few plastic chairs and an efficient lady in a pinny serving the customers. She unpeeled bananas deftly, feeding them effortlessly into the blender before adding ice and a little tinned milk, making the shakes for the thirsty foreigners.

Hannah asked for hers without sugar but Mel took it as it came – oversweet. They sat and sucked; there was too much ice and not enough banana, but it was cold, cheap, wet and would do.

"Soooooooooo," began Mel, "What are you doing here?"

"Um…Writing a book," Hannah gruffed unattractively.

"Oh coooooool! What's it about?"

"Well…it's a story."

Something about Mel's prying came across as disingenuous, and her straining to extract information put up Hannah's guard, so she ejected the conversation away from her onto Mel's more predictable affairs.

Mel was a personal trainer from London but there seemed nothing motivating about her. She had a form one could only describe as 'doughy', and the incongruence between her piercing eyes and fake smile made Hannah shudder inside: in fact, when her mouthy grin reached its peak, it looked like she wanted to eat you. Hannah hurried down the slurping of her shake.

"It's so cool that you're a long timer," gushed Mel, "My friend Jen's coming back from the US on Friday – you HAVE to meet her!!"

Hannah couldn't see that she would particularly like or need these people, especially if Mel's personality was anything to go by. Talk moved on to a more gossipy arena, "What do you think of the trainers?" asked Mel with seeming innocence.

"I'm not sure," replied Hannah, "I thought they were really sweet and earnest at first, but then Kam tried to touch me up at the chicken-stand, and I don't like the way Squishy Nose leers at me when he's holding pads…"

Mel was here on a 'permanent' basis, having persuaded the owner of the gym - big bad Don – that she could revamp his website in return for accommodation, food, a motorbike and pocket money.

As Hannah started to recount the incident at the chicken shack with the Thai girlfriend for afters, Mel shrieked with exclaims of surprise at her playful turn of phrase - questioning nearly every utterance for meaning. When Hannah had shed her load in full, Mel remained silent for a while - cold and calculating, then finally she spoke, "Hmmm, they can be a tricky bunch, but you and Tee seem to be getting along pretty well!"

"I suppose so, but I don't want to get involved with anyone right now – I need to focus on trying to write this book."

Mel looked down dramatically, as if to mark something, "They are *sweet* boys though…" She accentuated a pause, then looked up at Hannah in a slightly grotesque, suggestive manner.

"OK," Hannah got the hint, "who've you been screwing?"

Mel put her hand to her chest and gasped, taken aback by such forthrightness. Hannah remained still.

"Kam!" she finally announced, grinning proudly like a trussed-up turkey ballooning out her claggy feathers.

The mosquitoes had started their sirens of warning - the sun would soon set - and Hannah also felt close to expiration with the sweat, grime and exhaustion from boxing.

They got back on the bike and unsteady, slowly and wobbling they went. Hannah tried to stop Mel at the top of the dirt track that led down to the village – she wasn't sure she was ready to reveal her sanctuary - but Mel insisted, "I don't mind taking you all the way!"

Don't mind? You're giving me no choice unless I hurtle myself off into a nearby bush!

Hannah thought. She really didn't want Mel to go near the kind people who guarded and guided her, so at Salee Mart this time she insisted, "You can't go much further than this – it's slippery, here is fine."

Hannah hobbled home, the adrenalin-high from boxing having turned to an all-consuming knackeredness. It felt good to be back at Mama and Papa's Palace in the shower, with time for a feast on the roadside at Madame Kanchana's Kitchen. As she guiltlessly chomped on fried rice with an egg on top, she considered the day's events. There was something about the way Mel extracted information from her that she felt uncomfortable about. Mel was not a friend, not a good addition to her current energy, and not to be trusted.

13. Wandering Soles

The next day Hannah was lacklustre. She kept forgetting about her painful foot, and every time she attempted to hobble about her modest dwelling she nearly fell. In the early afternoon she was starving, so she stuffed on an old pair of jungle pants and a vest, grabbed her bag full of junk, left her shoes and picked her way ungracefully to Salee Mart.

"Hello! How are you?" the strong and steady Jeab enquired.

"Okay – hungry! I did Muay Thai yesterday – look!" she pointed to her left foot, which was impressively bruised in deep purple.

"Oh! Painful! *Jep Jep*!"

"Yeah, some horrible girl did it!"

Jeab smiled with a twinkle of mischief - they seemed to see eye-to-eye and to have the same disdain for the human race - people had to earn their trust.

"You take care!" she said.

Hannah started to walk back home, her questionable snacks in hand, but didn't fancy going straight back to Mama's, so instead she turned right at the guest house and made her way to the sea. She walked southwards without a clue as to where she was going, but it was sure not to be too far given her current impaired state. She passed the bar where she had sat with the sweet jungle Rasta boy on New Year's Day, and prepared for a smiley wave - but no-one was around. Old plump tourists in matching day-glo swimsuits waddled out of their overpriced hotels for an afternoon's roasting, a man lay on the sand in the lapping waves with his stomach protruding sky-high and sweet little semi-stray dogs followed her playfully.

She stepped into more unknown territory now and continued to meander with a dreamy look upon her face. A girl sat in the sand ahead, also dreamily looking out to sea, holding onto the leads of two dogs. Without contemplation Hannah whipped out her camera and took some photos of her, happy in the sand with her furry friends. The girl looked up, shielding her eyes from the bright rays of the sun.

"Hey!"

"Hi, I hope you don't mind me taking a picture - you look so content!"

"That's OK!"

"I didn't mean to walk this far - I only popped out for a banana but have ended up here. I love wandering – I'm always getting cabin fever."

"*TELL ME ABOUT IT!*" happily lilted the girl – who was American - "I'm Jen."

"Hannah," she replied, warmly extending her arm.

"I'm just takin' these pooches for a walk, I got 'em from the animal shelter. I'm so bored..."

Hannah took the smaller but more boisterous of the two dogs and the girls walked, laughing and chatting away. It was *exactly* what Hannah needed – this real person with interesting views and a heavy dose of humour and idiocy was tonic for the soul.

The sun had begun its descent into the sea as they reached the end of the beach.

"I didn't mean to be out this long! Look at me, I look like I've come out of a swamp - no shoes or anything!" Hannah exclaimed.

"Okay, girl, but you're comin' with me to take these mutts back to the animal sanctuary – the staff are evil bastards. Then I'll give you a ride home." It sounded like a deal.

On the track, one of the dogs suddenly lurched out into the road and a motorbike had to swerve out of the way. Pleased to have dropped them off unharmed at the animal shelter, Jen collected her motorbike outside a dubious-looking shack, and they rode home together to a sunset backdrop: two girls flying in the wind - new friends, refound sisters.

Jen drove her all the way up to Mama and Papa's and unlike Mel, Hannah allowed her to come inside and lollop on the bed whilst she took a shower.

"Sorry, I'm spreading myself all over your bed!"

"Make yourself at home!" Hannah hollered from the spray.

They decided to go and eat together on the roadside. Hannah put on a green t-shirt dress with an elegant gold-print design to make up for her earlier unkempt attire, and up to Kanchana's Kitchen they zoomed, to sit on plastic chairs at a wooden table and to be entertained by mosquitoes and Thai folk songs. Busy staff rushed about the small kitchen as hungry farangs clock-watched at every table. Jen looked at her phone.

"My friend Mel's coming – is that okay?"

Hannah froze, "Mel from the Muay Thai gym?"

"Yes! I haven't seen her since I got back from the States."

Hannah resisted the urge to blurt out her impression of Mel, sitting in ominous silence.

"D'you know her?" Jen pushed.

"Yeah, we've met…"

"Do you like her?"

"Not particularly - but you know, I don't really know her…" she attempted lamely. Taking it as a go-ahead, Jen launched into an impressive tirade about Mel – how self-centred she was, only talking about herself, and how she didn't respect Thai customs, just wanting attention from the boys.

Ten minutes passed and Hannah was hungry, "Can we order? I know it's rude not to wait, but it always takes a while."

Jen texted Mel for her order then proceeded to instruct the waiter in perfect Thai how she would like her hot and sour soup, blowing Hannah away.

"Your Thai is amazing! How did you learn it - I do try, but it's so hard!"

"Well, I've been here a while, and my boyfriend's Thai so…"

As they waited with slight foreboding for the appearance of Mel, Hannah was told all manner of intricate and bizarre details about Jen's slightly bonkers life: how she had just recovered from mad, feverish dengue, and rabies before that – and how as a result she was still prone to sudden and unforeseen raging outbursts. Jen was great fun – but sounded like trouble, the very thing that Hannah had been avoiding. Yet perhaps life had become a little *too* placid - maybe it was time for an adventure or two…

The food turned up but Mel did not, so they shrugged their shoulders and tucked in. Just as they did so a large, white shape wobbled into view - it was Mel, shaken and stirred!

"Guys! Guys!" she limply proclaimed from an impolite distance, "Sorry I'm late, I fell off my bike!" She presented her leg to them. It had been bandaged up and couldn't have been too bad - or she'd be in the hospital. Playing along with the scene, and knowing that the Thai way was to care, Hannah drew up a chair on which to rest Mel's leg - the staff in the kitchen nodding in approval.

Mel wore a woeful grimace – but there was nothing behind her empty, blue, shark-eyes. Hannah let Jen take over the conversation, faded out, and shovelled in her red curry. They paid the bill and she excused herself, leaving Jen and Mel to traipse off back southwards together. Going home alone for a quiet night in, she was happy to have met her new buddy Jen, but perpetually bothered by Mel's unstoppable presence.

14. The Golden Ticket

Posters had sprung up all over the island, proudly advertising this week's event – Saolek was coming to town! Saolek – the best Muay Thai fighter in the world!

SAOLEK!! FOR ONE NIGHT ONLY!!

The locals (who paid a tenth of the ticket price) excitedly asked: '*Are you going? Are you going?!*' At a hefty 2000 baht, a week's food money, she wasn't too sure - how grand would the 'performance' actually be, anyway? Don, the owner of *Talay Muay Thai Gym*, had purportedly paid tens of thousands of baht to reel him in - hence the expensive entry fee.

So, it transpired that on the day before the fight she *still* didn't have a ticket – despite every tuk-tuk driver and brothel girl trying to sell her one, and she wondered whether she would make it to the brawl.

Whilst walking home after a satisfying lunch at Uncle Lung-Lung's chicken shack, a familiar figure rode past her – the alluring silhouette of Tee. He growled in fake machismo, but as Hannah smiled sweetly, his face too broke into a shy smile, and he turned his motorbike around and pulled up beside her, "You come tomorrow?" he asked, in his low, sexy accent.

"Mai roo! Don't know!" she said, "Mai mee dang."

No money, as usual, the same old story - but a true one at that. He motioned with a jig of his head for her to hop on behind him, and together they went to the fitness centre. Don was loitering uselessly in the reception area - Hannah seized her moment.

"1000 baht okay?"

She handed over a bronze note, inscribed with the King's head, and received a ticket in return. Thanking Tee for his friendly favour, they went their separate ways - until tomorrow's big event. She might even let her hair down for once, get a bit tipsy and lead herself astray. She had managed two months here playing it safe; surely she could let herself go for just one night?

* * *

Koh Talay had a curious way of organising events: every establishment was allotted a different night to have its party, and this night never changed - woe betide if lines were crossed! Wednesday was Ladyboy Techno Night down on the deserted beach, Monday brought Rasta reggae bands from the mainland to Reggae Reggae Bar, Saturday sorted the jungle boys by the rocks and Sunday – well Sunday was Muay Thai Fight Night at Don's Stadium, followed by a sprawling aftermath at Charlie Chang's.

Hannah hadn't gone to any parties so far – despite the recent persistent nagging invites from Mel: '*Come on, it will be fun!*'

Bollocks would it! To Hannah organised parties were often a chore, forcing you to feign having a brilliant time whilst secretly dying inside, but tonight she *was* going to a party, and she was determined to have a ball.

She reserved her energy in the daytime - tonight's spectacle wouldn't start until after 9pm, and by then she was usually flagging from the heat and goings-on of the day. She kept in radio-contact with Mel, who was loudly proclaiming crass reports of Saolek's flawless body as he warmed up at the gym - rendering Hannah jealous and repulsed in equal measure. Annoyed, she made a note to go her own way this evening: good old Mel would have her uses – a free tipple or some inside information - but no-one would stop Hannah getting her rocks off.

After darkness fell, she squeezed on her costume for the evening – her ancient, ripped jean-shorts and a sequinned vest from Khao San Road - and headed to Salee Mart. She'd steer clear of the lethal *lao kao* rice wine and amphetamine whisky this evening - vodka seemed like a clean enough drink, and it might help keep her mind alert and produce a milder hangover in the morning.

On arrival at the shop in her glad rags, she found Jeab sitting behind the counter as usual on an old office chair, reading a book.

"Helloooo!" Jeab greeted, with cheery fervour.

"Hi! I'm going to buy some vodka for the fight night - can I sit with you and have a drink?"

"No problem!" she said brightly, putting down her book.

Hannah went to the booze section and dusted off half a bottle of Thai-brand vodka. She took some soda from the fridge, paid, and joined Jeab behind the counter - who stood up from her comfy chair, gesturing for Hannah to sit.

"No! It's your chair, I'll get one from the back!" she protested, but Jeab was having none of it - moving over and propping up her elbows on the cigarette counter, "I've been sitting all day, you sit!"

So, Hannah sat, pouring herself a generous measure of vodka before settling down to watch the world go by. Salee Mart was great for people-watching. It was the only shop in the little backpacker village, and long-stayers would pop in frequently - it being so convenient – to get a can of coke, or three more large beers, or to stand gawping at the peculiar toiletries section which contained nothing of use and was at least double-price. Jeab was a shrewd businesswoman. From time-to-time a local would come in: a tuk-tuk driver for an M150 power drink or the kind-looking schoolteacher, who was trying to give up, for three ciggies and a penny sweet. When they left the shop Jeab would tell Hannah their story, and whether they were *jai dee* – kind-hearted - or if they had caused trouble by sleeping with an ageing hippie's husband. Sometimes she would ask Hannah to judge on sight. The brothel girls came in too, for half a bottle of Similan whisky, soda and 20 bahts-worth of ice in a bucket. Everyone came and went easily and between whiles Jeab would sit with her book, smiling, passing comment, sighing or wiping her brow.

As Hannah drank, Jeab fetched watermelons from the back room, and using a knife cut them skilfully into succulent slices to sell. She liked to keep busy, and she didn't want to get fat or lazy. Two Canadian boys sat in front of the shop on benches drinking Chang beer and kidding around with one other, nodding over at the two girls behind the counter who also shared good times.

Half an hour later, and charged with stiff vodkas, Hannah was thinking about leaving for the stadium.

She had been telling Jeab how she could do with a bit of extra money and structure to her days, and Jeab let out a sudden '*Aah!*', jutted one hip out and stamped her foot softly, then made a proposal, "Come and work with me here in the shop! Just two or three hours a day - up to you! I pay you, we eat lunch. I think good for you – good for me! Good for customer. What do you think?"

"Yes!!" Hannah let her gut do the talking - how exciting - a curious little holiday job in a Thai minimart! "How many hours...when will I start?!"

"Up to you! I think I give you 200 baht for three hours, lunch, and you can take some things you need for your home."

"Are you sure? Do you have the money?" questioned Hannah – it seemed like a generous deal – some Thais wouldn't earn that much for half a day's manual labour.

"Of course! It will be good - we can see how it goes! Nothing serious!"

"Okay, erm, how about 11 until 2?" Hannah suggested.

"Up to you! Whenever you like!"

"Okay - not tomorrow though – I think mow kang!" she said – *hangover* - pointing to the vodka.

"No problem, see you when you like!"

And with an unexpected job and a few drinks under her belt, she jumped up, gathered her things, thanked Jeab - both of them grinning at the prospect of their new partnership - and went on her way to the Big Fight.

15. Tonight it's Party Time

Butterflies sprung up in her stomach, in addition to her rather empty stomach and the vodka. The familiar *thud-thud* of the warm-up music from the stadium emerged from a temporary darkness as she trudged up the track, glancing quickly from side-to-side at the threatening bushes, anticipating a rogue jumping out at any time.

With no more opportunity to compose herself nor hesitate, she turned the corner to uncertainty: the usually quiet road was chock-a-block with taxis, four-wheel-drives, tuk-tuks and farangs two-by-two in tie-dye apparel.

Thai people in their best jeans joined the swarm, which buzzed towards the stadium entrance, their eyes wide in anticipation and their gait a little nervous at such unfamiliar grandiosity: *For one night only! The Muay Thai legend! Saolek Soooooor Chokdee!!*

She recognised some of the locals and the expats – the straggly woman from the German deli, always highly-strung and stressed as she inefficiently struggled to make Emmental cheese sandwiches. Uncle Lung-Lung had been given an honorary ticket in return for a hefty heap of som tam for Don and his cronies. Lek from the office and her even heftier younger sister on the door, slightly less glum than usual, and just behind the trestle-table she could make out another familiar lump – Mel.

Hannah niftily approached the cliquey gaggle at the entrance, presenting her ticket with no haggling necessary, and walked straight on through to the other side. She poked Mel in her doughy back, which was

79

crammed into a badly judged 'princess' dress. The oversized bandage on her leg from the motorbike incident completed the look perfectly.

"Hiya! You look nice!" lied Hannah, attempting to get in her good books.

"Yah, um, yah, so do you! I like the holes!" Mel said, pointing down to Hannah's threadbare jean-shorts - those were no designer tears. Hannah grinned - she knew her appeal – the little blonde girl who liked to muck around with the big boys, in her thin, cheap but cheeky, sky-blue vest adorned with sequins outlining a pink rose.

Before they could continue this slightly underhand chit-chat, Don came over to ogle at Hannah and bark orders at Mel, and Hannah seized the opportunity for a quick exit. She didn't need to go to the bar - already having filled her trusty plastic bottle with left-over vodka - but she grinned up at Faa, who was gyrating to Beyoncé whilst plying farangs with bootleg booze.

"You look happy!" winked Hannah, "Anyone I know?"

Faa leaned in, cutely cupping a hand to her mouth, conspiring in a low voice, "There's a boy here - he fighting tonight! He see me at the gym and he say, 'I like you!' I been to Samui with him and his family already!" She let 'already' linger on in suggestive mischief.

"Ooooh! Nice one!" grinned Hannah.

As she went to find a suitable place to perch for the evening, she couldn't help but wonder if the object of Faa's affection knew the full story – they'd been on holiday with his parents - were the whole family accepting of her transgender status? Did they know? It was easy to understand why Faa could choose to not say anything – especially as he had *pursued* her – but one day that dream could come tumbling down. Well, for now that day hadn't arrived, and Faa looked so overwhelmingly happy that Hannah passed off her thoughts and continued looking for a seat.

The stadium was busier than usual and she wasn't sure if she'd get away with sneaking into the expensive ringside seats, already crammed with impatient farangs awaiting Saolek's grand entrance. As she wandered about trying to find a place in the hubbub, she bumped slap-bang into Keng Kam – the one who looked like Michael Jackson. Forcefully and without warning he drew both of her arms into his grasp, and stroking them, mewed, "Helloooooooooo, you beautiful! I fight tonight!"

"Yes!" acknowledged Hannah, a bit off-guard.

"*I!*" he repeated.

"Yes?"

"I! I fight - tonight!" Micky stressed again, rapping on his chest, his voice strained in a high-pitched strangled tone as he attempted to add more prestige to his announcement. His imploring didn't work; there was something about his botched nose job and lack of testosterone that turned Hannah off completely - though of course she wished him luck. He was an ex-champ, like most of the Muay Thai trainers, and although he still fought often, he was by no means the main event of the evening.

"Oh yes, chok dee!" she said quickly – *good luck* - wincing and wondering how to escape his awkward clinch. No sooner had she faked her enthusiasm than he had run off to the boxer's area, where wafts of excitement mixed with the zing of boxer's liniment, signalling adrenalin and nerves as it travelled on the breeze. Another familiar face now seamlessly appeared like an apparition, staring squarely into her own – Tee. Lovely, dark, alluring Tee, "Hello," he grunted through his nose sexily, still swaggering somehow whilst stood strongly rooted to the spot.

"Hi!" she grinned sweetly with a cheeky jaunt, knocking back a gulp of vodka before offering the bottle to him. He sniffed the clear liquid inside, screwed his face up in a disapproving grimace, and then thrust it back at her sniggering in disbelief: *This farang, swigging her own neat vodka from a plastic bottle in a fully licensed establishment! What gall!* Yet he appreciated her game, and she his – despite the heavy hint of cruelty: a power-play, a driven desire to tease farangs and an anti-imperialistic resentment at play. She liked him, but she couldn't trust him.

Suddenly, feeding off the atmosphere, Tee grabbed an old man that Hannah vaguely recognised.

"She! She! Gin lao!" pointing to the vodka he billowed his hands in an imaginary mist of fumes to surround Hannah in a forcefield. The old man sniggered creepily.

"This Papa Playboy!"

Hannah nodded, her face straightening in recoil.

"Say sawadee ka, Papa Playboy!" he ordered menacingly.

"Sawadee ka," she muttered reluctantly, her face stony and her tone flat in forced obligation. The old man bared his nasty toothless mouth at her and she turned to leave, but after a couple of steps a shrill, familiar voice clipped at her from behind, "Hiya! Having fun?!"

It was Mel, all puffed-up and baring her own toothy mouth whilst clutching a camera to her puppy-fat bosom. She motioned her head in ridicule towards Tee and Papa Playboy.

Hannah started to gruff out an answer - she didn't want to get stuck with the prize-pig all night - but her worries were unfounded as Mel charged off in the direction of the oiled-up boxers, eager to ogle them as she snapped away: tearing off pieces of their gleaming souls with her apparatus. Flashing at them, click-click-clicking with her sharp pincers, one evil eye fixed upon their tarnished yet flawless physiques, as she greedily licked her gnashers with relish.

Hannah exited the corner of incidence to find a place to settle, swig, and watch the fights - which were about to begin. She made a deliberate move to the far-corner of the stadium and spotted a small space on the end of a ringside bench next to the unappealing woman from the German deli. She nodded at her to budge-up, which she did - somewhat reluctantly. They exchanged a few words about Saolek - the deli woman hoping it would be worth the ticket price...

The fights began. In-between rounds, Mel's voice boomed from the commentary box in plummy Queen's English, announcing the after-party, "Don't forget to join us after the fights at CHAAAAARLIE CHANG'S-ah, CHAAAARLIE CHANG'S!! The official sponsors for this evening's event-ah!"

At the end of the first fight, Mel found her way to Hannah, "Alright?" she quipped brightly, tilting her head like a crow.

"Yes," drooled Hannah, skewed by the rocket-fuel in her hand. Mel frowned at her phone as it frantically beeped, "It's Jen - she keeps asking if she can sneak in, but you know what? I can't be bothered! I think I'll leave it."

Hannah shrugged – she didn't mind either way - the bigger the gaggle of girls, the less chance she had for creating havoc. She sent Mel to purloin some free vodka - obedient as a pooch.

The first fight was just a warmer to fill the fight card, but the second was worth something. The fighters were teenage boys in their prime, around 17-years old, who had not yet fallen prey to beer, whisky or yah-bah - habits that the backstreets of Gangster's Paradise offered. Both fighters gleamed under the streaming lights, with oiled bodies and embroidered satin shorts in hues of showy pink. One of them hitched his shorts high over his hips to make his kicks lightning-quick - no fabric between the air and his muscly thighs to slow down his sinewy limbs.

It was a technical fight which showed all of the signs of good training, hard work and great showmanship – one fighter dropped his fists every time the other went for a strike, as if to say *Come on! What was that?! I'm not scared, look – no guard*!' His face displaying the same sentiment; cocky and smirking like a joker.

Hannah was getting rather excited and the vodka was kicking in and, unable to sit still, she stood up and quick-footed it to the corner to yell along with the

Thais, *"OOOOOOOOOOooooo-eeeeeeeeeeeeee!"* when a round-kick missed, the other boy coming in with a low-kick to the inner-calf, striking hard. Then - with seemingly no lapse in time - they were around each other's necks, grasping onto strained muscle, clinching, kneeing each other's kidneys, pushing each other onto the ropes until the referee separated them to start the game again. She loved it. Tee appeared by her side, handing her his beer and cigarette to hold as he yelled out impromptu advice to the fledgling boxers. The older trainers, now jaded from their glory days, raised the new generation to fight for King and Country until one day they too would grow old and damaged, and retire to coach farangs in a jungle gym somewhere.

When the match was over, breathless from the hype, Hannah returned to the bench to get her bag to be faced by the deli woman, unashamedly gawping.

"He's my trainer," she explained, "I get to be his Thai-wife assistant as part of the deal." Hannah grinned, shrugging her shoulders coquettishly, and headed off to the toilet – a sorry affair on the far side, where Thai girls straightened their mini-dresses and powdered their faces, and farang boys released beery bladders into latrines.

A booming sound reverberated around the stadium as Hannah hovered above the discoloured toilet seat, "AND NOW!!" it announced, "The moment you've all been waiting for"....."Saolek.....Sor.....Chokdeeeeeeeee!!"

She willed the stream beneath her to dry up soon, and when it finally subsided, she made a mad dash back to the action - but it transpired that there was no urgency, for as she hurried out of the mosquito-infested cubicle a film began to unfold on the big screen: Magnificent Mel's powerpoint presentation!

It was, annoyingly, rather good. All foreign eyes in the auditorium turned to the deafening display – Saolek in pixelated 2D - but the locals just sat, oblivious and unimpressed, waiting for the legend to appear in the flesh.

Hannah hurried to take a seat. She'd had enough of the German deli woman and instead perched in the middle of a bench just behind the judges.

Here Saolek came, parading gloriously through the stadium: fierce, strong and oiled to perfection, his smooth, rippling muscles radiating in the electric light. He posed, flexing, and two rather squat men, also ripped and glimmering, appeared either side of him dressed in ancient fighting costumes, decorative mongkons on their heads and deadly serious expressions on their faces.

Saolek jumped over the ropes effortlessly into the ring and the crowd roared. Dramatic music sounded as they began their elaborate pantomime: the story of two small men in a forest encountering a mighty warrior – Saolek! Flying-kicks and double attacks from Saolek struck the men down. The pursuit continued but each time Saolek could not be beaten! Saolek Sor Chokdee! The mightiest warrior in the land!

Before ten minutes had passed it was all over and Saolek was gone, the lights dimmed backed down and the CD player turned off, leaving the crowd hissing a low murmur of dissatisfaction. The German deli woman walked past Hannah on her way to the bar, huffily remarking: "Well, I was hoping for more than *that* for my 2000 baht!!", and Hannah nodded but she didn't care – she'd paid half, was half tipsy, and was holding the trainer's beer in full view of the paying public. She felt important, she felt frisky, she felt mischief might finally be on the horizon.

Next to enter the ring was Faa's new man. It was his first fight and it could go either way. He seemed like a nice boy, full of energy and smiles, and although Hannah usually rooted for the Thai corner, this time she wanted him to win. It turned out to be an easy defeat – he struck his opponent down in the fourth round with a strong left leg kick to the ribs. A technical KO for a triumphant Swede, now off to claim his prize by way of the tantalisingly dressed Faa – his lady of the night.

Time had suddenly flown - the final fight was announced. Mel hobbled over from the commentating box to join Hannah. Mel kept checking her phone and dismissing Jen's texts while they waited for the intermission music to stop pumping which would signal the entrance of Kam – the object of Mel's desire. Hannah examined Mel's face; she was staring fixatedly at the empty ring, a troubled, little-girl-lost look about her.

"What's wrong?" Hannah slurred in rhetoric.

"It's Kam - Kam's fighting!" Mel gasped, "And, and I'm worried - he could get hurt – oh I just want him to do so well!" She over-emphasised every word, rendering them almost meaningless.

Kam entered the ring, suitably greased up, and began his peacock-like parade - an elegant *Ram Muay* dance directing the archer at his opponent. The other trainers from the gym gathered in the corner, ready and waiting to guide, coach and advise him. Mel's eyes glazed over like a frozen swimming pool as Kam bowed to each corner of the ring. When he faced the girls, easy to pick out on the front bench, Mel threw him a desperate, imploring look of adoration, to which he responded with a faint smile. This lit her weak heart on fire and she was happy now, even clutching one hand to her heaving breast.

"Oh come on!" said Hannah, "Look at you!"

In a whimpering voice, Mel retorted, "Don't be nasty! I'm worried - see how *you* feel when someone *you* like fights!"

"You looove him, you want to maaarry him!" Hannah chimed playfully, digging with a reassuring smile – was she 13 and at church camp?

Kam fought with strength and skill, his long limbs giving him an advantage over his stockier opponent to strike with front and round kicks, and he gracefully evaded the counter-shots by stepping back, then walking around the ring calmly: *No problem, try what you like – I'm invincible*! It was a clear win, and as he climbed out of the ring and passed the two girls, Mel reached out her clamouring hands to him, and he touched her lightly on the shoulder before leaning down and kissing Hannah forcefully on the cheek. Perhaps he had chosen his prize, and Hannah couldn't help but feel a little smug - oh, to be covered in winner's sweat, adrenalin and liniment!

The fights had finished, but the usual procedure of dispersing the crowd in rapid succession had been averted tonight in favour of continuing festivities at the stadium. Tonight was to be a party night, and Don had reached shallowly into his large pockets and paid for the local band – *Tarantula* – to entertain. There was to be music, dancing and drinking into the wee small hours! Only there wasn't - because Don lacked vigour in his promotional techniques, and even Mel's feisty attempts seemed to have been quashed, "Oh no!" she said, "They're all leaving! I *knew* this would happen, I kept telling Don…"   Shaking her head, she rushed off to the microphone booth in a last attempt to lure the crowds back in, "Guys! Guys! No need to leave just yet, we have live music from Tarantula! Yes, live music, and the bar is open!!" But no one was listening, they'd all gathered their things and were trudging off in a slow stream – miffed at the poor display that had been put on, having hoped for a more lasting impression of the great Saolek.

After a few minutes the stadium had almost completely cleared, leaving behind just a few scattered people. The band appeared and struck up their merry sound, grinning away as always despite a meagre audience. The bass player flashed his teeth at Hannah, and the others followed suit. Hannah, Mel and Faa stood to the side, chatting and drinking free vodka. The Thai boxers hung about nearby, and a table of animated local boys sat around a table whilst Lek and the other staff awkwardly loitered. No one was going anywhere – there was the music of the night to get through! Creedence Clearwater Revival's 'Bad Moon Rising' started up and Hannah got to it, lazily swaying her shoulders and moving her feet rhythmically. A few Thai men waltzed in and joined her – displaying physicality was never taboo on the dancefloor - the promoter jumping up and down like a forest creature, his arms high in the air and his hands in bird-like motion.

Tee joined her - although not one for dancing, he wanted to be near her now that he was happily drunk as a skunk. She put her arms around him warmly and he smiled into her face, before suddenly declaring, "Have girlfriend! Have girlfriend - England!"

Whaaaaaaaat? The music was loud, and the vodka was strong.

"Have girlfriend, baby, England!" he attempted again, successfully this time. "Oohhhhhhhh," nodded Hannah in understanding; he seemed to be implying that their imminent love affair could not take place due to his having a 20-year-old girlfriend back in England that he had knocked-up. Hannah didn't really care – she liked Tee, but she would never want to get seriously involved with him.

"Never mind, never mind!" she said kindly, stroking his arms. Mel glared at them – Tee and her did not see eye to eye, and it was likely Mel knew of his girlfriend. The boys on the back table stood up and started a snakey folk-dance: rhythmic, joyful and embracing the fun which Hannah loved - she hadn't had a good boogie since she got here, and now the vodka had brought her spirits up and she had Thai men to effeminately dance with. She hopped over to the table of boys and tried to pull them over to the dance floor, but immediately they tried to sit back down again, scared of the heathen blonde! Tee appeared at Hannah's side and quietly instructed her *That's enough now* - so Hannah went back to the bar, dancing all the while and putting on a show with all eyes on her and Mel taking snaps. Someone she hadn't noticed before approached the furore, jigging awkwardly. He held her hands briefly, saying, "Good, good!" then disappeared off as she too skipped away for more dancing.

After five or six songs, there was no denying a serious sweat, and it seemed that *Tarantula* had sung their piece, so nods all round signalled that they could move on. Faa was in a sunny mood indeed – her heroic boyfriend had won his fight - and they danced away from the limelight, sweetly and subtly. As the remainers made moves towards the exit to clamber on motorbikes for the onward adventure, Hannah watched Faa and her love leave arm-in-arm - his hand reaching down affectionately to tweak her bottom as they offed.

I wonder if he knows yet? she thought. They looked so happy together - they *were* happy together – so why should a gender issue spoil their chemistry? Hannah passed Tee near the exit, who was still standing, *just*, but swaying from side-to-side. He grabbed Hannah, "Where you go? I come with you! Have girlfriend, but no one take care of me! WHO TAKE CARE OF ME?" He motioned to his heart weakly, almost crying. *No one has to take care of you, you're 36 years old!* Hannah thought. And what about the poor girl and child at home? Who was taking care of *them*?

16. The After Party

Hannah walked over to the motorbikes which were parked on the turf outside. Mel was her only option, so with reticence on she climbed. The fleet of motorbikes whizzed along - some more wobbly than others – overtaking each other in random chaos as the road bent: farangs whooping on the back, Thais smiling as their sleek black hair flew in the wind. To Charlie Chang's, a concrete monstrosity a few kilometres away, for the after-party. Hannah hadn't ever ventured this far after dark and she was apprehensive at what she might find, but as Mel parked up haphazardly with her wheels skidding on the gravel, Hannah's worries were expelled. It turned out it was just a Thai bar filled with the previous occupants of the stadium plus a few bargirls and a prostitute she recognised from her little village, giving her a wave. You could sit outside and stare at the road rather than the dubious goings-on in the interior. Yet stare at the road she needed not - outside was buzzing with frivolity. She took a seat with Mel, Kam and a couple of gothy Thais who smiled and chatted to her in expert English. Nearby sat Faa and her heroic boyfriend, and all was jovial, chaotic, and very, very drunken.

Hannah felt happy – *everyone* was happy - merry and flirting, laughing around and taking it in turns to fetch random drinks for whoever wanted them. It had been a great night which was rapidly swirling into an intoxicated haze.

Mel sat fixated on the shifty Kam to her right, eyeing him up like an owl possessed. The story went that Kam would return to his hometown tomorrow in the far Northeast of Thailand, an area known as Esarn, from where Uncle Lung-Lung's spicy som tam hailed, and that he had asked Mel to accompany him. The whole situation smelt more than a bit fishy, and Hannah couldn't believe that Mel was seriously contemplating such a dodgy pilgrimage, so as soon as Kam disappeared to act on one shady deed or another, Hannah gave her a talking-to.

"Are you really going to go to the middle of nowhere with him? He's probably after your money and could well have a few kids and wives stashed away! The Thai countryside is quite remote – are you *sure* you want to go?"

Hannah's friend had visited Esarn with his boyfriend a few years ago, and it sounded pretty hairy – all goats and no comfort-snacks – certainly no wi-fi for Mel as she tapped away at her laptop. The thought of Mel in rural Thailand caused Hannah's mouth to break into a wicked grin, snapshots of her horrified in the arse-end of nowhere.

Yet Hannah's words made no dent, and when Kam returned from his 'errand', again Mel sat staring unflinchingly at him, boring her eyes of steel into his addled brain. In an attempt to lighten the mood, Kam leant over and pecked her lightly on the cheek, then got up to leave.

Hannah's eyes had turned towards the bar where a ruckus of some sort was unfolding – she could see manly arms pushing at a woman and hear raised voices - a shriek. As she tried to work out what was going on, the commotion suddenly died down and a darker mood enshrouded the bar. Out of this sinister calm came a hand on Hannah's shoulder: the hand was shaking. She turned to find Faa's beautiful face distorted with tears and emotion springing from her furrowed brow, as she panted and sobbed audibly in panic and despair.

They moved quickly over to a bench in the shadows and Faa recounted at speed, "A girl from the bar! She knows me from my hometown! She told him about...*me*! He angry! He VERY angry!" she cried some more, "SEE! Life for a ladyboy is hard!"

Hannah looked back towards the bar. The man of whom they spoke was bent over, pulling a plastic bag full of money out of his pocket and loudly demanding more beer. He staggered about, downed the beer, then ran to a nearby bush to throw up. The news had hit hard: his family had taken Faa on holiday, he was so into her - but now...now what? Faa wasn't a 'real' woman?! Betrayal and shock took its toll, Hannah wasn't sure whether to try and appease him. A gaggle of girls had gathered around Faa continuing to comfort her, and Hannah felt the urge to at least *try* and talk to him - she could try to show some understanding, or even explain Faa's side of the story a little?

She walked over with purpose and stopped just a few metres in front of him. She opened her mouth slightly then implored gently, "I know it's not easy, but Faa is my friend. She-"

"I don't know you! I'm sure you're very nice but please! Go away!"

He made his point well and she left - still relieved to have said *something,* just to reach out and try to bridge the gap between them. Back at the table people had rearranged themselves. It was getting late and the mood more relaxed, signalling the close of the evening. As she walked back from the bar, she could see someone sitting in her place. Impulsively she walked straight towards him, smiling ear-to-ear, him smiling back with equal vigour, magnetism drawing her in ever closer. At first she thought she recognised him as a Thai friend from the gym, but as she got nearer she saw a face she barely knew – it was the guy from earlier who'd applauded her dancing! Though she didn't know him she felt an instinctive trust – he must work at the gym – and he sat and beckoned her towards him, though she needed no encouragement. They smiled into each other's faces as she took a place on his lap – the move was automatic, there seemed a forcefield pulsating around them keeping everyone else out, they were drawn together with an irresistible, impenetrable magnetism. His face was beautiful and she continued to smile into it. He put his arms around her, a little bashfully.

"Hello," she said alluringly.

"Hello," he replied in a deep, gruff tone, "My name Kit!"

"Hannah," drooled Hannah. With her arms around his neck, they continued beaming.

"Where you go now?" he asked.

"Don't know," she said. Suddenly he broke the spell between, as he jerked his head away from her, "You and Tee - you and Tee?"

"He has a girlfriend in England," spoke Hannah, undeterred.

"I know, I know, but you understand him, he understand you!" He used his hands to indicate a closeness.

"I know, but he's no good - he has a girlfriend already!"

"But...but...I no speak English. Me, have wife, baby, gone now. But me, no good!"

"Drinking?" she asked. He nodded.

Drunk or not – no good or not - Hannah didn't care; Kit was gorgeous and she was in his arms. They continued to stare at one another, electrically charged, everything else fading out around them.

Mel plummeted in to destroy the ambience, "Come on chick, we're going!"

Hannah sat upright from her dreamy cocoon, "Where?"

"I don't know!" Mel replied, and hopped back over to flirt with an American, who wasn't looking too keen. Hannah turned to Kit with a quizzical look.

"I think I go gym, you go with your friend," he said. Hannah agreed - maybe it was far enough for tonight and best left here. She hopped up, smiled, and got on the back of Mel's bike. Without looking back, she departed, with Faa on a bike next to them, drunkenly shrieking Rihanna songs into the wind – it seemed she had already recovered from the debacle with the Swedish boxer.

"Where are we going?" asked Hannah.

"For noodles!" said Mel. The two bikes pulled up at Mr Green's – an all-night eatery – but for once it was closed, and the whole road lay in utter darkness.

"Chalerm!" Faa cried, as they continued on the road away from Hannah's room towards town. What the hell was 'Chalerm'? They parked up amongst dozens of motorbikes and strode towards the entrance: *Chalerm Rock Pub*, announced the sign.

The four girls entered stylishly in a party attitude and went inside to find a dark hall with a stage where a band had earlier played. There was a smattering of only 60 or so late-nighters left, sitting round tables sharing whisky and mixers. Hannah had thought the night to be over, but the change of scene unleashed in her a fresh energy. She went straight up to a table of folk she recognised - some 16-year-olds from the gym who made kissy faces at her till she scolded them gently. Her surrogate sons pulled up a stool and gave her whisky, ice and soda from their shared stash, happy to have a hot farang sitting with them. One of her favourite locals – a taxi driver with shaggy hair in skinny jeans and shades - danced on his own nearby to the muted beats of Thai hip-hop, looking cool and getting down with it, digging his feet into the ground. Hannah joined him on the dancefloor – finally off the leash! A funky track started up and Mel walked over to join them. She wasn't a *bad* dancer and could hold a rhythm, but without spontaneity or spunk. Hannah continued dancing, sliding and pulling moves, before they both got tired and it was time for more whisky. They went back to the table where Faa and a few more Thai faces she recognised were having fun. A few whiskies later and a soul classic had Hannah up on the dance floor again. She didn't care that she was on her own and exchanged grooves with other solo dancers. She danced with pure joy, feeling all eyes in the room on her. She glanced back at the table to see yet more faces had arrived - at four in the morning!

98

Wasn't that Kam? Didn't he have to be on a boat in the morning? Who was that guy with him? Was it...yes! Kit from Charlie Chang's! Hannah flashed him a quick smile which he took as a go-ahead, and he shyly bopped his way over to her with a strange dance - a high school step-tap with Muay Thai arms!

He had only to perform this awkward display for a moment, because as soon as he reached her, he grabbed her and planted his succulent lips onto her face. She kissed him back, but it was *so* embarrassing – even after all the whisky - so she led him back to the table where he put his arms around her waist, as if still at the high school disco, and she stood awkwardly waiting to be jibed by the rest of the gang. Yet no jibes came - instead Faa's friend clapping and whooping in excitement whilst taking photos! Kam sat quietly and still, and before long everyone was too drunk for anything more.

"Shall we go?" asked Mel.

"Yep!" chimed Hannah - better to call it a night when you were still having fun and could make it home unassisted.

She turned to her fancy man, "I'm going now!" He looked hurt and panicked and followed her outside. He remained by her side as Mel fetched the bike.

"You not come with me now, okay?" Hannah said.

"Yes but...where you go?"

"I go home. I see you soon," he looked disappointed, "You train me, okay?"

Kit's face lit up - she had clinched the deal; first he had snogged her face off on the dancefloor, and now her official trainer!

She left, quickly. Mel was even wobblier on the bike than usual, and blurted at Hannah over her shoulder as they rode, "Kam only came because Kit was so drunk! Don sent Kam to look after him!" Hannah nodded and grinned – she'd had such a brilliant night: when was the last time someone had danced over to her to go in for a high school snog? It had been a while, that was for sure!

At the top of the dark track leading to the village, Mel stopped, "I won't take you down...I'm worried about my leg – *you* know..."

Even though it was gone four in the morning and the bushes held creepy secrets, Hannah didn't care - if she died tonight she would die happy – and the whisky had given her a delicious bravado. She made it home and turned out the light, passing out into a heavy sleep.

17. After the Party

She cautiously opened one eye and checked the time – 9ish, acceptable - she could snooze later. Time to assess her hangover: not tooooooo bad. She rolled off the bed and onto her feet to use the toilet, and sitting there she didn't feel so bad – no headache *as such*, but everything seemed a bit bleary – *still drunk*, she thought, and *hungry*.

She boldly shoved on her swamp pants and vest and went to the lobby to see if Mama and Papa were still serving breakfast. She was slightly afraid of being reprimanded by the stern Mama, ever since the time she had lost her keys after playing with the jungle boys on the beach. Mama had come out of the darkness like a spectre, with fierce, wide eyes, shrilling: "YOU'RE DRUNK!" Hannah had, in fact, been smoking bamboo bongs.

In the lobby now, she ordered breakfast and sat down as quickly as possible. The hotel was busy, so Mama paid little attention to her disposition. Hannah sat looking at her fry-up - she could swear the eggs were looking back at her – she let out a short, maniacal laugh before digging in.

She wrote a ditty about her night on Facebook – the river-dancing, the whisky, the Muay Thai and motorbikes - and saw a message from Mel. They chatted back and forth about last night - Mel jibing Hannah about snogging on the dancefloor, and Hannah jibing back about Mel's mooning eyes over Kam. It was good fun at first but Mel started to change tack, talking about how much fun it was at the gym today and how she had knocked over a moped whilst talking to Kit. Hannah's curiosity grew: she was being sucked in by what she might be missing and she hated that feeling. Jealous of Mel's position close to her new man in the heart of the Muay Thai world, trickling snippets of information but never quite enough, Hannah was hooked. Mel continued to attempt to lure Hannah to the gym – claiming that everyone was still drunk and it would be funny - but Hannah had other ideas. Training could be fun, but it wasn't 'funny' to her – she was there to learn; not to loon about.

'Anyway, Kit says he's leaving tomorrow to see his daughter, so there's no need to be paranoid,' wrote Mel.

Oh, thought Hannah flatly, *Oh well, he can't speak English, and we did decide that it was best not to go there, but what a pity to waste such attraction and magnetism! Not to be continued further, just a harmless bit of fun: time to move on.*

But they had been so *drawn* together, surely there was more to their story? Back to Krabi he would go to see his daughter - the romantic image of the doting father presenting even further appeal. It hadn't felt like a one-off last night, and he'd agreed to train with her - he couldn't do that from a remote distance! Hannah reminded herself not to trust Mel's words – to just read them lightly then dismiss them, she still hadn't earned her trust.

Hannah's delirium increased as the day went on. The aftermath of a romantic frisson rolled within her and her mood had uplifted with the dose of serotonin from the high school kissing - a welcome tonic from her constant fretting over writer's block. It was something else to waste her time on - a beautiful Muay Thai man. She lolloped about on her bed, allowing herself to dream. Kit didn't seem like the other two-timers; he seemed like a simple man with a kind heart and sense of humour with a mature head on his shoulders. Genuine and traditional - no playboy, no *jao chu* - not the type to play games or be deceptive, although of course she didn't really know him. He must be better than the sly Kam, stringing Mel along for her doughy thighs and money.

Kit...

At nightfall she drifted into semi-conscious sleep, hazy images of a beautiful, smiling brown face swirling before her closed eyes, quiet flutters in her heart at what she might find when she went training tomorrow, holding on to the hope that he hadn't yet 'gone'.

* * *

The following afternoon she was rejuvenated and ready for action. A tuk-tuk driver offered her a free ride to the gym, and she did her best to hold a conversation in Thai with him in exchange for the lift. She walked the last part of the track, letting him go on his way. The gym dogs danced up to greet her as she turned the final corner down to the corrugated building in which she loved to box.

The gym was busy and roaring hot, and she glanced discreetly about her for the subject of her desire – perhaps he'd gone to Krabi to see his daughter after all. As she passed the ring Squishy Nose gave her a sleazy nod as usual and she marched briskly to a tyre to warm up. Mel must have spotted her from the office, and rushed out at once to greet her, standing claustrophobically close to her as Hannah continued to bounce. She exchanged a brief pleasantry but wasn't going to let Mel stop her from training.

Then, from the back of the gym where the trainers ate together and showered, strode a familiar figure – a short, almost stout figure, a man proud of who he was and of his work – Kit. Hannah tried to dumb down her delight as he marched masterfully to the ring to hold pads and instruct, and she went over to the bags to practise her technique where she could still watch him.

As he turned sharply to demonstrate a move, she caught his eye and from his focused face a sunbeam shone through just for a moment. She was happy, she was dreamy – she was sweaty - and now it was her turn. Kit made himself available to train her – no more cutting her legs on Squishy's evil pads, and he nodded at her to come and join him.

"Kaaaa!" she said in thanks.

With shy looks between them – her coy behaviour surprising even her – they set to training, moving swiftly without intermission. She saw faces watching her as she flew – instructors and boxers resting against ring corners - taking in not only her powerful roundhouse kicks but the chemistry between them.

In-between rounds she drank water hungrily from the cooler, going outside in the hot afternoon sun to pour some over her head – her whole body in fact - seeing as she was soaked through already. Then returning to her man, his eyes encouraging and full of optimism.

When three rounds were over Hannah thanked him politely in Thai and bowed out of the ring through the ropes - women weren't permitted to go over them. As she stretched down on the mats a shadowy figure appeared, looming over her - Mel. Hannah had seen her skulking around the ring earlier, her eyes narrowed in blatant envy, staring at her training before quickly scuttling out of eye-shot, back to her desk.

"Hiya!" said Mel with a fake lightness.

"Heeeey!" Hannah was tired out but buzzing.

"How was training?" asked Mel with pursed lips.

"Fantastic!!"

"What you doing now?"

Hannah looked back over her shoulder at Kit instinctively, unable to help herself, "Erm, I don't know!"

"Come back to mine? We can have tea and gossip, then go for Esarn food?"

"Okay!" agreed Hannah. She had half-planned this likely occurrence, knowing that Mel would be feverish for gossip, so she had packed her best swamp-pants and vest in her training bag. Mel had a hot shower, tea, and access to Kit. Hannah was aware that her two-faced behaviour would likely bring no karmic reward, but it was all she had to work with right now. Mel would get her fill, feeding off Hannah's mind like a parasite. They traipsed back to Mel's bungalow - just a little way up the hill, and halfway Mel's face suddenly turned from a persevering bravado to sorrowful mourning, "It's Kam!" she gasped, "He's gone!" She grabbed Hannah in an embrace that was hard to escape before entering

105

Mel's small abode. Hannah filled the kettle and they sat on the floor. "He's gone! I knew he was going back to Esarn - but it's true, it's all true!! Everything everyone said about him - he *does* have a wife and child! He wanted to take me with him, and Faa told me he was going to stash me at his sister's house!"

They sat, Hannah nodding throughout Mel's heartbreak saga, "What a cunt!" she offered, "How horrible! Smuggle you to Esarn and hide you in someone else's house!"

Hannah continued to console Mel over tea. She did feel a *bit* sorry for her – but it was closer to pity. At least Kam had gone now and Mel could lick her wounds alone.

"Come on," suggested Hannah, "Let's go to the beach!"

"I don't usually go there at this time of day!"

"Come on, it's sunset - you need to sit and have a good think."

So off they went on Mel's motorbike. As they rounded the corner Hannah turned to see Kit still training his students – he could wait for later.

The girls turned down the track that led to the beach. Ramshackle scenery surrounded them – a bar that had seen better days jutting out onto a rocky edge. Boulders rose out of the sea, which lapped rhythmically to the going down of the sun. Hannah plonked Mel down on a rock then walked along the shore, taking in the fresh breeze and pink panorama.

As the sky began to darken and the cicadas commenced their song, the girls turned and looked at each other – it was time to go. Silently they walked back together to the motorbike and set off in search of som tam and grilled chicken. Hannah felt relief to be somewhere different - this end of the island had a different atmosphere.

"Here," said Mel, and they parked up next to a modest food stand where a couple smiled cheerily as they made dinner for the locals. Hannah walked in, politely greeting the chefs, who nodded back at her. Mel ignored everyone and stomped over to a table, turning her nose up at the mess left by the previous customers.

Still standing, she looked over at the owners expectantly, her impatient gaze fixed and unfaltering, and the woman hurriedly finished mixing together her som tam ingredients and rushed over to wipe the table, uttering a *'sorry, sorry'*. Hannah smiled and said, "Mai ben rai!" – *Never mind!* - but Mel just cleared her throat and sat down heavily on a plastic chair.

They ate grilled chicken and som tam, and Hannah added a barbecued egg for seven baht, Mel following suit. When they were done, they went up to pay. Hannah smiled brightly, reciting in near-perfect Thai that they would like the bill. The man totted up the food and asked for the money.

"Oh, not together!" exclaimed Mel, "Separate, separate, we want to pay separately!" It only amounted to peanuts, but no, they couldn't split it! The man laughed – Hannah's was three baht cheaper. He rummaged around for some change but Hannah waved her arm with a – 'No, no!' - who wanted three baht?

"I'll have it," Mel snapped, the man looking at Hannah in awe at her unwieldy farang friend. Did she really want him to go and search for three baht? Yes, she did.

"I want whisky!" announced Hannah, as they walked off onto the dark road. They crossed over to the '555' store where Hannah went in and joked around with the shopkeeper, whilst Mel sniffed around the aisles looking for bounty. When she reached the till, Hannah was already standing with a bag full of whisky and soda.

Laden with drinks and snacks they zoomed back in the darkness to the Muay Thai gym. Hannah hadn't been there after dark before and was excited to see what went on. Though past seven, some of the more serious students were still sparring with trainers, preparing for their fights on Sunday. It was magical to watch from high up the track, figurines in the bright lights set against the dark sky with its luminescent stars: kicking, moving, clinching, then separating again as they learnt from their masters.

Mel went into her bungalow and brought out some glasses for the whisky, and they sat on the porch. There were no chairs – not even a cushion - so they sat against the wall of the bungalow with their legs stretched out, taking in the night scene with its swaying palms and astronomical sky, pleasantly and in silence. Mel took a whisky, and soon the girls loosened up and started to laugh and joke about the Kam debacle. Mel put her music on and demonstrated some unconvincing African dancing she had learnt from her former lover, Kwame. She told stories of how her exes were deeply in love with her but it could never work out for one reason or another:

English being their second language, for example - and Mel unable to speak any other.

They topped up their glasses and opened up the snacks, Mel near-inhaling them, and as the night continued Hannah started to turn her attention away from Bungalow Six and towards the gym - where training had finished and a certain someone was settling down for the evening. So close and yet...

Quietly Thai boxers emerged from their shared quarters onto their porches for a daily digest, sharing tiny shot-glasses of local booze and chatting away over life's discrepancies: passing the night away *sabai sabai* – relaxed, happy and chilled - and sleepy after a hard day's work.

Mel didn't seem to notice Hannah's 'meercat' behaviour - she was too busy staring into space in heart-wrenching self-pity, as she dreamed about what should have been with her sweetheart; the now-departed Kam. Hannah was becoming twitchy - where was Kit and what was he doing? She ached to be near his smooth brown skin in the night-time, and she needed to know him.

"What do you think the boys are up to?" she chanced.

"Boys?" balked Mel.

"Yeah...you know...Kit!" she grinned sheepishly.

"Oh, they'll just be at their bungalow - he doesn't go out, in fact, I've only *ever* seen him here!"

"Do you ever drink with them?"

"No not really, I mean, at the stadium sometimes on a Sunday..."

Could Mel not reach the frequency of Hannah's deafening hints? She ached to see him, and the sooner, the better.

"I'd like to see him," she finally admitted.

"Well, why don't you go down there?"

"I feel a bit...awkward," Hannah uttered, awkwardly.

"Well, how else are you going to see him?"

"I suppose I could take him down a whisky and soda?" she proposed, knowing that Thais would usually receive any gift humbly and gracefully.

"Yeah! Why not?! That could work!"

Hannah stalled for a few more moments, but with a slug of whisky for courage she prepared her love a glass of grog and made her way down to Bungalow One. She trod carefully – the ground was uneven with a jungle feel – she carefully placed one foot in front of the other for fear of making noise, falling or spilling the whisky. She passed Bungalow Five, Four, and now she was nearing and her heart was racing – she didn't get why she was quite so nervous - she'd approached men before - but had she approached a Thai man in the dark brandishing whisky? A bush provided momentarily relief from her wobbling and she stopped for a second, controlling her heartbeat. When she commenced the final descent, she recited aloud, "Trouble! Trouble! You're inviting trouble!"

So well-behaved this whole time, but about to offer her head to the lion's mouth. She spotted the lion a few metres away, sitting on a brightly lit porch with a lanky friend. She walked straight up and he turned his head, smiling widely at her and shifting sideways to make space for her as she grinned back,

110

then reaching out his arm in invitation. She sat on the cold tiles next to him and he put his arm around her reassuringly. She presented to him the whisky, which he set down between them for all of them to share.

"Hello," he said.

"Hi."

"Okay?"

"Yes."

The lanky man peered at her scrutinously, "What you doing?" he asked, in a creepy, low English tone.

"Drinking whisky with Mel!" she said, feeling quite nervous.

"Mel," he said.

She thought she'd seen his build before, lurking at the back of the stadium.

"Okay, we come in a minute or two, come have a drink with you and Mel, yeah?"

"Er... okay!" It seemed like a reasonable plan.

"I like Mel," he boomed, "But I not a *bad* man, want to take it step by step, little by little, friends first, you know what I mean?"

"Oh," Hannah responded, this being a forceful introduction and far from the 'little by little' of which he spoke: He seemed hungry for flesh, but at Kit's side she felt completely safe.

She made it quietly back to Mel's bungalow, to find her still staring into space in melodrama, contemplating her lost love.

Hannah grinned, "They're coming up!"

"Who?" asked Mel in alarm.

"Kit, Kit and that other one...don't know his name. He's lanky and a bit creepy."

"Ake?" suggested Mel.

"Yeah, I think he likes you, he kept talking about 'step by step' - a bit weird."

"Hmmm," Mel voiced, contemplating the new attention.

They sat in anticipation, five minutes turning into fifteen, when a sudden movement arose from the bushes: Here came the boys!

Mel and Hannah shuffled about making room for them to sit, and they formed a circle, sharing whisky and Mel's sugary snacks. Kit politely accepted a biscuit, chuckling to himself.

"Not like sweet!" Ake explained: a savoury mouth, just like Hannah's.

They settled down to more comfortable lounging arrangements. Kit pulled Hannah over onto her back and rested his head on her lower stomach – his arms resting on her muscly legs in a reversal of gender roles. The carefree pair smiled, their heads turned towards the stars, the murmuring of Mel and Ake providing background sounds for their nestling. It felt good to cradle him. He squeezed her thighs and turned cheekily to her, "You – poochai! Me - pooying!" *You are the man and I am the woman!*

She grinned back, feeling completely at ease. Forgotten feelings roused in her from long-gone times, releasing happy hormones – to hold and be held: had the west forgotten such a thing?

Hours passed. They finished the whisky, the night sky adorning a velvet-black canopy above them. Mel and Ake played chaperones to Hannah and Kit, still quietly intertwined, smiling up at the moon which rose high above the gym and the dark and silent trees.

It was nearing the hour of sleep, and the vibe shifted to a more practical tempo as all parties brushed themselves down and collected the glasses and leftovers up in preparation for bed. Ake leaned towards Mel and rasped salaciously.

"Want to take it step by step, little by little!"

Tempted by his crude allure but still smarting from Kam's fresh surface-wounds, Mel dismissed Ake and turned to grin at the lovers, before winking and disappearing inside her room, closing the door behind her. Hannah and Kit were now alone in the semi-darkness, already used to each other's bodies from the long caress. The presence of silence drifted in - but not for long - as Kit moved up against a pillar and pulled Hannah onto his lap. He commanded her physically, pulling her astride his lap and arranging her arms around his neck. She was hesitant and coy from the forcefulness of his actions, but she turned to look at him and he kissed her as quickly and frantically as the night before - his full lips succulent and stinging as their mouths joined. She wanted to take them in all night, tasting their fresh, wet juiciness, a tongue or two. She attempted to calm the pace to a more tender, seductive tempo but there was no slowing his desire. After a minute or so, he was grabbing at her body: up and under her vest he exposed her tits to the moon. Alarmed, she made another attempt to quench his fire - who knew what prying eyes were watching from the jungle surrounds.

"No," she urged softly, "Not here! Cannot!"

He looked up at her, "Why? You come with me!"

"Where?"

"Gym - room above gym - we go there."

She was not up for that, and the quick change from idyllic, seductive caress to frantic grope rang alarm bells. She didn't want this dreamy night to end with a dirty baptism in a filthy back room. With more force this time she firmly prised him off of her, "Not tonight, okay?"

"Okay," he muttered breathlessly, still full of fire. Together they stood up: him breathing heavily, his face open and wanting. He pushed Hannah to the side of Mel's bungalow and again the entanglement began - her vest up, exposing her body to glare white in the shining moonlight, his hands wandering rapidly under her waistband, attempting to venture further south.

She stopped him, grabbing his hands and pulling them away. Firmly, like a schoolteacher she reprimanded, "Not now, okay?"

Indicating their open surrounds, she continued, "People can see! Not here! Not now!" She knew that the moment she gave his hands permission to wander that she wouldn't be able to stop proceedings. Once more he spoke quickly, his face close to hers, imploring her to go to the back room for a bunk-up. Swiftly Hannah administered a final kiss, grasped his smooth hands and bid him goodnight, then watched his exit back to Bungalow One.

Flustered from this erotic rollercoaster and giddy from the whisky, pleasantly tired and smiling she quietly opened Mel's door and tip-toed into the room.

"Alright?" a familiar voice chirped from the darkness.

"Yeah," sighed Hannah contentedly, flunking onto the bed next to Mel.

"Been snoggin' ya boyfriend?"

114

"Yeaaaaaah," said Hannah, "He was trying for more than that!"

"Good kisser?" asked Mel, adding to the high school jeunesse.

"Mmmn," said Hannah, rolling over. A few more slumber-party style mutterings and the girls lolled into sleep, each in their disparate worlds, till morning.

18. Sunshine on a Rainy Day

BANG BANG!! HAMMER HAMMER!! DRRIIIIIIIIIILLLLLLLLL!! screeched the construction site: '*Don's Condominium! Come and see today! 29 new apartments in jungle setting! Only 1.9 million baht per condo*' bragged the posters.

Hannah had forgotten that Don was building a monstrous concrete high-rise, for rich and foolish farangs, adjacent to the gym. At 7am, Burmese workers in skinny jeans piled in and clambered up the incomplete steps over menacing iron girders and debris. They brought with them everything they needed for the long, scorching day: cotton wide-brimmed hats to protect them from the sun, flasks of hot tea and food in metal containers: fuel to work like horses for baht to feed their families.

"Ohhhh!" groaned Hannah, rolling over and stuffing her face into a pillow to muffle the sounds.

"Morning!" shrilled Mel, half-naked. She was up and out of bed, bright-faced, showered and now getting dressed.

"What are you *doing*?" Hannah asked with half-closed eyes, catching a glimpse of her creased reflection in the mirror.

"Off to work!"

"But...it's so *early*!"

Mel just shrugged and, not wanting to be left in the noisy den, Hannah rolled off the bed - still in last night's attire - shoved on her sunglasses and then bolted off. With lightning speed, she marched up the hill and away; not turning back to look for her beloved in the fear that he would see last night's dinner in this morning's bin.

She tripped and traipsed along the path and emerging out of doziness found it a novelty to be out in the sun so early. Everything looked so different in the subtle morning light - and though groggy and grumpy at the early rise her disposition was light and there danced a spring in her step: the flippant spring of a new love affair fluttering inside her. She tried to put these clichéd feelings aside but they remained, effervescent in the sunlight.

Love songs swam round and round her delirious head: she had only kissed a Thai guy, and he couldn't even speak English, and yet somehow her feet sprang lightly from the ground. She passed the French Bakery that Mel was always scoffing about but didn't stop along the way. Instead, she went straight back to Mama and Papa's – who hadn't seemed to notice her overnight absence.

Her passport lay dishevelled amongst her things and reality presented itself brashly: her visa would expire in a week and her rent was up too - a plan was needed. Lying on her bed procrastinating didn't produce fruit, so she showered, changed and headed out into the bright sunshine, balancing along the hardened clay ridge in her bare feet to prevent slipping into the sludge below.

She called in on Jeab, who was sitting with her legs stretched out in front of her, reading a book and mopping her brow with a wet flannel. Hannah chose a strawberry yoghurt drink and sat behind the counter with her. Across the path she could see Pom-pooey practising his fire dancing.

"Got to go to Krabi," said Hannah, "Need a visa extension!"

"Oh easy!" said Jeab, "Just call these people, they will take you there."

As they candidly chatted, they decided that Hannah should start her new role as shop-girl on her return. She left the Mart and continued up to the road in search of eats. At Kanchana's Kitchen she sat in a bamboo stand watching the world go by, supping on her complimentary iced water. Approaching from the right was Jen on her powerful motorbike, whizzing round the bend with expert precision. Hannah waved her arms about, frantically grinning, and Jen stopped, dismounted, walked in and threw herself on the seat opposite, "I'm in *such* a mood, my boyfriend Mon is on the booze again, and we've been arguing all day. I can't handle it!"

Hannah replied with happy squeaks.

"What's up with you, Missy?"

"Nothing," Hannah replied with a wry smile, "Just been having a bit of fun – I saw that guy..."

"The Thai one?"

"Yeah."

"Did you sleep with him?"

"NOOOO!"

Hannah recounted the high school disco happenings of the night before with aplomb, excited to share her secrets with an ally. Her food arrived and Jen stared at it enviously. She didn't eat until she was absolutely about to drop - a manageable eating disorder designed to avoid exercise of any kind - which no-doubt couldn't help her constant fevers and rabies repercussions.

"I've got to go to Krabi for my visa extension," garbled Hannah between mouthfuls.

"When?"

"Friday."

"I'm gonna be there Friday!"

Jen had a teaching job three days a week in Krabi, which she had taken to get respite from her twisted relationship and the confines of Koh Talay - and to fuel the hope that she might one day meet a farang to sweep her off her feet and make things less complicated.

"Stay with me at my place! Have a little holiday - oh go on! IT WILL BE FUN! I need some entertainment!"

A place to stay and a personal guide who spoke fluent Thai – perfect.

19. Packing Up and Shipping Out

Thursday night found her surrounded by belongings in her room at Mama and Papa's Palace. It was time to move on – first to Krabi - and then to a new abode. Mama and Papa's had served her well, but she longed for independence – not having to sneak through the lobby at night after a few too many whiskies. She still wanted to stay near the village - her new job in the shop would start soon and she was in with the local folk. Yet she had no idea about accommodation in the area that didn't have rats or wasn't vastly overpriced.

She had arranged to stash her stuff at the gym with Mel whilst she was away - of course Jen was a much better friend, but her boyfriend had the unpleasant habit of selling foreigner's belongings for moonshine.

Her optimism for the sojourn to Krabi made packing easier and, as Mel would pick her up from the roadside later, she could afford to shove her stuff in any which way. She stopped and hovered at the plastic washbowl she had carried back from the port: it may have been cheap but had come in so useful, and she had grown attached to her daily ritual of rinsing out her smalls then hanging them out to dry on her balcony. It was *her* washbowl, and with no real home here possessions meant more - it was coming with her!

After a last lay on her old bed, she gathered the strength and mounted the bags upon herself like a donkey. She crooned a sweet goodbye to Mama and Papa – an *au revoir* - and traipsed up to the road with a cumbersome yet satisfying struggle. Mel was to pick her up from Reggae Reggae Bar and take her to the gym to stash her stuff, then they'd go for Esarn food nearby.

Hannah plonked herself down on a platform at Reggae Reggae Bar, and prised the bags off her laden body. A sweet jungle boy came and sat with her, strumming sweet love songs as she explained in her best Thai that she was going to Krabi for a while. He nodded and continued to strum. Mel was taking her time and Hannah was getting hungry, but she put her stomach on hold and enjoyed her present company.

Mel's unwieldy form eventually emerged, wobbling from the darkness. She walked up to Hannah briskly, keys a-jangling, and barked an over-loud "Hello!"

Kristine, the owner, bid Hannah a warm farewell and Hannah nodded at Mel to introduce herself, "Hi," she clipped, stiffy, "So you own this place, do you?"

"Yes!" Kristine replied with a stony stare.

"Off we go then – I'm starving!" diffused Hannah. She turned to nod at the lovely jungle boy then hoicked all her belongings single-handedly onto Mel's bike.

The ride was slow: not only were they weighed down and it was dark, but Mel's driving skills required patience at the best of times. Still, after twenty minutes or so they made it to the gym.

Hannah niftily grabbed her stuff and they went to Bungalow Six, where they set about tucking her things way down the side of the bed, her trainers in the cupboard and the washbowl in the bathroom. Hannah was grateful that her things would be safe.

Straight back out for food - but no barbecued eggs this time - instead to a quiet stand where a young couple tended to noodles and pork, long beans and spices. After soup, chicken and sticky rice they went back to Mel's bungalow for a cup of tea and a chat, then Hannah would be on her way – off on her little adventure.

In the room they chatted about this and that; Mel seemed to be over Kam and was mentioning Ake a fair bit. Outside on the porch there was a stirring, so they went outside, and out of the darkness a spritely figure was bounding up to the bungalow – Kit - come to see her of his own accord, wearing nothing but a pair of lurid Bermuda shorts.

"I hear your voice! I come see you! I sleeping! Then I hear you!" he beamed and panted. Intuitively they walked towards each other, meeting in front of the door and embracing warmly, holding onto each other's wrists and gazing at each other.

"Why you not come train?" he asked, "Me no good?"

"No - you good!" she said, "Me no good!"

In honesty, she'd been doing other things, and although Muay Thai was her great passion, she didn't train every day - partly to save her from injury – and there was no use trying to explain herself in the limited language they shared.

Instead, they sat, and Ake bounded over to join them when he saw them settling, "Anyone want anything from *Seven*?" darting his eyes about like a lemur before hurtling off on his motorbike. Ten minutes later he was back, with whisky and snacks.

"Oh, just a little bit of whisky for me," said Hannah, "I have to go away in the morning." She said the last part slowly, with weight, so that Kit might notice.

"Where you go?" he immediately demanded, panting in slight panic.

"To extend my visa!" said Hannah, "I'll go to Krabi for two or three days, I don't know."

Kit nodded in understanding, "When you come back?"

"Don't know," she said kindly, smiling with mischief in her eyes. *Keep the intrigue alive...*

The foursome sat: Kit and Hannah entwined and fooling around, Ake translating and Mel detached - up against the wall. Ake continued, "He not normally go with farang, but he like you!"

Hannah narrowed her eyes - he was choosing his words too carefully. Suddenly, Ake blurted out, "You not trust me!!"

"No! I not trust you!" Hannah confirmed, "But it's good that I can tell you!"

Ake's lanky frame sloped over to the wall and loomed over Mel. He closed in on her, offering her slimy beef-balls on a stick before plopping them into her wanton mouth.

Hannah's man was in her arms, skin smoother than satin. Letting go felt impossible, but leaving was imminent. They started to rouse beneath the stars, and Kit suddenly stood up abruptly, rushed down to his bungalow and returned with an ancient Thai-English dictionary. Together with Hannah's *Lonely Planet* phrasebook they attempted to communicate. Kit fumbled through his aging volume and pointed out a

sentence: *'I don't want you to go, I will miss you.'*
One wondered what kind of dictionary it was, and to whom it had belonged previously, but it was sweet all the same.

Missions accomplished, it was already 11pm and she had to be up early. Hannah didn't fancy chancing a ride with Mel, unattractively drunk, but out of the darkness a few students from the gym staggered outwards towards the motorbike parking area. Though stinkingly drunk themselves, they were out to party more, and so Hannah took her chance and approached the biggest, strongest man.

"You're not driving to Yao Beach, are you?"

"Yes we are!"

"Could you give me a lift?"

"Yah sure!"

"Are you drunk?"

"Of course!"

"Can you drive?"

"No problem!"

Drink-driving was the only transport option at this time of night, and at least he looked powerful and sturdy. She looked down at Kit's confused face which seemed to say *'Off so soon? No time for a quick grope around the bike sheds?'* Yet he understood the need to get home, and with a quick embrace she was gone.

It was fun riding with the hunky He-Man blonde, who smelt overpoweringly of Western aftershave. He drove fast, the thrill of speed and his enticing scent a heady mix.

Hannah hopped off at the fitness centre and made her way down the path for the last night in her current home. Salee Mart was still open – Jeab's husband Yim had arrived to collect her and was helping her pack up the postcard stands in a leisurely manner, whilst a stream of drunken travellers purchased their last-minute beer. Hannah decided to pop in to pick up some snacks for her early morning journey. She walked into her favourite shop grinning, with an empty rucksack to pack for her visa trip. Jeab and Yim looked up brightly in unison and Jeab pointed at her, exclaiming loudly, "Look like sea gypsy!!"

Hannah looked down at her crumpled vest and hippy balloon trousers. Jeab was right - these two months had reduced her to a sea-gypsy - but she felt exultant: a vagrant - a gypsy adventurer - buying trashy snacks in the jungle shop at midnight.

20. The Immigrant

In the early morning a gleaming minivan pulled up to Mama and Papa's - who both waved Hannah off joyfully. A good forty minutes of trundling around picking up holidaymakers, then finally reaching the ferry port – whence upon the van boarded a creaking, antiquated vessel that would take them o'er the sea to the mainland. The stink of oil and metal stang the air, and the loud chug of the engine promised not peace but at least progress.

When the cars, vans and motorcycles were parked and the engines dulled, Hannah clambered over the tourists and out of the minivan and hopped out of the sliding door onto the cracked concrete deck. She turned back to see enquiring faces – *should we all get out?* – but slammed the door with speed behind her.

The early morning light radiated through the hills behind, casting white light on the deck. Hannah made her way through the bumper-to-bumper vehicles to the side of the boat - away from the noxious fumes - to join the Thai people, who stood about smoking with cloths covering their heads to prevent heatstroke, or worse still, a tan. Young lovers on motorbikes and Muslim girls in shawls added to the fresco. They glimpsed at her as she approached, but soon ignored as she continued to gaze at the surrounds. The clime was pleasantly cool, and this vignette an unexpected relief from the journey.

Hopping back into the van, they disembarked and started on the highway to Krabi Town. Quaint little houses lined the open road which turned into a concrete jungle. Through an industrial district, hundreds of dishevelled and dirty Thai workers digging up the earth and climbing bamboo scaffold, wiping their foreheads with their shirt-sleeves, their heads covered in wide-brimmed hats. Then signs of a bustling town - food markets and clothes stalls; a post office - teenage boys on bikes running errands or up to no good. The road stretched for miles and the scenery hurtled by: *Pineapples – 3 baht a piece*!

They took a left turn further into the town centre and to the right of them a river stretched out, snaking into the distance. Shiny, happy people chatted at coffee stands and backpackers breakfasted at quaint cafes. Hotels, bookstores and hippy paraphernalia built up the surrounds, and all the while a cool breeze ran through.

The minivan stopped at a small office - it was as far as this driver would take her. Disappointed, Hannah got out and looked around - folk seemed so happy here! Perhaps being in a town was what she needed; though she loved Koh Talay, sometimes the world closed in on her. She thanked the driver warmly and searched about for her next ride. There only seemed to be motorbike-taxis, so she strode up to one, haggled on price, clumsily attached a helmet, mounted the back, and off they drove to the immigration office. The roads were busy and chaotic and she was glad of the helmet, should they collide and be thrown onto the tough, sun-baked concrete at speed. They passed two guitar shops and Hannah gulped greedily with desire, then zoomed past a large school, kids shrieking and laughing at play in their neat uniforms.

She had enjoyed this journey and had forgotten how new experiences - changes not rests - could be the fuel of inspiration, and her writing-mind started to ruminate. A semi-conscious commentary ran though her, a steady torrent of words beginning to flow, and she did her best to store them for later.

She paid the motorbike man with a smile, and he helpfully ushered her to the correct door with vigour before zooming off. Here was the difficult bit – remaining calm when touristic chaos abounded all around. She entered the building, squeezing past panicked and confused people - scrabbling around with incorrect paperwork, scribbling out details with half-inked pens – and the energy entered her. She hadn't quite thought this process through: another 30-day stamp should be easy to get, surely?

A gaggle of farangs crowded around a cramped desk, shoving their forms at a glaring clerk and demanding information, grabbing pens and crossing out errant details. *Forms*: yes, she remembered now! They weren't just going to take her passport and stamp it, for goodness' sake, she had to *apply* to stay in the country.

The woman behind the counter didn't look at her, instead she pointed outside with her arm outstretched, "Fill in form!"

Not wanting to waste any more time, Hannah marched outside, grabbed a form, then plonked herself down on a stone bench in the heat and began to scrawl haphazard inaccuracies on the paper. It wasn't quite clear what they were asking for, and the Thai script was misaligned with the English, so who knew what she should write in 'tambon'? Normally an expert form-filler from her days working in social housing, here she was flummoxed. Presuming everyone else was in the same boat, she continued as best she could. She wasn't *entirely* sure which port she had just come from, or her next port of disembarkation for that matter, but the woman in the office would surely know; she must have had to deal with far worse strung-out lunatics in her time. Hannah's previous optimism for new experiences siphoned its way down the drain, forced by the hand of bureaucracy.

There was no organised queue - order seemed governed by survival of the rudest - and right now she joined the competition! She needed this visa stamp, and AS SOON AS POSSIBLE! As she waited, she snorted sharp exhalations of breath – a hot, sweaty, impatient farang was she.

The woman behind the counter didn't look up as she grabbed Hannah's documents and hurriedly sifted through them, "You have photo?!" she demanded. Hannah's jaw dropped – she'd completely forgotten about that, but the officer said nothing more, leaving Hannah's documents on the counter and turning away from her to continue processing the mound of paperwork in front of her.

Was Hannah supposed to just wait and, if so, for what? Her forms weren't actually 'handed in', and the pile was growing by the second. *Help! I need my visa!* her internal organs cried.

The woman looked up at her, finally, with a stony stare, saying quietly with grave intent,

"Look, I working! See? Not lazy. NOT LAZY! WORKING!!"

After another few minutes, Hannah's mantra of forced calm not taking hold, the woman pointed to a plastic chair above which was a sign, *No have photo please sit here.* So, in front of everyone, in that office, on this sweaty afternoon, Hannah sat for her mugshot -

the other applicants twitching and fidgeting in agitation, glaring at the stupid girl without a photo who was making them wait their turn.

She looked into the camera's lens. The officer said nothing, but the loud electric *zoom* noise confirmed that it was to be very close-up. Hannah submitted, staring placidly with strength at the woman on the other side, who glared back at her with disdainful eyes, taking her time purposely.

Scared that she might not be granted further passage in the country, Hannah rasped, "Thank you," and scuttled over to the waiting area.

Another girl sat down in the executioner's chair. Hannah smiled at her knowingly, as if to say, *'I know how that feels!'* Yet this time, the executioner's air changed entirely and, grinning, she retracted the camera's zoom, chiming, "Smile!"

The woman returned to her desk and inserted the camera's SD card into a strange contraption, and moments later the photographs popped out of a slot. The other girl got hers first.

"Oh GOD! I look AWFUL! That's what not sleeping for three months does to you!" Hannah took a peek – the girl looked fine to her. Hannah now glimpsed at her own picture to be met with a gypsy refugee from the 1970s - as close-up as the camera

131

would allow! The immigration officer had officially won.

"Look at mine!" Hannah shrieked at the other girl.

"You look fine!" said the girl.

Finally, with their forms handed in, it was back to sitting on a bench and waiting.

Hannah and her new compatriot sat chatting in lowered tones. It transpired that the girl lived here, in Krabi, and was dating a Thai boxer! Save for Jen, Hannah hadn't met many girls she got on with since she arrived, and it was a great relief to chatter lyrically and freely about her situation, and to compare notes.

Hannah didn't have any naughty tales, as such, but she could feel herself heading into something. She normally steered clear of relationships back home – preferring a warm equilibrium peppered with affairs – and the other girl said the same; yet somehow, she ended up back in Thailand for a few months each year, and back in the arms of her Muay Thai man.

Time now passed quickly, and at intervals the girls took it in turns to check the 'done' tray. Hannah's came first and, abandoning her new friendship, she rushed outside to phone Jen, who had been teaching at the school nearby.

"Hey girl! How are ya?" drooled Jen casually.

"Okay! Bloody visa office was a bit of a nightmare!"

"Yeah, it always is. I'm just having a coffee, I'll come pick y'up."

And as quick as that, with just enough time to check the new date-stamp in her passport, she was free: for another 30 days, at least…

21. Dr. Flameheart

Jen whizzed up expertly to the pavement, and without word Hannah strode up to her, grinned, sniff-kissed her face, and they were off. Two girls on the road – like Thelma and Louise – and Hannah hoped Brad Pitt would be hers. On the way to Ao Nang beach, where Jen had a condo, they passed more music shops and at Hannah's excitement, Jen parked up at one of them and they went inside. The staff were friendly but had no clue, and the way the beautiful wooden instruments were laid out was more like a museum than a shop. They were a bit pricey, too, so after a few glances and nods they left. Yet as they headed out to the road, Hannah could hear a faint strumming nearby: it seemed to be coming from the coffee shop opposite.

"Hang on a minute," she instructed Jen, and ran over. Inside she found a smiling, laid-back Thai Rasta man, strumming out some tunes.

"Excuse me...Where did you buy that guitar?"

The man stopped playing and put it down. He chuckled and pointed, "Near school! Near school! Turn right, big…!" He made giant circles with his hands.

"Roundabout?" guessed Hannah correctly. Though his directions were vague, she thanked him and took the chance that Jen might know the place.

"He says there's a shop near the school - turn right at the roundabout – can we go?"

"Yeah sure, it's not far!" said Jen, and off they went, seamlessly weaving in and out of the busy traffic, past the bustling school with its kids joyously running riot in the playground. Just a few doors up they could see a few guitars in the window of a small shopfront. Jen pulled on the brakes and they trotted in; perhaps Jen's fluent Thai could help clinch a deal?

Hannah's intention to barter evaporated as she fell in love with all five guitars strung up before her on the wall. She looked with ravenous longing at them, touching their bodywork before gingerly asking to try a few.

Some were shiny, some matt, some a bit plasticky and twangy - which would be hers?

She eliminated a few by their bulk and weight, narrowing her choice down to three: a light blonde number, perfect for Country and Western, a lurid, blue rock demon– *why not? It's Thailand!* - and a shady, sexy number, black splaying into red-gold towards its centre. To be sweet, lurid or sexy? This was the question.

A teenage boy, just in from school, was there to help. He passed her each guitar carefully and watched as she sat on a small, plastic stall and had a strum. Though self-conscious, she needed to not be rash - only to get home and find out that she wasn't in love after all.

The first gave good sound - standard, *sensible* almost. The second felt twangy and out of control. So, to Mr Black and Red-Gold – Dr. Flameheart! Oh yes! He slipped and slid through her hands like satin - so light, so easy to play - his sounds reverberant, bright and clear. A happy chappy with a golden chest who loved being held close to hers – invigorating!

The shop boy knew this guitar was special and looked upset to be letting it go. He took it in his own hands and gave it a last seeing-to – perhaps with regret that he hadn't fully appreciated its beauty before - but always knowing that it would go to someone someday soon...

Jen managed to barter him down to 2000 baht, and Hannah was jubilant. She paid 400 extra for a leather holdall and the girls were back on the bike – this time with their new friend, the flame-thrower. Overjoyed, Hannah giggled and chatted as Jen smiled back at her in the wing-mirror, driving carefully and skilfully away from town and onto the open road.

＊ ＊ ＊

Spectacular scenery panned out to each side of them: the road to Ao Nang a scene of stunning beauty permeating Hannah's every sense. Majestic karst rocks rose from the fertile ground around them, planting her in a land of giants. It was Hannah's first time on the open road on a motorbike - just her, Jen, a bag and her new guitar; a heavenly taste of freedom, hair streaming behind them in the wind.

They were getting nearer, and finally they turned a bend to find civilisation springing up around them. The small apartment Jen rented was in a block owned by the family on the ground floor: dogs, kids, bikes and tour desk included. Hannah was over-courteous on entering but Jen just marched straight in, motioning for Hannah to follow her on a climb to the top floor.

They unlocked the door to find a tiled floor strewn with a chaotic trail of scarves, leather and underwear. A TV sat in the corner, and beyond it a balcony with two chairs. They slung their things on the bed and went outside. It was still a few hours before darkness would huddle in like a warm blanket. Hannah was happy, if a little jaded and sweaty from the visa debacle and day's travelling.

"D'ya want anything?" enquired Jen out of politeness.

"Yeah maybe, what've you got?"

"Ummm, well…there isn't a kettle," she rummaged through the whirring fridge, "Soy milk?" she offered, examining the half-opened bottles for passability.

Out on the balcony they drank the soy milk, and Hannah tentatively plucked on the strings of her new beau – Dr. Flameheart. She felt a little coy - her hands didn't know this instrument yet, and she was out of practise. The balcony overlooked a small courtyard and some other apartment blocks, in the middle a small place cooking up dinner for the locals. After a rest they mused over their next move.

"I don't want to get drunk," said Hannah, "But I wouldn't mind getting out and doing *something.*"

Jen agreed, so they freshened up in idle fashion and, leaving Dr. Flameheart behind, trotted back down the stairwell and onto the bike.

"We could always walk?" suggested Hannah. Jen recoiled her neck: *no one* walked in Thailand! If you had to go somewhere, you did it on *at least* two wheels. Yet after a moment's consideration, she shrugged her shoulders, "Yeah, why not?"

Hannah loved to explore; not the tourist spots or mountains, no, she just liked to wander down unknown paths - her own version of 'off the beaten track' – often into trouble of some kind. There is a lot to be found in the industrial estates of London's East End, just as in the donkey-forests of Kerala.

The two girls walked in single file as occasional bikes hurtled past, staring at the two fair farangs on foot. They headed towards 'town' - wherever that was. Hannah didn't have a clue even in what direction they were facing, having let Jen whisk her about on the bike to get there, and enjoying the wild breeze and scenery too much to notice nor care. The roads they now trod were unremarkable – bushes, an odd corner family-store, brothers lounging about on chairs out front - but after ten minutes or so they came to a junction and turned left to see the mighty ocean!

They followed the road along the coast - still no tourists in sight, just a scattering of Thai families enjoying dusk-lit picnics on the beach. The vibe was different to the microcosmic bubble of Koh Talay, and she supposed that people actually 'lived here', not just there to make money from the tourist trade. Krabi town was nearby, so these must be Thai day-trippers.

As the road continued, the first signs of an area catering for tourists appeared: a cramped row of clothes stalls, restaurants and bars lined the path to fulfil your every desire – pizza, cheap vests, happy hours, yet retaining a flavour of 'real' Thailand with a row of street food stalls opposite. Hannah and Jen sat down at one of them and ordered grilled chicken and som tam. They sat, as the sky grew dark and the cicadas started their song.

It was only supposed to be a little jaunt and Hannah didn't quite feel equipped for night-time: her swamp-pants and vest a key giveaway. Jen pointed across the road to a hideous neon arcade full of bars, discos and night-clubs, and Hannah shook her head at the thought of going in. Jen hovered for a bit, but finally accepted her refusal and they continued on. Hannah suddenly stopped, "What are we doing?"

"Don't know!" Jen replied, "Shall we have a drink and then go back? We'd better get a taxi, it's not that safe here after dark."

"Mmm, okay," Hannah concurred. They'd come all this way, so a quick tipple would mark the occasion nicely. Yet except for the neon lights their options were limited. Without announcement, Jen marched into 7-11, pointed at a bottle of red wine behind the counter, paid and came back outside. They sat together on a low wall and opened the bottle. In front of them, two cheeky kids started a breakdancing show for the tourists and pocket money. Hannah and Jen watched, swigging red wine.

After a while of watching and drinking, the girls got up, polished off the last of the astringent red liquid, and continued their meander. Around the corner was a group of schoolkids, sitting on a wall strumming an old, beaten-up guitar, with just a rubber-band and a screw holding the neck in place, and one string missing. Hannah sat down next to them as they unashamedly bashed out unrecognisable, out-of-tune chords from a dog-eared book, wailing along deliriously in different keys arrhythmically. She reached into the zipper of her crumpled handbag and pulled out her special toy – an electronic guitar-tuner on a key-ring - and proceeded to help them make the sound slightly more melodic. The tuning pegs were rusty and couldn't turn properly, so one boy ran into his parent's shop to fetch a tool, and there they sat, tuning a guitar with a wrench.

As Hannah and the merry band caterwauled away, Jen popped her head into a few shops and chatted with an earnest man holding a monkey. Hannah didn't feel self-conscious of her tatty appearance anymore; the red wine had settled in nicely with the spicy papaya and chicken legs. They continued on their little expedition.

"Can we go to a bar up there?" Jen said, pointing into the darkness, "It's a really cool reggae place."

"Well, I wasn't really going to drink, and I want to check out the Muay Thai round here tomorrow, and...look at me!!"

"Yeah well, I just kinda need to go in there. There's someone I need to see... He kind of did me a favour."

"Right...?" said Hannah, waiting for it to make a little more sense.

"Yeah, well...he's a hitman, and - remember that time I told you about – that time the psycho stalker rammed me up against my friend's doorway?" Hannah nodded - Jen was full of such stories.

"Well, he was basically going to 'sort him out' for me. I had a woman in the shop down the road who I could just call, and then he'd come and...and so...really, I just need to say thank you!"

With no room for protest, off they went. From the outside you could tell that this reggae bar was serious business. Tourists and locals alike sat smoking joints on benches carved from tree trunks, and various shirtless Rasta boys wandered in and out. Inside a commotion sprung up as two fire dancers twirled their sticks with wild abandon. Hannah felt a little out of her depth - at least out of place - in her pyjama pants, like a little girl lost. She tucked herself away inconspicuously whilst Jen weaved in and out of the throng, looking for the hitman. Through the crowd Hannah could see that she had stopped and was talking to a sweet-looking Thai guy with ratty dreads. A rather small man with a slight paunch - was he the one?

Jen and the man moved towards Hannah and she followed their signal and moved towards them to meet in the middle.

"Hannah, this is Mot. Mot – Hannah, a good friend of mine from Koh Talay."

Hannah nodded sweetly with strength. Mot furnished them with extra-strong cocktails – it was hard to say no to a hitman. When he was out of sight Jen took the opportunity to explain a bit more, "He just got out of prison, but he's a good guy really, I just needed to come say thanks." As they drank, a reggae band started up in the basement – and they were pretty good.

They smashed *Roots, Rock, Reggae*. The lead singer was older but handsome, and the drummer entered fully into the vibes, with a strange rotund man pulling out a fiddle and ripping up a solo Irish-style. Hannah filmed them, slightly wobbly now from the booze, and Jen bopped about like a cute American – somewhat disappointing to Hannah who hadn't seen her move before, and *somehow* there was another drink in Hannah's hand, and caution had been thrown to the wind, and here they were – dirty, smelly, sweating and skanking along to the rhythm. Hannah

140

took the opportunity to stand right at the front of the stage, grinning and enjoying the band's captivating energy.

Jen appeared by her side, "I used to date the guitarist," she whispered, "We went everywhere together. But he had a wife!"

My God! Was there anything this girl hadn't done?

They got more and more drunk and when the band took a break, Hannah went on autopilot and started to enthusiastically blither on to the band about what she liked, how great the drummer was, how funny it was when they lost their way but didn't care! Though they welcomed her there was a distinctly stiff edge – and Jen pulled her away after a few minutes. She didn't resist - Jen was a good judge of when to run she reckoned, or she wouldn't still be here. They slurped the dregs of some evil-tasting bucket and tripped back up the wooden stairs to the street.

"Wooooooooo!" exhaled Hannah.

"Yeah!" said Jen, galloping along - two giggly drunkards in the night air. They stopped for chicken-on-sticks, then stood on a corner near the sea.

"How're we gonna get home?" Jen said, more to herself than to Hannah, "Should get a taxi - yeah."

There weren't any taxis.

Hannah staggered about in the road searching for vehicles – she usually managed to find a ride home. Eventually a teenage duo hurtled rounded the corner on their motorbikes, and Jen and Hannah stepped closer, peering at them inquisitively. They stopped. The leader grinned at his mate behind, who didn't seem to see the funny side.

Jen switched to damsel in distress mode, and spoke to them in Thai: *We're two girls stranded – you live nearby, right? Give us a lift?* Again, the lead guy was game, but his friend behind crossed his arms reluctantly.

The girls climbed on anyway – Jen took the chirpy one and Hannah the sullen. As they hurtled through the blue night air Hannah realised that she couldn't be much drunker – or happier! The boys dropped them right at the apartment entrance, and the girls waved them off – Jen's one still friendly and fun, Hannah's still a grump. As they tripped up the stairs to the top floor Jen laughed and fell about, slurring.

"I quite fancied my one – he wanted to take me to the beach!"

"He was about twelve!"

"Yeah, I know - that's why I didn't go!"

"And you *have* got a boyfriend."

"Yeah, yeah, I know, but you know...we've got problems and..." Hannah nodded her head in understanding - a wry smile dancing over her lips briefly. She didn't really care – it was Jen's moral call, not hers - and she had probably done worse. She was so grateful and relieved that Jen had led her astray tonight; every cell of her body wanted to dance with hitmen every night and ride with Thai strangers through the dark, milky moonlight to an apartment in the middle of nowhere. The thrill of the unknown and the pull of wild abandon, the addiction of hedonism on the road. With these thoughts lingering in the indigo haze around her, they zonked out on Jen's double bed: rancid, stinking but satisfied.

22. Trumping on my Parade

They slept well through sunrise and into late morning, finally stirring at around midday. Jen leapt immediately into action: she had to teach a class at 2pm in town! She got up, had a 'top 'n' tails' wash, then gathered her things for school. She needed to do a load of photocopying but there wasn't time now. Hannah wasn't ready to unleash herself on the world in her dishevelled state, so she stayed behind.

She wasted the next few hours away; drinking coffee, showering, playing Dr. Flameheart and relaxing, then she noticed a message from Jen.

'Oh my god, just got this from Mel: Hi, I'm coming to join you. It's all gone tits up - Ake's wife just turned up at the gym, I've got to get away!'

And just when Hannah was starting to enjoy her escape! She replied and made her feelings clear.

'Doesn't matter', wrote Jen, *'We can go to Ton Sae tomorrow – that little hippy beach I told you about.'*

Hannah wasn't keen on the tourist trail, but Jen needed a partner in crime with whom to misadventure - and hippy heaven was more attractive than a threesome with Mel. Hannah's hangover suddenly kicked in, and this afternoon's newsflash added to it a feeling of glumness. She waited for Jen to come back from work, sitting on the balcony and strumming melancholic tunes. The boys from the soup-stand below gawped up at her, and the owners came out smiling and nodding in approval at her melodies.

Jen returned – flustered – in the late afternoon. On the way back from town she'd had a call: one of her friends had been involved in a tussle outside 7-11 and someone had sliced off her finger - insanely unbelievable but completely true. Jen was a mess, and Hannah didn't have the stamina for the chaos that seemed to strike Jen daily.

Hannah calmed her – reasoning that although it was bad, she had enough troubles of her own - and it would be okay, the girl was in safe hands at the hospital.

They ate at the soup-stand and settled in for a 'girlie night', watching terrible period-dramas that Jen knew all the words to, and that Hannah didn't care for one bit. Mel would arrive sometime around lunch tomorrow. Going to Ton Sae was a great idea: she couldn't stomach three of them in that room and she had come here for a break - not to be subsumed in Muay Thai dramas from the all-consuming Mel.

In the morning they went straight into town. Jen took a massage while Hannah swam in a hotel pool accompanied by Jen's friend 'Sunstar'. Hannah sat next to her on a sun-lounger, trying not to stare at Sunstar's unkempt pubes, which spilt out of her bikini. They talked about Hannah's book - a conversation she usually avoided - but Sunshine was probing.

"Well, it's kind of about some animals living on an island, only none of them are pure-bred as they've been mating with each other for so long," Hannah began, outlining the events and characters of the story so far. Sunstar nodded along but she didn't really seem interested. In truth, neither was Hannah – she could feel something else growing inside of her, and the urge to spew it out onto the page was growing fast.

Her experiences in the last few weeks - the Muay Thai world she was becoming entangled in, the overwhelmingly annoying Mel, Jen's hilarious out-of-this-worldliness - these were the things impacting her right now, these were the things that made her feel alive, and *that* was what ignited her writing - not genderless animals. An internal monologue had started, but she tucked the prose safely away for later; she couldn't write by the pool, nor with the thunderous arrival of Mel, and certainly not in some 'hippy haven' - it would have to wait until she had settled back on Koh Talay. In a new room she could settle down and let it all out. Perhaps it would be nothing – a diary of sorts – or perhaps it would be the beginning of a delectable plot.

Jen appeared from the massage parlour laughing - her masseuse had wanted to send some rice over to Hannah, reasoning that she must be starved after thrashing out fifty lengths in the pool. Feeling gloriously thin and victorious, they drove back to Jen's apartment to await the inevitable arrival of you-know-who.

At around 1pm the frantic texts and calls started - '*I need a lift from Krabi Town!*' - but Jen wasn't playing, "She can get a motherfuckin' taxi! *She's* invited herself here!"

After what seemed like far too long, and another bowl of delicious soup from the boys downstairs, there was a hollering from the street, "Hellooooooooooooooooo! Hello?" whined Mel.

145

Begrudgingly, Jen went down to collect her while Hannah stayed in the room. Instinctively, she sprawled herself out on the bed – claiming some territory. Mel entered with a thud, looked around with visible distaste, shoved Hannah's stuff aside with complete disregard, and made space for her own things.

"So...you've left the gym?" enquired Hannah.

"Yes. I had to get away – it was AWFUL! Ake's wife turned up – someone must have told her about me, or she wouldn't have come!"

"Yeah, I reckon someone tips off the wives at the gym," remarked Hannah, "I suppose however good friends the Thai people seem, they look after their own first." She rolled over, trying to ignore Mel's fussing and re-arranging. Hold on a minute: if Mel had left the gym and packed up all of her things, then where was Hannah's stuff?!

"Is *my* stuff okay?"

"Oh yes, yes," Mel dismissed, "I put it on the shelves in Lek's office - of course it's okay - I wouldn't just abandon it!"

"Where's my washbowl?" remarked Hannah suddenly - the last time she had seen it was in Mel's bathroom.

"Oh, yes...erm, the washbowl. No, no, sorry – it broke!"

"Oh," said Hannah in surprise, "That's some strong Thai plastic there – I wouldn't have thought it *could* break!"

It may have only been a washbowl, but it was the story behind it that bothered her. Mel had told her before that the Thai staff had bought her nail varnish which she had immediately smashed, so perhaps she was just clumsy - or perhaps she liked to destroy that which was given to her, and husbands too, from her latest performance.

Hannah took the opportunity to sneak outside and play her guitar gently, leaving Jen to do the talking. Mel had invited herself to stay for ten days or so until her visa ran out, when she would have to go to Malaysia to apply for a new one. As they chatted, Hannah opened her laptop and took the opportunity to put down a few ideas for her novel - details she might not remember later – then rested for the evening, drowning out their squawks and exclamations.

As soon as Mel was in the shower and out of earshot, Hannah hissed at Jen, "This is *our* holiday, I want to have fun! Who does she think she is coming here and…and MOVING IN? Shoving my stuff in the office at the gym!"

"Yeah, she's annoying alright, I'm gonna get some rent money off her whatever the excuse."

Hannah was miffed, "Let's go to Ao Nang tomorrow, and let's not invite her."

"Well, I've mentioned it already so-"

"Please, if she comes, I'm not going - I'm not even going to make an excuse. I literally CAN'T spend any more time with her – she's really annoying me and encroaching on my space - look at this room!" Hannah dramatised.

After another period-drama the girls slept – Mel angling for the bed, but Jen firmly announcing that her and Hannah were sharing it, and that Mel could make up her own bed on the floor from whatever she could find. Moodily Hannah turned over and slept – it was hard to keep up the sour act, but she wanted Mel to pick up that she was put out. Hannah was an independent woman, whose every molecule cried out for freedom. True: Mel had been Hannah's initial route to Kit, but now she would be away for the next few weeks maybe Hannah could form a relationship with him on her own - without Mel's interference, control, gossiping and jibing.

Considering this, and with the prospect of stowing away in the morning to Ao Nang, she could finally sleep.

23. Island Getaway

All went according to plan: Mel left early to train Muay Thai, and the girls drank powdered coffee downstairs with the Thai family, then slung on their backpacks and went to the pier. They waited for the longtail boat at leisure, and when other tourists arrived and it was getting full, a bright and nimble man quickly walked them to the shore to board the small wooden vessel for the short journey to another isle.

Hannah and Jen sat at the back slurping cola, Hannah snapping away at the emerald sea and the craggy, majestic rocks which rose from it. Above her the boat man steered the craft, smiling with an open face to the wind, a Thai flag blowing in the breeze behind him. Hannah was happy at sea – her grandfather had been a captain during the Second World War, and she liked to think she had sailor's legs. They turned the corner, circumnavigating a steep cliff, and it was then that their destination revealed itself – Ton Sae.

The passengers clambered ashore – Hannah in her swamp-pants, dragging in the saltwater. She hitched them up around her knees and squinted in the midday sun. Jen marched straight up to the bar ahead of them and enquired about a room: 400 baht for a night - more than she recalled paying before, but for ease they took it.

The barman led them through woodland surrounds to a small hut at the back of their plot of land. It was built on short stilts; the door didn't fit properly and the mattress had an almost visible stench rising from it: the once-white fabric now brown with dust and sweat-stains. The gappy wooden boards creaked every time they moved. Hannah crawled out to inspect the 'bathroom' - a toilet bowl with no cistern, set into cement in the open air. Sweaty and bedraggled they threw their bags on the bed and went out in search of a feed.

Hammocks swung and reggae boys played football, farangs in filthy fisherman's pants walked tightropes between trees and flung poi balls around in spiritual passage.

Jen and Hannah just wanted food. They reached the far end of the beach and turned inland to a row of food stalls. Hannah budged in on a table with two hairy Spaniards, and Jen ordered chicken and noodles. The boys introduced themselves - they were different to the strays on Koh Talay, charming, good-looking and very much at one with their unkemptness, their unwashed feet smeared the colour of soot. Hannah could hardly preach in her three-day-old harem pants, but what was so 'woke' about being unclean and smelly? She'd had her days of squats and hippies and communal meals that gave you the shits because of dirty fingers and the odd 'harmless' piece of pink chicken. In Thai culture cleanliness was revered: the floors must be clean, as must your hands and feet; as much out of practicality and to keep the bugs and disease away as anything else.

They wolfed down their soup with glee and bid farewell to their new hippy mates, who in truth had spiced up their lunch a little. Now it was time to explore.

Jen knew the terrain well, and they started out on the path that led to the famous Railay Beach. The road was man-made and detracted from the cliffs and shorelines that dumbfounded you at every corner. Nearing Railay, they passed under an arch to find a man perching upside-down above them in a crevice, his hands and feet seemingly gripping onto air itself!

"They call him the monkey man!" explained Jen.

Silent and absorbed in his own world, he carefully considered the terrain before him, powdering his hands from a small leather pouch on his belt to strengthen his hold, swinging from edge to edge as he navigated the rocks, oblivious to the gawping tourists below, and mesmerising.

They turned the corner to a small inlet, and as the tide was out the girls could clamber over the rocks to discover ancient hidden Buddhist shrines. It was so peaceful, and the coolness from the rocks provided a welcome break from the burning sun. Just a short distance further and they arrived at the picture-perfect beach with its immaculate white sand and colourful longtail boats. Hannah was a little disappointed; in a place of such dazzling beauty, why did there have to be so many shacks selling overpriced fried chicken?

The afternoon was nearing its end and though the breeze was sublime there was an air of closing-down, so the girls decided to turn back to their beach. Nearing home, the path took them over rocks and, slipping and sliding through sinking-sand, they arrived on shore covered in dirt. It was thirsty work and they were in need of refreshment.

"Let's go to the top of the village," said Jen, "There's some cool little places."

She seemed to be re-tracing the steps of a previous life, Hannah a live spectator. She hoped it didn't mean more hitmen...

They walked through rows of bungalows up to a road lined with leather stores, restaurants and bars. They stopped for two happy-hour cocktails. Soon Jen was speaking in hushed tones, explaining to Hannah in garbled English that she used to stay at this bar with the owner - whom she now believed had gone to prison. Jen nodded at the woman behind the bar who she believed must know the inside story, and slyly started probing –but the woman said nothing, just stared back, polishing glass with a cloth.

A heavily pregnant but painfully skinny white girl appeared – it was the owner's new moll. She served them drinks and chatted with Jen curtly and with caution. Every utterance from Jen bleeped out a code: '*I know you know I know, just tell me something!*' but the girl shrugged back, claiming not to know where her former lover had gone; nor what had happened in the lead-up to his apparently innocent disappearance.

Hannah sat slurping away, trying to remain uninvolved.

After the drinks they left. Jen launched immediately into a tirade, "I know she knew, the BITCH!"

Hannah remained quiet – it was best not to feed Jen's rabid fire. They stopped at another bar.

"Shouldn't we eat first?" suggested Hannah.

They ordered two vodkas from a cheery large Thai man who was more Western than both of them put together. In a rock t-shirt with a boy-band haircut, he chatted to them in a perfect cockney accent. A band struck up and before long they were grooving along to country covers, a Lenny Kravitz tune; they weren't half bad, despite their microphones being fixed to stands with gaffer tape.

When the music turned from acceptable to deafening, Hannah turned to Jen and announced that they were going to eat. They grabbed their bags and wandered along looking for food.

"Here," said Jen, and they wobbled up to look at the menu. They couldn't figure out what most of the dishes were, so Hannah made a move and ordered some 'chicken no name':

"What's that?" asked Jen.

"It's bad, but it's very, very good. It's food. It's fried. It's delicious, and we're on holiday."

They went to the bar next door and nodded for the staff to bring it over when it was well and truly fried.

Jen knew all of the bar boys here. Hannah's mouth had spun off its hinges from the booze and was barking outrageous things every time it opened. The boys lapped it up, joining them for a few shots of whisky, and before long Hannah was prising one eye shut so that things weren't quite so blurry.

The 'no name' arrived and rescued them a little, Jen gobbling it up exclaiming *'Why hadn't I heard of this before!'* Hannah just raised her eyebrows in reply - she'd curse herself in the morning but right now it tasted gooood.

Jen reached over the bar to grab a game of *Connect 4*, "You like this?"

"Do I?" replied Hannah. At university she had endlessly beaten her boyfriend at the game, and having a mathematical mind, believed herself to be quite good.

"I used to get free drinks all night playing *Connect 4* against Thai people," Jen said, raising the stakes. As they played, a Thai audience grew around them. They both knew the ropes; where not to go, how to build the game until your brain split apart for fear of the wrong move and it all being over. When they ran out of playing-pieces they continued with what they could muster: a finger here, a finger there, until the board was full and nobody had won - a truce! Hannah was glad it was over – every time she moved something flew off the bar – a water-bottle, her bag, her scarf - she didn't even think she was moving.

"Let's go," she slurred, and they wobbled off their stools and traipsed back in the direction of their bungalow.

"One last drink! One last drink!" implored Jen.

"Okayyyyy!" staggered Hannah.

The next bar was livelier, which helped Hannah to perk up. A band played away on the wild beach for a small hippy crowd of drunken farangs who were dancing the night away, the waves crashing behind them. Jen propped herself at the bar, chin in hand, and fixed her gaze intently on the barman - who was at least forty and looked curiously back at her.

Hannah bought a bottle of water and wandered off into the crowd. She spotted a tall boy with a sweet face and curly brown hair, dancing alone and absorbed in his own world.

She weaved through the crowd to him and moved subtly in time with his rhythm. He moved closer and they danced together. Eventually their faces met and he smiled and put his hand on her waist. They chattered in each other's ears and soon decided to move away from the bustle of the crowd towards a boat marooned near the shore. Jen remained at a distance, grinning in approval. As soon as Hannah stepped into the boat and they were alone, everything came into focus. The boy's name was Christophe and he was a rock-climber with ambitions of opening up a business on Ao Nang.

"You're joking, aren't you? You want to own a business in Thailand that could put the locals out of pocket? Rather you than me!"

Christophe rolled a joint and they lay not too close together, laughing as they became inebriated from the ganja. When the joint was done, Christophe moved closer until Hannah was in his arms, gazing at his face, still chatting languidly. They talked about love: Christophe used to have a girl but their dream died here in paradise. Hannah told him of her own situation – a potential new love, but in unfamiliar territory. He caressed her further and though it was tempting Hannah suddenly stopped, "I'm not going to kiss you."

"Wha-hat?" he said, surprised - they had come this far.

"I know it sounds stupid but I do really like the guy on Koh Talay, and I don't want to muck it up before I've given it a chance…" She was drunk, she was stoned and she was lying in a boat with a lovely French man, yet she didn't succumb, and so with a shrug they headed back to the bar where Jen was sat keeping watch.

"Ooooooooooo, lovebirds, back so soon?" she crooned.

"Yeah," smiled Hannah. Christophe went to get a beer to get pounced on by his straggly friends, who gave him the third degree.

"I'm not interested," Hannah told Jen, who was surprised.

"But, my god! I've *never* danced like that with a guy!"

"It *was* great dancing," said Hannah, "And he's really nice, but I'm not bothered - I've done it all before! Come on, let's go!"

Christophe and his posse followed them and they fell in step with a few Thai guys who had been working at the bar. Halfway to their hut the Thai guys gathered and sat on a rocky patch. Jen went over and sat with them and Hannah followed, reluctantly. Christophe's friends had disappeared but he stayed close to Hannah – hoping for a last-minute change of heart.

The bar boys made a bamboo bong and passed it around. Hannah accepted a few puffs before passing the bong onto Christophe who hesitated – he wasn't used to such contraptions. He tentatively took a drag then passed it on and now appeared heavily drunk and a bit wasted. Hannah chatted to a guy on the other side of her, who suddenly grabbed out in the pitch darkness and squeezed her arm. Enough was enough. She shuffled over to Jen, "I was just being friendly to that guy but he touched me – let's get out of here." As they staggered off, Jen confessed that she was getting ready for a ruff-n-tumble in the bushes with whomever so wished for it.

They crawled into their insect-ridden hut and somehow laid themselves out straight. They didn't attempt a blanket nor even shut the door before both of them passed out heavily.

* * *

Morning glared at them. Hannah rummaged around for their bags – they were still there, unopened. She emptied her bowels in the outside toilet then Jen announced they were leaving. Both a little broken in a way that no bucket-shower could fix, shielded by sunglasses and shawls, they went to catch the boat.

After a short wait the longtail arrived to take them back to reality, and from the town they hailed an open-backed *songthaew* wagon back to Jen's apartment. Mel had already gone to Malaysia to get a new visa.

"Right, we're going!" Jen announced.

"What do you mean?"

"Well…we can wait another whole day to get back to Koh Talay, but we may as well go now - we'll be back in time for sunset."

Hannah liked to take her time over travelling, but Jen knew the drill and would get her home - hangover or not - she just had to follow along.

After a shower which improved things tenfold, they packed their things, said goodbye to the Thai family and got to the bus station. It was by now late afternoon and they caught the last bus of the day. Nobody else boarded the bus, but as the driver lived on Koh Talay the three of them went on their merry way, singing along to the radio in the golden light of sundown, the now-familiar scenery whizzing past -

rich people's palm-lined houses, the stranded ship from the tsunami - then a short wait for the ferry and finally to Koh Talay; home, sweet home! What a feeling!

Jen's boyfriend Mon collected the girls from the bus station and they rode three to a bike, dropping Hannah off at the top of the dirt track. She shuffled her way down in the clay taking care not to twist an ankle and hurried into Jeab's shop.

"Welcome!" grinned her good friend.

"Sawadee ka!" replied Hannah, "Can I leave my bag here while I find a room?"

"Sure! You want to start work the day after tomorrow?"

"Yes," smiled Hannah - jaded but glad to be back.

She needed a room just for the night but didn't fancy back-tracking to rat-villas nor to Mama and Papa's - who would surely overcharge. There weren't too many other options, especially at short notice and after nightfall. The closest and sturdiest huts belonged to 'Monkey Bungalows', who had a reputation for unfriendly staff and consequently usually had rooms free, so she headed to the beach where she knew a woman from the restaurant:

"Kor..." she began, '*please...*' The woman made no signal, just briskly grabbed a key saying, "101 - you know where?"

"I know where."

It was one of the huts away from the beach, near Salee Mart, and it would do. She wearily lugged her bag to the hedged entrance of Monkey Bungalows. It was dark and she had to squint to make out the numbers – the nearest started with a '3'. She ventured two rows further back and there were the '1s', starting with '123' and working backwards. A few scraggy hipsters sat on their porches, giving Hannah a vague nod as she trudged past. At last, hut 101: at the end of the row and farthest from anywhere.

Opposite was a shack where some Thai men were building a fire. Perhaps they were the night watchmen - she hoped they weren't watching her! Inside the room was bright and clean with the biggest bathroom she had seen yet, furnished with hot water and fresh towels.

She luxuriated in a long shower, before heading off for subsistence - Kanchana's Kitchen was the easiest option. She was shattered and it was heaving, so she shared a table with a young Austrian couple who didn't interact with her until the food came, when the girl asked her questions about where to stay - as everything in Yao Beach was full. Hannah had been lucky with her room it seemed. She apologised to the girl for being strung out and the girl assured her in reply that they were all tired.

After dinner she headed straight back to her temporary dwelling and switched off all psychological alarm bells, knowing that at least someone would hear her if she screamed. She had a mission in the morning to complete: to find a new safe haven.

24. Housewarming

Early the next morning, stuffing her belongings back into her rucksack, she went in search of shelter. She decided to follow her feet rather than reason and started - past Mama and Papa's then through the rough trail inland. Five minutes later she emerged from the brush onto a road that led to the sea. To the right was a diver's shop, and she recalled a faint memory of someone telling her, '*If you want a long-term room, ask the divers – they should know*!' She took a few steps into the shop, feeling ill at ease, and quickly scanned the staff. The friendliest one, who seemed to command an air of responsibility, smiled at her.

"Hiya!" he said.

"Hi! Somebody said you might know of some long-term rooms? I've looked around before but not really found anywhere I like."

"Oooooh…" the man put his hands on his hips, "I don't really know anywhere around here – I stay out the back!"

She waited while he had a quick word with his colleague.

"Someone said something about a yellow house on the corner - I think a few people have stayed there before - it's about eight grand a month or something. You just go up to the main road and turn right, it's kind of on the bend."

"Yellow," repeated Hannah, "Definitely to the right? 'Cause I remember a couple-"

"Definitely on the right, I'm pretty sure it's the only one before you get to the ATM, it's pretty easy to spot!"

Up to the road she went.

Though she knew the area well, it was further along than her usual stomping ground – past Lung-Lung's chicken shack, Reggae Reggae Bar, Kanchana's Kitchen, the boxing arena. As she walked south, she spotted the coffee shop she had visited in the rain all that time ago, and directly opposite was a three-storey lurid yellow building – that must be it! She had gone past it many times before, but not given much thought to what it might be. A sign saying *Talay Clinic Lap* jutted out into the road – so it must have been some sort of hospital in the past. On the ground floor was a hair salon with four kittens rough-and-tumbling outside, and to the left of that a store where women in traditional Muslim dress sat behind a desk surrounded by bottles of petrol, dried grains and dusty hair accessories. She must have to ask them: the entrance to the rooms was unmarked and there was no other sign suggesting it was accommodation – perhaps it was word-of-mouth only?

The women behind the desk didn't look too welcoming - more defunct gas station than guest-house – but Hannah had limited options, so she gathered some bravado, slipped off her flip-flops and approached the be-gowned ladies. They might have smiled - she couldn't be sure – she just saw four sets of eyes peering at her, narrowed, as if to say, 'Yes?'

"Er hi, my friend from the diving shop says you have rooms?"

The women nodded and glanced at each other; their eyes slightly panicked – English wasn't their strong point. One ran out to the back room, and leaning a little so that she could peek out the back, Hannah made out layer upon layer of hijab scarves, hung high upon the wall - there must be quite a few people living here!

A smiling woman in regular dress appeared from the back and announced to Hannah in perfect English, "Can I help you?"

"Yes, I'm looking for a room – my friend said it's 8000 baht for one month?"

The woman said nothing, just took a key from a hook and strode around to Hannah, "Come with me!"

Out of the shop, through the entrance and up the baking-hot stairs to the second floor. The woman showed her two rooms – one at the front of the building with no balcony that smelt damp, and one in the middle of the corridor – 203. It had a better feel - certainly a more pleasant smell - and a tiny balcony that opened onto the side of the building, housing an air-conditioning unit but with just enough space to stand next to it and hang out the odd wet t-shirt. There were all mod cons: a TV, fridge, clean bathroom, big bed and clean linen. It felt grown-up, it felt right, it felt a bit like an end-of-the-road motel; and Hannah loved the trailer-trash ambience. The woman instilled confidence in her, with her good English and efficient manner, so as they walked back down the stairs Hannah checked the price before announcing that she would take the room, handing over the cash immediately.

It wasn't where she thought she'd end up – a disused medical centre run by alarmed Muslim women who didn't speak English and sold petrol out of bottles - but she loved it already, and from her side-balcony she could just see the twinkling fairy lights of the coffee shop and the pond the owner had crafted with care, along with the pretty shop sign and the carved wooden bar and stools.

Next to the coffee shop was an empty restaurant. She could just make out some figures in the kitchen – also in Islamic clothing. This area felt slightly wilder than the beach village, yet still safe, and in the distance she could just see the thatched booths of Lung-Lung's chicken shack.

She had a home but she was far from settled – all of her other possessions being somewhere at the boxing gym - and though drained, she still had stamina for this mission; not least because going to the gym might mean seeing her beau, with no Mel to intervene.

Nearly two weeks had passed since she snogged him on the dancefloor and canoodled with him on the porch. She hoped he had missed her - like he said he would, using the big old dictionary – still, she had no idea if he would even be there.

After a shower and fuelled by nervous excitement, she pulled on her Thai boxing shorts and started the journey on foot to the gym. She was already relishing in the sensation of independence her little room had brought – she felt somehow older and wiser - and ready for some action away from the shelter of the village. Jen was back safely with lover Mon; all forgiven and forgotten until the next drama, and Mel was away in Penang. The sun was lethal, but Hannah protected herself with a shawl - a fitting look in her Muslim neighbourhood. As she turned the corner a loud wailing commenced – the call to prayer – and eventually she spotted a tall pole with a loudspeaker atop, reaching into the sky, directly opposite her room.

No one she knew drove past to offer her a lift, but the forty-minute trek would be worth it; knowing that she would be reunited with, at the very least, her bags and, at the most, her man. She knew that she could potentially be making a big thing out of potentially nothing, but her heart lent itself to such. Everything here seemed out of this world – she had to pinch herself every morning just to check she wasn't in paradise, that or *The Truman Show*.

As she grew nearer her heart quickened – soon she would turn the corner and see what she could see: was Kit even here? She held onto hope, and though the bright sunlight blinded her as she approached, she continued to stride in a straight line towards the gym: fierce on the outside, cowering and nervous inside. She didn't have to endure suspense for long, for as she walked into the hangar-like space there was a stirring from Bungalow One behind her. She turned her head – it was him! He grabbed his shorts from where they had been drying on the balcony, hopping on one foot to pull them on quickly, and started to run towards her. Pretending not to have seen him, she quickly stepped out of eye-shot, nodding at the other trainers. As she did so Tee screeched from the corner of the ring, "Take me out tonight! You! Take me out!" whining like a schoolboy.

"Mai mee dang," she shrugged – *Got no money*. She didn't have much - it was true - and certainly not enough to take naughty Esarn boxers on a night out; there was more important business to attend to.

Onto the tyre to warm up, and in strode Kit, his chest rising and falling after rushing in - his girl was home. She smiled in his direction but he didn't turn to look, so she continued to switch her feet with her guard up, working up a sweat whilst checking in the mirrors that she hadn't turned into a complete monster during the walk there. She had twisted her hair neatly into a gypsy-style bun and her face was bright, clear and expectant. Kit was in the ring holding pads for a hefty Swedish man - beer belly and all. This time, when she smiled, he caught it – returning a bashful grin that flickered over his face for a split-second - before continuing his work. She went to the far side of the ring to watch his skillful instruction as he manoeuvred the man around the ring, completely consumed in and hard at work. She stretched out her legs one by one, feeling a pull in her inner-thigh, and finished with a quick limber in the splits: left, right and centre. Those dancing days had done her good.

She started to work on a bag. Kit's student took a water break, and without sound they walked towards each other, he in the ring and her below; in what seemed like slow-motion, and at the same time a single heartbeat. With no inhibitions he reached his arms through the ropes, and she too, grasping onto each other's forearms, smiling warmly into each other's faces, the sunshine flooding in.

"You back! You back!" She nodded, unable to control the beam that projected from her face. After holding her for a few more moments, he was back off for another round of pads and she was walking over to the bags to practise her technique: walking on the outside, skipping, leaping and jumping inside.

She worked hard, her mind consumed in the physicality of training but her spirit in wild la-la land, her heart giddy. As she worked away – jab-jab, cross, a body shot, a right hook and step back for a killer round-house – there he was, approaching from her right, a little uneasy on his feet and nerves audible in his voice, "You, you go to Krabi?"

"Yes!"

"You have good time?"

"Yes," she said, "went to Ao Nang – good!"

"Ah, yes, good!" he agreed.

She looked back towards the bag, stepped a little to the left, twisted from the hip raising up on her left toe and dug a kick sharply and swiftly into the bag before ensuring a balanced land. She was in mid-flow, and Kit stood, not quite knowing what to say, having run out of English. She turned to smile at him one more time, but he was already back in the ring, standing against the ropes observing the duets of bodies – trainers holding pads for foreigners who hesitated before they kicked, or who nodded in slow comprehension as the trainers shouted 'Jab, jab - good! More twist…good!' in perfect Boxer's English.

Now it was Hannah's turn to enter the ring. Through the lower ropes she swooped – agile and professional, her palms pressed together in a *wai*. Kit was smiling and ready for her: he seemed confident this time – his girl had come to train. With a nod and touch of gloves, they were off. She focussed solely on Kit's instruction, and in doing so an endless energy flew out of her. In between rounds she drank from the water machine, looking around the gym; a few western lads were leant up against the ring staring at her, and though she attempted to remain poker-faced, she hoped that she had made a lasting impression. She knew she looked good whilst training; yet kicking pads with precision doesn't mean you'll triumph in the ring, and though it felt nice to be noticed there was no place for ego - she was here to learn, learn, learn.

When three rounds were down, she was out of breath and wired with adrenalin. She stretched on the mats and eased off with some yoga poses, stretching her shoulders for writing, and headed into the office.

Lek was plonked there as usual, but her mouth upturned a little as Hannah approached. She pointed to a small shelving unit close to the floor where Hannah's things had been stored. Anyone could see it and have a pick through, still, it looked like it was all there. She thanked her, then heaved the bags off the shelves, sweat dripping onto the clean tiled floor, the icy air-con turning her wet body into some kind of preserved waxwork, before getting back into the heat of the gym, dragging her belongings with her. She lugged it to the exit, feeling awkwardly conspicuous, and half-expecting Kit or one of the others to come and help her, but no chivalrous chaperone materialised.

Once in the glaring sunlight she dropped her things in the dust - out of the boxers' view but in full view of anyone else milling about their business; pervy Papa Playboy, some teenage kids home from school - goodness only knew who they belonged to. She didn't know how to get home – she had sort of presumed that Kit *might* take her but didn't know if he had a bike. So instead, she just stood there: if no-one came to help, she would go back to ask Lek for help - perhaps this time her baggage would warrant her a lift.

As she turned her head to see if Lek was in the office, contemplating an imminent move, a revving sound came from out back - and within seconds a shining red bike appeared, complete with a shining Thai man. Yes! Kit had come to save the day, like a movie star - a brown James Dean, and just as good-looking, his clear features and full mouth directed towards her. She mounted the bike without hesitation. Kit put her backpack between his legs and they rode off into the nearing sunset, past the half-built condominium with its spectacular view to sea, then zooming off towards her new home.

"Here, here, *tee nee!*" said Hannah gently. Kit pulled over, swerving expertly to park. They both dismounted, and she looked to him – was he going to come and help her with her stuff and would that mean...did that mean...what did that mean?!! She was wet through and sweaty from training and he the same, though wearing it better than she, but before she could attempt to ask, and without word, he picked up her stuff and marched into the building. She led the way up the stairs, one set then another, then nodded for him to follow her along the corridor. She slipped her key into door 203 and there they were.

It wasn't exactly a mess, but it wasn't exactly the scene you'd paint when inviting a man into your home for the first time. They looked around for where to put her bags, and Kit neatly stacked them against the back wall. Hannah sat on the bed, looking up at him: *Would he go now*? She stood up and indicated towards the shower.

"Okay," he said, "you shower, I wait". She stood up to go, but he stopped her. Pushing her onto the bed, he kissed her with urgency, pulling at the clothes that clung to her clammy body. Momentarily she stopped his advances - she was covered in dirt and sweat and they didn't need to hurry - but there was no deterring him, so she gave into the struggle and instead entered into this after-school romp, briefly instructing him to wait as she rushed for a condom. With no qualms at the interruption - and no protests thank god - he slipped it on and was back, at an angle on the bed, her beneath him as tradition might have it.

This was no wedding night; no drunken fumble either. She enjoyed it despite its urgency; it was a little as if he was getting the first time over with to confirm their status. She was still slightly in shock, in fact, when it was over – it would have been so much nicer to be beautifully groomed for such an occasion - but that could come later. She sat up, exhausted.

"Okay, NOW you go shower!" instructed Kit.

She smiled, gathered her clothes up off the floor and trotted over to the bathroom, and as she did, he added, "I go now - come back later!"

"What time?"

"Don't know. Er, nine - or ten!"

"When?" she asked again – she was better if things were planned carefully.

"Er, nine, think nine!" With that, he darted out of the door looking quite perplexed.

25. I Bring You Milk

She lay, flat out on the bed, as he closed the door behind him, smirking to herself at the strangeness of the situation. However odd, she had in theory got what she wanted: returned from her mystery sojourn to win the heart of her man, who had driven her through the wind on his gleaming beast to heroically help her move in and then delivered an impromptu housewarming present.

She searched through a pile of things she'd tipped out of her rucksack and found a towel and some soap. She wrapped the towel around her then sat back down on the bed for another think. It all felt surreal, and she laughed out loud because she loved the unbelievable, and life often didn't bring enough surprises. Words from a distant poem she had written came to her: *'Nothing much phases me, but nothing much amazes me'*. It was about the state of inertia when life doesn't make you feel alive and the magic isn't there – you are suspended in mediocrity.

Yet some kind of magic was with her now, and the shower could wait. In a mischievous mood she opened up her laptop and sent a message to Jen, who most likely had no internet access, phone credit or power as usual, and was probably crying on the floor after another argument with her crazed jungle boy who liked sharp knives. She sent the message anyway, *'Training was good!'*

And lo and behold one came straight back! Jen was studying in the restaurant that Mon worked in, *'Cool, so, how was he?'*

'He's just left my new place! He drove me back and then...'

She remembered that Jen had advised her to make him wait, but Hannah had little patience, as well as not much choice in the matter.

'He's coming back later!'

'Cool, well I've nearly finished studying so we could hang out for a bit at yours?'

'Yes please, I'm a bit nervous about it, and you can see my new place x'.

Now it really *was* time for that shower. She didn't bother with special clothes – he'd already seen her in her bedraggled gym gear – and, settled in homely attire, Jen arrived to gossip. Though it had only been 24 hours since their wild night in Krabi, still Hannah had missed her. Jen lay on the bed, making it her own, whilst Hannah twitched about frantically. She preferred impromptu meetings in bars or a clinch at the end of a party – dates made her nervous - and now she felt trapped in her own circumstance.

Jen remained on the bed, slurring in sleepy Californian that all would be fine. To add to Hannah's neurosis, she hadn't yet eaten – there hadn't been time earlier, and now it was nearing nine.

"Go! Go!" she suddenly rushed Jen, "He's going to be here any minute! It'll be weird if you're here!" She thought again, "No, no! Maybe it's better if you *are* here! My friend popping round, yeah cool! No, no!" Jen got up lazily, "I gotta go anyway, Mon's cooking me food at the restaurant." And, earphones in, she slouched out of the room. "Enjoy your date!" she winked cutely.

174

Hannah shut the door and sat on the bed, breathing shallowly, actively waiting. She thought better of it and turned the TV on – waiting was a terrible pastime. Frantically she switched channels in search for anything suitable - should he arrive right then – but there was nothing on. It was 9:15 already: maybe he wouldn't come! She didn't have his phone number and she would be too chicken to call anyway, and he looked at computers like a man from the 1950s. You *could* say they had the ill communication.

Doubts started to mess with her head, and she wished she'd washed her hair earlier as well as *gin kow* – had dinner. Maybe she should put on some more make-up or try to sort her hair out. She jumped up and went to the bathroom mirror – every second racing against an indeterminate clock, a moment nearer to a potential knock on the door - which might never come, or which could come NOW!

Still, he didn't materialise, so she remained nervous, uncomfortable and unsatisfied with her appearance but accepted her lot and pretended to stare at the Thai telly in rehearsal for his arrival.

She was starting to get over the whole thing fast - the anticipation was killing her! Like a teenager waiting for her new boyfriend to call the home-phone she paced about in agitation. She tried to calm herself by switching off the godawful blare of the TV, and instead put on some mellow music. She couldn't give a toss what she looked like anymore either, and it was nearly time for bed - which wasn't a bad thing - at least if he *did* show up they wouldn't have to force too many late-night chats with the twenty words of language they shared.

At 10.25, sleepy, exhausted and hypoglycaemic, she was nudged alert by a knock on the door. She feigned a pause, but the door was only a few metres from the bed, so she got up, reminding herself to 'act naturally', and opened the door: There he was - her new man - come to warm her new house for a second time!

He stood proudly presenting himself, in a pristine white t-shirt and shorts, freshly laundered and starched and smelling of sweet fragrance. His chest was puffed out in pride or fear, and optimism shone from his warm face. A peculiar outfit, if she was honest, but the smell of fresh linen and the smartness of his appearance was respectful at least. He presented her with a small bag from 7-11, like a pleased kitty brandishing a mouse. She welcomed him in and, both still standing, he unpacked the bag one item at a time, like a Christmas stocking! He presented each precious gift to her anxiously, looking to her for approval.

The first: a pint of 'Dutch Mill' creamy milk - a little strange, but lovely, she stifled her laughter and instead grinned widely. The second: a highly synthetic chocolate brownie, vacuum-sealed - good for a moon mission or apocalypse, and lastly, something she couldn't quite figure out – she had to look at it more closely.

"I think, I think, maybe you like this?" On further investigation she made out the words 'crabstick-flavour pizza' - packed with luminous colours and tasty preservatives. Delicious!

Quickly, to emphasise their insignificance, he pulled out the two more items: condoms and a packet of Juicy Fruit chewing gum, from which he took a piece and began masticating. It dawned on her that he had put some thought into these things: what might a farang want for her new home?

"Thank you!" she said finally, as a show of appreciation – though the gifts didn't really make up for his lateness, they were sweet and thoughtful, 'proper' somehow.

Kit dived straight onto the bed, flopping outstretched in exhaustion, and flicked through the channels hastily: settling on a Thai pop channel.

"Like this one!" he said, pointing, and started to sing along noisily. The song was called *Khao San Road*, and the video showed a boy band hanging out on benches, having fun together - attempting to be a 'crew' - but looking more like old-timers on a reunion tour.

Next up, a love song with a pretty Thai girl on a bus, staring through the window wide-eyed as she left her man. Hannah gave up her inner battle and tried to enjoy it. Kit flicked channels again to a Thai talk-show. Two cute girls with dimples sat making jokes on a sofa. Hannah couldn't understand a word of it. Kit pointed to the girl on the right, "She! Sexy! I think sexy! She!"

Hannah's neck came visibly out of joint and she quickly recoiled it. Of course, there was nothing to be jealous about – she was just a girl on the TV, and he was just being honest - but looking at herself she couldn't have been any more different. She told her head to take a hike and fetched her laptop.

She quickly checked her messages then showed Kit a few pictures: perhaps they might explain who she was a little more? He glanced, but clearly had no affinity with computers, so she put some music on instead. After a few songs, it was time for bed. With the lights out, and clothes off, it was time once more. Their bodies bonded beautifully, Hannah finding it easy to wrap herself around him, finding comfort in his warm, smooth skin. He moved without pause – no rush either - manipulating her into positions, guided by her twists and turns: both wanting the same.

After each delicious round he would shower, leaving her in a high, heaving, sighing mess, blissing out. Once or twice, she popped in for a quick wash - holding onto the wall for balance, weak with no energy left - and he giggled and laughed at her, mimicking her post-orgasmic sighs as she turned and grinned at him with good humour, slapping his firm buttocks.

She was noisy – loving to embrace the sexual experience in full - and she relished every drop, but after three beautifully constructed lays it was time to rest. Kit took one blanket and she the other, and they loosely arranged them about their persons, with access for a boxer's leg to drape over her slender hips - an arm suddenly reaching out - a moment of closeness between their faces as they breathed in time.

* * *

When morning came, his mobile phone noised off a pop-music alarm and he sat up, slowly but steadily. Hannah was pleased to have no hangover - just a satisfying post-coital relaxedness – she guessed that Kit might be a little tired at work today. She turned her head in his direction but chose not to open her eyes fully – 7am was a time she didn't do. Fuzzy logic reasoned that if she wasn't looking at him, he wouldn't be looking at her either: crumpled in the morning.

Kit got up swiftly, pulled on his clothes, walked back to the bed, lifted her body up effortlessly in his strong Muay Thai arms, deeply sniff-kissed each cheek and kissed her once on the lips so that it almost stung.

"I go gym now," he said, and he left. She flunked back down in her lover's lair to dream.

26. Giddy in the Morning

Hannah was due in the shop at eleven for her first shift, so she rested until nine when hunger got the better of her. She opened the fridge: A small amount of curdling milk, a few sachets of sugar and jam from Kanchana's Kitchen weren't going to cut it. Yet what was that stuffed in the bottom of the fridge? The radioactive chocolate brownie and 'crabstick pizza' – the housewarming gift from Kit! She opened both and took small nibbles of each alternately - the brownie overly sweet and dry, the crabstick pizza congealed and slimy. Both revolting, but still technically 'food' - and she had a job to get to.

Full of hormones and happiness she put together her best costume for the imminent transformation into a pretty and meek shop-girl - a flared short cotton skirt and vest. She did her hair and face as best she could in the baking heat and left her new home. How things had changed; she felt grown-up all of a sudden, as if she had come of age from a tourist wonderland into an adult world full of hope and the unknown - hell, she might even buy a kettle.

Skipping down the steps, Hannah exited the building, waving to the lady in the hair salon then walking quietly with her head down past the Muslim shopkeeper crew, who were sat as usual behind the desk, with Granny on a bamboo platform out front. She could just make out Grandpa in his wheelchair in the background, in the room where they kept the headscarves. Uncle Lung-Lung stood smiling and singing as always at his chicken stand and, just beyond, the kitchen staff were hard at work at

Kanchana's Kitchen. Hannah turned left and continued down the mud path to her old neighbourhood where Salee Mart glinted in the morning sun. The Brothel Ma'am sat lazily swinging her legs on the massage platform, nodding at Hannah through her preoccupied gaze. A tuk-tuk driver whistled, shouting 'Souaaaaay!' - *beautiful*. It was only a cheap skirt, but it always fulfilled its purpose.

Now for the new shop assistant's grand entrance. A tiny flutter of nerves passed through her, but she smiled brightly and drifted in, walking on air: a new man, a new house, a new job - life had taken a fresh turn.

Jeab was nowhere to be seen, but Hannah could hear rummaging out back from the storeroom, so she poked her head around the corner: there was Jeab, shifting boxes of snacks whilst wiping her brow with a flannel.

"Helllooooo!" she warmly welcomed.

"Hello!" Hannah brightly returned, and they set to work. Hannah wrote prices on sticky labels for kit kats and mars bars – she'd forgotten there might be temptation here.

By the end of her shift, she was drenched in sweat and exhausted, but satisfied. It felt good to earn her keep. Jeab put together a house-keeping pack for her - coffee, yoghurt and cashew nuts - paid her 200 baht and warmly wished her on her way.

Back at the yellow palace, Hannah wondered if she'd make it to training – there was still *just about* time - but she couldn't muster up the energy. When would she see Kit again? Would he knock on her door every night? Was this a shared bed? Time would tell, but betweenwhiles she could romanticise about the fair maiden in the yellow corner house and her handsome hero at the gym. The anticipation was a strange kind of fun, emanating nervous energy and a time to dream.

After a flop on the bed and time wasted trying to connect to the internet, it was starting to get dark. There was nothing to do apart from slurp down a bowl of soup, and she was aware that if he came to her room and she wasn't there he wouldn't have a clue where she was. He didn't know much about her life here – or who she was back in England - but those details didn't seem to matter; they could be together in the room making sweet squishy love together – why complicate matters with complex thought? She was good at persuading herself, her head in the clouds. She *loved* romance – impossible romance - and she was good at the dreaming part; there was just the reality to be worked upon.

She smiled more than usual as she ate at Kanchana's Kitchen, treating herself to a 90-baht glass of foul chilled wine, the new waiter there attending to her meticulously. She was always happy there, eating alone and people-watching. Hideous tourists didn't really go there – it looked 'dirty' - and to be fair, the odd rat or mouse *would* scuttle through the bushes next to her table. But she hadn't gotten ill off the food yet, it was cheap and delicious, and the place was bustling. The open kitchen displayed unabashed mayhem and cheer, an ingenious and quite confusing system of teamwork, and an ordering system beyond comprehension.

Back at home she stuck the telly on for company. *'What shall I do? What do I normally do?'* she wondered, and she couldn't remember. Ah yes, of late she would be invaded by Mel or the calamitous Jen, hurtling in with some drama or another, but Jen was back in Krabi and Mel was away for at least a few more days. Should she...should she...try to write? Yes! In between the punching and the kicking and the falling in love, she was here to write.

She opened up *book.docx* – the story she had started writing about the animals. A couple of phrases made her laugh and she enjoyed the style she had adopted, with its whiffs of Vonnegut and Steinbeck, but she had no passion for it; she liked writing about 'real things' – things that struck her core. She could write about a piece of chewing gum if it *meant* something to her, and her blog audience had always come back begging for more. What did 'being a writer' mean? Did you *have* to write a book? Did she even *dare* open up the Pandora's Box that had been whizzing about behind the scenes in her brain? What if she started writing and couldn't stop? Yet she was here to write, and what else did she have to get up for in the morning, save for a few hours' work in a shop with a friend?

She took several deep breaths then opened up a blank document. She wasn't sure where her story began, so she started from the part when it got interesting – right about the time she put on that spangly vest top, downed a bottle of vodka and leapt around with the Thai boys and Saolek Sor Chokdee. Right about then.

How enjoyable - an emptying! She tap-tapped away, all the while darting her eyes to the clock and the door alternately, which gave an urgency to her writing: *What if...what if...her little man should come?*

9.30pm passed - the time she might expect him - and she checked herself in the mirror at ten-minute intervals to make sure her face was holding up. 10pm came and her heart sank a little. She was flagging, forgetting how much mental energy writing consumed, and how much her arms felt like they were going to fall off. At around midnight she started to stray onto the internet again. She moved to the bed, taking a few gulps of whisky for stamina, but there was no rejuvenating - she was done with writing for tonight – 6000 words on.

She had set the scene with a fair dose of excitement, and the early damning of Mel – my, how it felt good to get that out! Right now it was more like notes or memoirs than next year's bestseller, but she hoped it was 'the biggie', so she carefully saved the document - 'real book' – smiling in deep contentment, before flopping down to sleep: still with her make-up on and still in her little cotton skirt, just in case he should come.

27. Don't Save a Prayer for Me Now

She woke up alone to Sunday – no different than any other day - with the exception that tonight was the weekly fight night at Don's Stadium, and guess who would be there?

She made the counter-intuitive decision not to go – she didn't want to hang about her new lover awkwardly like a spare part - and besides, he'd be working. Thai culture did not approve of public displays of affection and Hannah might find that particularly difficult, being the affectionate human being that she was, and having an uncontrollable urge to be near Kit at all times. She'd stay at home instead, away from the ogling eyes of Squishy Nose and Papa Playboy, who would be curious to know what she'd been up to: playing it cool felt much better. Secretly she hoped that Kit would be expecting her, as he whizzed about cornering for his fighters and performing his role of Master Kru: brother, teacher, friend and supporter.

The daytime passed effortlessly. Her second shift at the shop saw more locals stopping by to witness the spectacle behind the counter - shocked boys stammering for cigarettes - Jeab laughing all the while. *You work here?* they enquired. At first Hannah nodded and smiled sweetly, but when the shop was empty Jeab turned to her conspiratorially.

"You must say you not work here! We are friends and you are learning Thai." Hannah nodded obediently; she loved her good friend but would

187

definitely never mess with her – Jeab yielded an almighty power.

She explained further, "You need work permit - the Police can send you to prison!"

Though that didn't feel very likely in this peaceful paradise, from now on whenever anyone asked, the answer remained, "We are friends, we have a good time, I learn Thai!" with a jaunty bob of her hip. They knew – they *all* knew - but this was the arrangement, and her Thai *was* indeed improving, along with her confidence to speak it, as she whipped banknotes in and out of the till with ease.

Bags were politely offered, but not if they didn't need them: why add to the bulging, burning plastic heaps sending their poisons into the beautiful blue, or to the mountains that gathered in the sea and rivers, choking the ecosystem. Must paradise always be lost?

Now she could automatically think of numbers in Thai, and all thanks to Jeab - who gave her lunch, a little cash in her pocket and some groceries for home after each shift. Neither of them knew how long the job would go on, so for now they just worked side-by-side – safe in their mutual understanding that it would last just until it no longer served them both.

In the afternoon she swam in the sea, the waves lifting her body in rejuvenation, wild and choppy. Wading back to shore she wrapped a sarong around her waist and walked home past Uncle Lung Lung's and the coffee shop, musing to herself: *not a bad life.*

She took care not to venture near the stadium that evening, standing firmly by her decision not to attend fight night. This also meant not eating at Kanchana's Kitchen - which was slap-bang next door. She loved

Uncle Lung-Lung's chicken, but he had closed early; and anyway, she preferred to sit on the road in the daytime watching the world go by. On her tiny balcony, the aircon unit whirred, spitting out thick dirty water, and she gazed up the road for inspiration. Nothing presented itself, but she couldn't survive forever on pot noodles and sugar sachets.

Across the road she could just make out a dim light, coming from a place she had passed many times but never stopped at, the menu written in poor English and the expressions of the staff blank and apprehensive. Well, what of it? She was famished and it was *her* neighbourhood now – time to forge some new relationships.

She hobbled down the steps of her apartment in a shawl and crossed the dark road. She walked in, bowing her head respectfully, eagle-eyeing the least conspicuous table. An open-mouthed girl came to serve her, her face white from bleaching-cream, her petite body dressed immaculately with a hijab covering her hair and her eyes shining in beauty. She approached Hannah nervously, clutching a small notebook.

"Noodle soup? Beef?" Hannah guessed. The girl nodded silently before quietly stepping back into the kitchen. There weren't any other customers tonight, and numerous members of the family sat around a monstrous TV, blaring out a dramatic Thai soap opera. Though

Hannah couldn't understand it, she fixed her gaze in its direction to ease her awkwardness. She didn't suppose many foreigners came here, with the peculiar service and unwelcoming facade.

189

The soup came – dark, sweet and brothy, Muslim-style. She slurped it down and instantly felt better, the tables around her coming into focus. A little girl played out the back of the roomy wooden residence, her Mama gently scolding her for being too excited; a condition likely caused by the luminous pink soda she sipped through a straw. Men occasionally appeared from around doorways, peering at Hannah - inspecting the new specimen. She finished her soup and waited ten minutes or so for it to go down, still 'watching' the TV drama in which a doctor cunningly plotted to inject a poor, beautiful damsel with poison. After paying - which took some time – she smiled at everyone she could see in hope of approval, then hurried back to the safety of her home - her *bahn* - to set up camp for the night. Away from the bright lights of the boxing stadium she could while away some hours catching up on her writing.

If there was any chance of a visit from her man, it would be around midnight when the paying public got turfed out of the stadium and the bikes hooned off to Charlie Chang's. Yet midnight passed and, sleepy, she got into her favourite muumuu - the one with the blue flowers - and hit the pillow hard: no more sleeping in vests and skirts.

At around 7am she stirred but remained horizontal, figuring out her state of mind and mood - rested yet hazy.

Suddenly came a frantic knocking on the door. Alerted, she swung her legs around and sat up. With nowhere to run and nowhere to hide, she legged it to the door, pulled it open with force and leapt back onto the bed. Kit strode in enthusiastically like a gallant puppy dog and threw himself down beside her. She looked to him in bemused confusion.

"Sleeping!" she said.

He placed one arm over her body and talked quickly, but with little sense, "Oooooh, *mau mau*! Last night, last night…I fight! I…I fight!" He indicated to himself frantically.

"Oooh!" she mirrored back, trying to summon up excitement from her morning docility.

"I win!! I fight, I win!!" He was clearly still drunk but in a happy way, in yesterday's clothes, come straight to her after the last whisky had been drained from the bottle. She smiled now and slowly she got up to open the back door for air and sunlight. She sat down beside him as he continued, "Today I not work! Have holiday!"

'Wow,' she thought – were they to spend the day together? How would that go? He embraced her but they remained fully-clothed, without even the first clamours of arousal.

"You okay?" he checked. She nodded, but she was in truth embarrassed at her morning attire, him seeing her yet again at her worst – but him not seeming to think anything unusual of it. Had she gone to the stadium last night she could have taken home the prize fighter, but instead she had vouched for soup and safety.

They sat on her tiny balcony while he filled her in on his victory; he had knocked out his opponent without even having trained! He was high, happy, drunk and sweet. When they went back inside, he managed to string a rehearsed sentence together, "I go see daughter, Krabi, I come back tomorrow."

She wondered if he would stay a while – if they should perhaps go and eat breakfast together - but she needed wonder no further, as he abruptly announced his departure. He threw himself over her, hugging her mid-section tightly, "I like you very much!" he piped out rapidly. She smiled back at him as he left.

"I come back tomorrow!"

Tomorrow was February the fourteenth - her sweet lover would return!

Now she started the day for the second time, a little bewildered but with a certain sweetness: her funny valentine.

28. All the Lonely People

Valentine's Day arrived, and though Hannah had conditioned herself never to expect too much, her man was coming home! How wonderful it would be in the arms of a fresh love on such a day! She rushed through her shift at the shop, reserving energy for the afternoon. *This* time she wouldn't stay away – she was going training to see her lover, reserving his arms for the night.

Excited and with extra effort put into looking sharp in her Muay Thai gear, she arrived at the gym around 4pm. It was busy, and there was no air of the romantic about it at all. She went to get her card stamped in the back office then warmed up on a tyre. There was Kit – on the far side - busy sparring with a young western guy she hadn't seen before. He was good – *very* good – and Kit didn't even glance around at her as she bounced. She couldn't wait to see her man but she felt that something wasn't right. She put it down to shyness and got on with training, but after bag-work he *still* didn't approach her, so with a resigned nod at Squishy Nose she climbed under the ropes and suffered three rounds of gruelling pad work. She could feel her shins being battered, and as she looked at Squishy's pads she could see that they were hacked-up, with sharpened pieces of leather jutting out: that was one way to teach the farangs.

Throughout, she kept looking over at Kit who was on the floor mats. Squishy smirked at her – he knew her game. Why couldn't everything be merry and gay as it was supposed to be?

After three rounds her sinister trainer muttered simply in a low, sinister tone, "Jut jop," – *finished* - the end. It felt more loaded than just an instructor's words, and Hannah felt suffocated in this impenetrable gym and its scathing, watchful eyes – even with Mel still in the arse end of Malaysia filling up on masala dosas.

Jut jop it was then?

She hung about for a while, watching the new boy throw spectacular head kicks, but Kit had disappeared out back. Could he be borrowing a motorbike to carry her home?

Kit didn't reappear, however, and she knew that as soon as she walked away from the dusty doorstep of the training space that she would have even fewer answers, so she sat on a bench waiting.

When he finally appeared, she rose slowly to her feet, looking at him deliberately. He knew she was on the approach and to avoid a commotion he moved towards her but with no smiles or eye contact. Hannah's voice came out in a strangled moan, "Can you take me home?"

"Not have motorsai."

"Can…can you come later?"

"No have motorsai!!" he repeated with an exasperated shrug.

Defeated and exhausted, it was time to put her tail between her legs and tread the long path home alone. She couldn't help but look back as she started the ascent to the jungle track, just in case…*just in case*…but there was nothing but Swedes at their bungalows and boxers milling in and out of doorways - a clockwork toy universe, fully cast with all the

194

characters needed – no part for her, and no invitation for a call-back. She hoped that it was just a technicality, but why should something so magical and full of promise suddenly become something so sad? She had come to expect disappointment from love, but there seemed no *reason* for this - she hadn't done anything wrong – and it seemed such a swift change of heart from 24 hours ago.

Hannah hit the road and started the long trudge home in the fading heat. At 7-11 she made a sudden decision to call in on Jen, back from Krabi, who lived nearby in a small row of conjoined shacks which served as low-rent homes for downbeat locals. As she approached the track, she could see that the ramshackle door was wide open, and inside that she could just make out a crumpled figure, a little heap of a figurine-like woman, mourning on the ground.

Jen looked up as she approached. Her hair was beautifully tied back in a twist, and her make-up so pretty - yet her face forlorn.

She summoned up a whimper of a smile as Hannah sat on the floor beside her.

"I've been so sad all day," she began in a rapid and jumbled stream, "Mon didn't get me anything for Valentine's and I made him a leather bag, and it's been awful and we had a fight and I've been crying all day."

There was no trace of the aforementioned Mon - that unromantic rogue. Hannah comforted her gently and listened to her Valentine's woes, before recounting her own tale of pitiful rejection.

"We could go and get some food?" Hannah suggested - perhaps in their rejection they might find solidarity, hope even? But Jen was staying put to thrash out her drama, so Hannah bade her leave and went quietly on her way, very much alone but reassured a little by their sharing of sorry tales.

Perhaps she could write. She opened up her laptop and managed a tenuous connection to a wifi point somewhere in the distance. She settled down to a solitary night with nothing but social media for company - still holding out for that knock on the front door – and as it happened, she turned out not to be alone: 86 other lonely hearts on Facebook chat were turning to any remote connection to get a fix of love on Valentine's. Now she felt less desperate and alone she placated herself, rationalising that this might be just another three-week fling to end in fear or miscommunication. Perhaps it was better not to tumble into another mad love affair: perhaps the story ended here.

She posted a link to Roberta Flack's 'The First Time Ever I Saw Your Face', and a few ex-boyfriends reached out to her in support, but as she stumbled into a troubled sleep in the pretty skirt she had vowed to no longer wear at moonset, she decided that she needed to be a woman of action.

29. Gypsy Han

Not so bright and breezy, Hannah got up, shook off her lethargy and shot out to get things done. Armed with a memory-stick, she took herself in search of a printing shop to make some flyers for tarot readings. She had brought her cards with her from England and knew them quite well; besides, she could rely on her mystical acting skills to get her through. After much mishap and technical duress, she was the proud owner of ten colour posters, two laminated signs for the coffee shop and Jeab's store, and a hundred flyers to be flung around – starting with Happy Printing Shop itself - who gladly propped some up proudly on the front desk.

It was hungry work, so in the afterglow of success she visited the bustling German Bakery to order a congratulatory feed of strong coffee and porridge – substantially perfect with its banana and honey - and looked over her pile of flyers. A voice hollered over in her direction, "Oh…Aaye!" She pointed her nose up briefly to find a rather ungainly, cheery-looking mass before her.

"Where'd ya get yer flyers from? Can't find a photo-shop anywheres!" Nothing could mask the unmistakable drawl of a Queenslander on the road, "Me name's Macca, pleased ta meet ya!"

Though about to head off, she was always happy to help a traveller in need, so she stood up and indicated, "Happy Printing's just along the way, they have some camera stuff."

"Fancy a ride?" He offered. So before she knew it, she had mounted his bike and they were back off to the printing shop on the lookout for a tripod.

"Into photography, are you?" Hannah enquired politely.

"Yeah, y'know, I try an' that," shrugged Macca.

"I'm a writer," said Hannah.

As they whizzed past a gigantic poster for Miss Ladyboy Koh Talay Beauty Pageant, she had an idea. Pointing at the garish and gargantuan billboard she proposed, "Fancy going to that contest with me tomorrow night...take a few snaps for an article I'm writing?"

It was true that she *did* have a contact in Bali who would pay for Asian news, and the competition *did* look like ridiculous fun.

"Sure! Sure!"

"Stop! Here!" she said, near her room yet not too close for him to know the exact location.

Yet he carried on, closer to the *bahn itsalam* where she sheltered, where again she instructed him to stop.

"Nah...nah, I'll drive ya to yer door!!" insisted 'Macca'. She explained to him that as a lone girl on a crazy island there had to be rules, and then he understood. She arranged to meet him at his bungalow at sunset tomorrow when they could ride together to the ladyboy event of the year.

What a tonic to meet a new friend. Now she not only had set up her new tarot venture, but had an engagement for tomorrow night - when the writer, the photographer and screw-loose Jen would let themselves loose on a field full of hopeful beauty queens.

* * *

That night she tried writing, but it felt like a hopeless distraction - seeing as the plot could already have expired. Impatient at the best of times, she wanted answers: Where was Kit? Why did he not want to be her beau anymore? As no words sprang forth, she attempted to purge the emotions out of herself.

She opened google translate and began constructing an imaginary letter to her make-believe love:

Dear Kit,

Sorry I didn't come to see you at the gym, but I find it hard when your friends laugh and make jokes around me. I thought you might come to see me, but maybe it's not what you want.

I like you and feel happy when I'm with you, and think you're funny too, but do you want us to be together? I enjoy training together and hope we can again.

Tomorrow I will come to the gym.

Yours,

Hannah.

A little weak, but research had revealed that the Thai way to ask for answers was to say little and nudge gently – not to boulder-blast in, no matter how strong the desire.

She edited the note intricately which took her some while – re-writing it over and over in search of the true essence of her heartache. It was clear that she now needed to know if there was a future for them –

or whether she had quietly departed from his consciousness. She still felt weak, but condensing her whirling emotions into an inhumane translation tool trimmed a little weight off her mind.

After the purge she wrote about Macca and the kindness she had experienced that day – Mama and Papa who had gladly unburdened a bundle of tarot flyers from her.

In the late afternoon sun, she wandered out to try and buy some wine from 7-11 in Klong Kung. Next door was a store that sold cheap sunglasses – and as Hannah's were a bit old and tatty she went in and chose some oversized wayfarers. As she handed over the money, the overbearing sales assistant thrust a flyer into her hand, reading: '*Miss Ladyboy Koh Talay, don't miss!*'

"Oh yes," said Hannah, "I know!"

"You come?" asked the frighteningly pushy woman.

"Well-"

"I sell tickets! You buy! I bring many, many *katoey* ladyboys from the mainland!"

With nowhere to run she purchased her ticket – tomorrow was on!

With her imaginary love-letter painstakingly punched out, her ladyboy article notes scribbled down and a few stray book notes, that night she showered carefully then donned her blue moo-moo for a good night's sleep. She would need to be rested for her mission tomorrow, moonlighting as a journalist for a gaggle of ferocious, transgender, wannabe beauty queens as soon as twilight fell.

30. Hot off the Press

She was a little lacklustre on her shift at the shop - Jeab could tell that something was afoot – yet Hannah still served with a smile - if a little empty. On her way home, Faa came rushing out of the Fitness Centre, shrieking at her directly, "I'm so excited about the competition tonight!"

Wanting to share in her jubilation, they went inside so Hannah could buy tickets for Jen and Macca, watching as Faa carefully and proudly tore along the perforated lines, gushing with sheer excitement, "Mel said she might come!!...Yes, she back today, she said she try to come!"

Mel, who would refer to Faa as 'Oh you mean the *ladyboy*!'

Indeed, Mel had been fishing about all day on Facebook for gossip - but had also informed Hannah that one of her Muay Thai 'contacts' was fighting in town and that she'd agreed to go, so her false promises were likely to let 'the ladyboy' down.

The afternoon proved long and there was only so much napping that could be done. Eventually, Hannah turned to her laptop whereupon Google Translate stared her in the face, along with the love letter she had strung together the night before. She re-read it: though not exactly life-changing, it wasn't half bad, and with a heavy dose of hesitation she copied it into a word document and went off to seek out a printing shop.

The first place was useless - the computer couldn't convert her version of word - but she spotted a man across the way, sitting behind a desk with his feet up

201

on a chair. Behind him was a row of PCs lined up against the wall, and there was no one else around. She crossed the road and slipped off her shoes at the dusty entrance. The man welcomed her in, flapping his arms excitedly. His slacks were from the 1970s, and his wily expression suggested that he had seen some living. She plugged in her USB and opened the document - a crazed font stared her back in the face. She called the kooky man over from his lounging-counter, who peered at the screen in scrutiny.

"Ohhhh..." he spoke, "You write this letter in Thai?"

"Yes. I just want to print it."

"Oh...no...no!!" he said, his limbs shaking with seriousness, "No good!"

"I know but-"

"You write 'pom' not 'chan' – you a man!" He fell about laughing - perhaps he had better take a look over it after all.

Together they sat, the man - strange in his clodhopper sandals - carefully asking Hannah exactly what she meant by each phrase, in a high-pitched nasal tone. She explained the best she could which only proved to highlight the glaringly apparent meaninglessness of the whole debacle, and carefully and deliberately the man set to work, crafting his version of the situation, giving her letter his own voice – that of an effeminate eccentric, shrieking from time-to-time in Italian as he slid his slippers on and off.

"No! In Thailand we not say like this! This 80%! You need 30...40%!"

The strange man continued, "I was a writer! Agony Uncle – me - big magazine! Had to stop!" he flapped his arms about chaotically, "Too much smoking, too many late nights, too much for this!" he said, whirring his hands at his temples.

And so it was that Hannah and the Agony Uncle re-wrote her imaginary love-letter to Kit; now in a gentler style: more *rescue me* than *fiery farang*. Two hours passed and she wondered what the hell they had done, but it was printed and ready to go. Why she had put her trust so completely in a bonkers stranger was another matter, but in some way she was beyond caring. He offered up some final gems of advice, "You must not give it to him, Thai always need middle man! Through a friend, through a friend better!"

Not wanting to change her mind, she whizzed straight to the fitness centre - maybe Faa could give it to Kit before getting ready for the pageant. She peered through the gargantuan glass doors but couldn't see her anywhere. In her place sat a younger boy that Hannah recognised from her first days on Koh Talay. He was alone. She drew breath and marched in, presenting the unmarked envelope, "You know Kit, yes?"

The boy's face lit up with mischief and excitement – he did indeed know Kit and was thrilled to be appointed Cupid's messenger. Convinced that he would complete this most serious deed, and, with a wave of her finger – NO PEEKING! - Hannah rushed back home to fashion a suitable costume for the sequin-spangled extravaganza that next awaited her.

31. Miss Ladyboy Koh Talay

The unlikely threesome handed in their cheap paper tickets and swaggered into the dank field haphazardly. Empty plastic chairs wobbled around metal tables, and food stalls lined the dark, mulchy path that led the troublesome trio to their table in the front row.

"I'll warn you in advance," Hannah warned, "I'll probably go into serious writing mode shortly - and when I start you can't stop me!"

The other two nodded, Macca laying out his various lenses on the wobbly iron table and the eternally erratic Jen sitting dormant, for now, under the pretence of obedience. Here was a dubious table of professional con-artists amongst the performers, who were somewhere to the side fussing about with layers-upon-layers of face powder and false eyelashes. Shielded from the public eye only by a flimsy canvas canopy - put together no doubt by moustachioed locals at three in the morning for a bottle of Hong Thong - the stars of the show awaited their entrance.

Hannah shifted about in her seat, preparing her notepad and pen in an imitation of efficiency, still waiting for the creative flow to burst forth.

With a few high-pitched squeals from the PA system, onto the stage milled an intriguing collection of Southern Thailand's most lovely ladies, led by a hideous creature in a bolshy, strapless dress that looked like it had been lurking behind a cheap leather sofa. The various array of nervous, garish beauties filed in haphazardly, forming a wonky line. Each held a number card in front of their plumped-up breasts: some hormonal, some puppy-fat, some stuffed, some silicone.

Hannah let out a yelp of excitement as she identified Faa, who was tentatively trembling in galactic high heels, her lip juddering with nervous tension as she attempted to brave a smile.

"She looks so nervous!" whispered Jen. Hannah held the tip of her pen to the page - still waiting for inspiration - and the compere began her commentary in Thai. Jen howled along to it as she interpreted, "She keeps calling number three Monkey Face!" Nobody could deny that number three - now sporting a venomous scowl - did look a little primitive.

After much parading and a dance routine from a troupe of misfits, it was time for the intelligence round.

"Question 1: You can have a handsome man but small, or an ugly man but big: which would you choose? Question 2: If you die, what do you want the people to do with your body? Question 3: You must pick one man: one will love you but get hit by a car, one loves you but has HIV, one will love you but hits YOU with a car, WHO WILL YOU CHOOSE?!!"

Things were starting to get juicy. Macca was enjoying snapping away as self-appointed paparazzi, Hannah pretended to write meaningful notes though her mind remained firmly at the Muay Thai gym. Jen, meanwhile, had joined a scattering of adoring friends and family at the front of the stage, throwing 20-baht roses at the immaculate Faa.

Without warning, the dramatic event came to a sudden halt, as the heavens opened and heavy pellets of rain crashed down onto the stars and audience alike. The aghast lovelies shrieked, scarpering off the stage, and everyone else speedily gathered their things and dashed about looking for shelter. Stagehands appeared, hastily stowing away the electrics.

Hannah and her two amigos grabbed their various wares and, after a hesitation, nodded in agreement – the best place would be under the canopy just over there...

They entered the canvas cocoon to find warming floods of lamplight enveloping the contestants, stylists and crew. Hannah crept in further - Macca and Jen followed suit. Gently Hannah tapped Faa on the shoulder. She turned, with an expression that quickly switched from disappointment to hope - for here they were, her farang supporters!

"You look beautiful!" gushed Hannah.

"Really? They put on too much white - I don't like it!" Faa replied, referring to her complexion - and she had a point; up close her ghostly make-up resembled Plaster of Paris.

Some queens re-touched their garish faces, whilst others gossiped excitedly, eating noodles from polystyrene trays. All sheltered from the storm and prayed for it to pass, but a failing momentum fizzled into sure defeat as the lights were turned off over the waterlogged field: there were to be no grand prizes, nor glory, for the girls. As the colourful troupe started to disperse, the snap-happy three scurried ahead, exiting before them.

Through the pitch-black, sodden field they tripped, yelping and squelching, happy at such fun as Macca played cameraman to their frolicking. Then to a lit shelter across the road which served them Thai food from a tatty menu. Jen and Hannah ordered morning glory in oyster sauce and chicken noodle soup, and Macca feasted on fried delights.

Afterwards, racing against the rain they rode in tandem, swerving around the red-clay curves, Jen safely depositing Hannah at her Muslim door and returning to a more placid Mon.

As their delicious mini adventure drew to a close, Hannah felt a familiar pang begin its beat from within. If this night was over, and if Kit had received the note, then the next chapter of her story must be waiting – come high hope or disappointment.

32. But How?

She turned the key and entered her home-from-home. With TV for company and her laptop wearily blinking away at the half-ready, she flung down her wares and peeled off her wet costume. She braved a quick, cold shower – tensing under the icy spray whilst keeping a keen ear out for a knock-knock-knock.

Settling down in rainy-day comfort clothing, she stared vacantly at the television screen, on which monks chanted in a hazy glow from the tenuous aerial connection. She sighed – she sighed a lot, but at least it was late and sleep would soon come to finish the day. She took some satisfaction from the semi-accomplished mission to *Miss Ladyboy Koh Talay*, and now she could attempt to write the magazine column.

Just as she began to drift into semi-consciousness, it came. The almost unfamiliar knock! Just three metres away behind the insecure wooden door: her lover was here!

Her internal world rapidly evaporated as she made split-second preparations: rushing quietly to the bathroom mirror, she checked herself – she looked okay. She wished for more time to compose herself, but without any she twisted open the rattly knob and allowed the door to swing freely open. Too bashful to stare her fantasy in the eye, she turned back towards the bed, but made no headway, as a perplexed and fumbling Kit stumbled into the room with panicked urgency, catching her, turning her around and putting his short, sturdy arms around her. He continued to trip and stumble into her, and still she could not look him in the eye. He held her still, and panting with worry, he breathed, "Solly, solly, solly!!"

"It's okay," she said shortly, walking out of his embrace over to the chair to sit at her desk, leaving him to arrange himself in the space. Overwhelmed by the unexpected dramaturgy of his entrance, she closed off her body to him, along with her emotional availability, in an attempt to gain composure, and continued tap-tapping away at her computer like a Western fool, unsure of what had made him burst in so urgently.

He sat on the edge of the springy bed with his knees wide apart and his nervous hands clasped together. She could feel his stare piercing through her so, though uncomfortable, she turned her body to face him.

"But...but...!" he forced out in troubled perplexity, "We together? How?" He made the Thai gesture for togetherness, drawing two fingers together to touch in front of him.

"I don't know!" said Hannah, idiotically.

"When...When you go?...What happen?"

"I don't know! I have one more month but I want to stay longer."

She smiled a lopsided, cowardly smile that offered no solution to the man before her. The securing of relationships had never been her forte and, indeed, he was no more reassured.

She knew this: she wanted him – slowly, the panic of his sudden arrival subsided and the room came back into focus. She went to him, sliding her arms naturally around the body she had so missed, and lowered herself down beside him, allowing the embrace to unfold, a kiss and a holding of the face. This was how they could be together now, this their only understanding.

After the act of love, they went to Hannah's tiny balcony and lounged comfortably together, peering around at the night scene before them – an odd dog cautiously treading his path home in the dark forest surrounds, a tuk-tuk ridden by Muslim lovers who clutched on tightly to one another as they flew through the night jungle mist.

"I like Koh Talay," said Kit.

"Me too," nodded Hannah, appreciating both setting and dialogue - the calm composure of post-coital release, all tension now evaporated. These were the only words needed.

It was already bedtime – there would be no need for the fuzzy pop-channel tonight. They took their respective places – Hannah on the left, and Kit on the right. He arranged the blue fleece blanket around his cold limbs but Hannah stayed uncovered - too hot with her Western blood. With their arms around each other, smooth and close, they drifted, kissing, Hannah's face shining in perfect contentment in the dark.

33. Butterflies

At 7am her man arose, letting her snooze but sniff-kissing each cheek warmly. The sun streamed into her room and Kit opened the back door to let in some air, then quietly bid his leave and left for work. When the door was firmly closed and his footsteps had echoed off down the stairwell, Hannah allowed herself to wallow in the delight of her man coming home. She allowed her heart to brim over with glee and indulged in the illusion that she'd never been perplexed – oh how the heart erased! She held onto 'yes' for now, and bathed in the warm afterglow.

As Hannah got up and dressed to go to her own workplace, her mind shifted to a more realistic plane as she replayed the 'making up' conversation over and over. There wasn't a lot to over-analyse, but she had a good go at it. She now felt embarrassed at her awkward, childish responses, and vowed to fix it somehow – to try *for once* to confirm a relationship. She should probably spend more time at the gym - perhaps even *move* there - oh wouldn't that be the dream! Her plus lover in a Muay Thai community on a hill, in their cosy little bungalow - a simple life, languidly writing in a sweeping sarong as Kit masterfully instructed the farangs, winning the occasional fight in his full glory.

Somewhere in the damaged part of her heart she knew that it was only a dream, but perhaps reality was sometimes made from dreams. After all, hadn't she made her journey here to this magical, mysterious island of endless intrigue from a dream? Couldn't she take it further - couldn't she make it all the way?

On her walk to Salee Mart she floated like a butterfly past Uncle Lung-Lung who was waving and smiling, and the brothel girls who sat around munching on snacks, bored in their dreaded wait for dubious custom.

Past Madame Kanchana, who shone with a busy smile, down the dry, dusty track. The Brothel Ma'am yelled out to her, so obediently she went to sit on the edge of her bamboo platform. The Brothel Ma'am produced a cigarette, smoking thoughtfully with a conspiratorial look on her never-telling brow.

"You!!" she said, sticking her chin up at Hannah, "You!!" Drawing two fingers together, "You! Together or not?"

My, how news travelled fast. Hannah smiled and shrugged – you could tell something was up with her from the way she flounced around in lovestruck delirium.

"Mai roooo!" she said playfully: *I don't know!*

The Brothel Ma'am sat nodding stealthily, chewing on a piece of dry grass. She butted her nose in the air, signalling permission for Hannah to leave.

At the stiflingly hot shop Jeab stood beneath a fan, slicing pineapple for the fruit trays. Exhausted, she wiped her brow as Hannah approached.

"Got period! Oooooooo! Bpuat tong!!" she said, clutching her stomach.

"Mine's finished already!" replied Hannah. Jeab took a piece of pineapple and dipped it in chilli and salt.

"Don't like the taste, but good for period. Yes! Good for cleaning the blood!"

214

As Hannah wondered about the validity of this folk remedy, she refilled the Wonder Dang cigarette-shelf and served a few stray farangs.

"You use the tampons?" asked Jeab in low-toned curiosity.

"Yes," replied Hannah, "Thai people don't, do they?"

"No, no," concurred Jeab, "Except prostitutes - yes! They use them so they can work when they have period!"

Hannah shuddered at the very thought. As they considered topics for today's lunchtime debate, a slip of a young girl wandered in, as lost as a lamb. She turned to Hannah head-on and stared at her with icy-blue pools of trouble.

"You are Hannah, right? You read the tarot?"

Hannah was taken aback, "Uh...yes!"

"I need a reading!" She was more demanding than enquiring.

"Okay! How's your English?"

"I am Cherman but I can understand for everything!"

The girl stood there acutely, her face sucking in Hannah's brain like a vortex.

"Today? You can?"

"Uh-" Hannah had been so pleased with the achievement of making the flyers, that she had forgotten someone might *actually* want a reading.

"Yes, okay. Actually - can you do tomorrow? I finish work at 3pm, we could meet outside on the bench?"

Hannah needed a day to digest; it wasn't that she had any particular plans for today - she just wasn't quite prepared for such abrupt confrontation. The girl went away happily. Hannah turned to Jeab, pulling a face.

"Maybe you can do *my* tarot!" suggested Jeab. It beat pricing up mars bars, and meant that they could sit and rest, so Hannah cleared a small space on the laminated counter-top and began the reading, taking mouthfuls of Jeab's home-made jungle curry in between cards.

Tarot was in its nature a little awkward – ruminating over someone's inner life without any *real* knowledge of their past - uncovering potentially uncomfortable truths; ones she might rather not know about!

Jeab's reading revealed a lot of strong female mental energy surrounding her - perhaps *too* much – which could be stopping anyone getting through to her. Jeab concurred – she only counted two women on the entire island as close friends, and she didn't trust many people - especially with her personal business. Delving deeper still, the reading focused on her husband Yim, and Jeab's stubbornness in the way she communicated with him.

Jeab didn't say much at first, and Hannah hoped she hadn't offended, but suddenly it all came tumbling out: Jeab had only ever loved Yim, they had been childhood sweethearts from the same neighbourhood. He was a simple, local boy and had always been true to her – except once when her daughter Salee, after whom the shop was named, was young and he had 'been a butterfly', but this was apparently quite normal for Thai men, Jeab advised, and when she told him to stop, he did.

Yet Yim was lazy and couldn't think for himself. True, he was a good Papa - but not a good husband. He couldn't handle his finances nor the little seaside restaurant that he ran, and he hung about with losers who were going nowhere. There didn't seem much between them in terms of partnership.

The story felt quite sad. Hannah already felt part of the family, and Yim greeted her so warmly when she trudged in for her nescafé in the mornings - now she felt obliged to look at him from a different side. The cards spoke more.

"You are strong and you have had to be strong in your life - and look at what you've achieved! You've supported and held together your whole family, but you go too far. You are allowed to be soft: you can be a softer, more sensitive woman - especially with Yim. You can take that chance."

Jeab thanked Hannah and told her she would pay 100 baht for one final question. Hannah shook away the money, but Jeab was insistent.

"Okay! What's the question?"

"It's not for the cards - it's for you."

Hannah's internal organs jumped into her throat: Jeab was a strong woman and close friend, and Hannah didn't want to pull the wool over her eyes, but was petrified of offending her.

"What do you think of me?" Jeab announced strongly, fixing her large brown cow-eyes on Hannah's small blue oceans.

This question she could answer, "You are a strong, true family woman who doesn't suffer fools, but your heart is immense. You are clever and sharp, and an excellent judge of character. You know that looking

217

after family comes first, and you take enough love in return - but nothing compared to what you give. This is because you know that what you give comes back by way of karma." Hannah stopped, "Was that enough?"

"Yes!" said Jeab, happy with her answer. They sat together contentedly for the rest of Hannah's shift, eating chunks of pineapple with chilli and salt.

When she got home, she didn't have the energy to do anything productive, so she lazed about on her laptop, chatting with Jen about Kit. Things were going well with Mon, and the girls decided to go on a dinner date to celebrate both their successes, and each other.

Jen picked Hannah up and they set off in search of food. The British pub that Jen recommended that always seemed so dark and eerie was closed, so they continued to ride past Klong Kung and its quiet whorehouses, ending up in the harbour.

At night, the usually bustling port became silent. A few tourists meandered, sleeping in boutique B & Bs before catching boats to the mainland in the morn. Pretty artists' studios lined the path to the jetty.

"There's some great falafel around here somewhere," said Jen - both of them hungry for Western food. Nearing the ferry ticket office, they found it - a quaint wooden bookshop built on wooden stilts, complete with languidly lounging cats, that opened out over the water into a restaurant. The staff were brisk and unfriendly, but that didn't matter – they had the hummus, the falafel and the flatbread. The girls chose a table close to the water's edge, sailboats bobbing on the wave, a fresh night breeze flowing through. With gin-and-tonics in hand they chinked glasses. Just as contentment filled their hearts and bellies, just as they started to relax and puff out sighs of relief, a short beeping noise transmitted from Hannah's bag. She took out her phone and retrieved the message: It was from Mel, who was back in town: *'Jen's phone not working. Going to get Esarn food. Korner Bar later. Kit coming.'*

Jen put her head in her hands – Mel had already been hassling her from any angle she could: emails, text messages, missed calls… Hannah's nose slid out of joint at the carrot she now dangled: *'Korner Bar later. Kit coming.'*

Little did Mel know, of his blessing her with his presence whilst she was away. With a few deep breaths, the girls persevered with ignoring the unwanted interruption, and continued to feast, intermittently slurping on G and T.

They paid and Jen announced that she had to go - it was her and Mon's official Valentine's night after he'd made a pig's ear of the real one. Earlier he had presented her with a pearl bracelet – 'the bracelet of guilt', she called it - and after he finished his shift at the restaurant they would spend time babbling and cooing together.

Outside it was starting to spit with rain, but calmly enough the girls slid through the night, sweeping in curves around corners, back to Hannah's *bahn itsalam*, for a warm embrace, good luck and good night. Satisfied with the day, Hannah let herself into room 203 and settled down for an evening of Thai soap operas and contentment.

    * * *

An hour later came the knock. In strode Kit, wet from rain, in t-shirt, jeans and cap.

"Hi," he quipped casually, "Wet!" before matter-of-factly peeling off all of his clothes, leaving him in only his blue briefs. Hannah defied the temptation to stare at his pants, averting her eyes from the Mowgli-like vision. Kit's round chest was proudly pumped out as always - a neat package of a man – and he strode about her room attempting to hang out his clothes. Hannah took the opportunity to intercede and, playing wife, propped coat hangers up on the back of doors upon which to lay his soaked apparel.

"Where did you go? Mel said Korner Bar?" Hannah enquired, as they lay themselves down on the matrimonial spread to get comfortable.

"Mel? No!" he said with a self-conscious chuckle, putting his hand on his forehead as he always did, shaking his head a little and darting his eyes downward as he grinned, coy and embarrassed around the Caucasian girl.

"Rain!" he said, stretching out his arm towards the wind-warped back door, "Go eat with Don! Eat a lot, drink…drink, little bit!" He turned to face her and to run his sturdy arm over her body's profile – from her ribs to her waist to her muscular hips. She smiled - it was all she could do - she couldn't help herself.

They kissed, movements sliding naturally into playful exploration, leading to a turned-on engagement - Kit now taking his place above Hannah, her happy to be taken, knickers eased down and the lighting adjusted, a condom seamlessly grabbed from the side-table, light from the muted TV accompanying the white flashes before her closed

220

eyes as she sunk deeper into ultimate bliss: kissing, conjoining and rocking together in slow waves – breathless gasps from Kit, fully on-board, Hannah willingly journeying with him. Never happier and wholly present; a small sprite whispering in the back of her mind over and over: *'Take me - I'm yours. Break me - I don't care! Just take me, I'm yours.'*

34. On the Cards

The German girl looked deeply into Hannah's eyes, as they glanced between the tarot cards and back to her unblinking gaze, the blue sucking her in like a whirlpool; the girl on the muddy riverbank clinging onto any reeds she could find so as not to get swept away. Intense. A sweet, country girl from Germany with a heart and mouth full of deep, unanswered questions. Serious – and, at the same time, full of air.

It was hot sitting on the uncomfortable stone bench outside Salee Mart. The girl had a dilemma to face, and it was Hannah's job to help the girl interpret the cards, giving guidance and advice, but without putting too much of a slant on things. Often the tarot seemed to offer answers to questions that hadn't been asked: *'What are your true underlying fears? What problem really needs to be dealt with here and now?'* And so unfurled her story: The girl was married, but her husband was back in Germany. She wasn't sure if she was still in love with him and had flown away to start a journey of self-discovery – alone.

Well, *almost* alone. A certain Indonesian tour guide Skyped her daily, promising notions of love and commitment. As she showed Hannah a picture of him Hannah's nose crinkled immediately into a sneer – she had heard this story before, and it was no bestseller. To add to the cacophony of potential disasters, this girl had forged close acquaintance with the insipid Pom-pooey – the sleaze from across the way - whom Hannah trusted as much as a broken chair.

It seemed the girl needed to become a better judge of character - before her hippy tassels got singed by the kerosene flames of romantic tourism - and to stop mistaking cheap mountain thrills for exotic love. Hannah tried to deliver this revelation without pooh-poohing the girl's life. There were three questions to be answered: *What is actually real? How would it work with the tour guide? Is your husband really so bad?*

The girl started to cry. Another half hour of her honking out her washing line of despair and they closed the reading - Hannah agreeing to payment by massage - and so it was that they packed up their troubled cards and trotted back through the little village to the girl's bungalow. Her meagre shack was tucked out back, and though it symbolised nature and simplicity to a starry-eyed traveller, to Hannah it meant rats and mosquitoes.

They took their place on a deserted wooden platform nearby, which fitted the two of them perfectly, and the girl set to work with her warm fingers, kneading Hannah contentedly.

Ging - a good-time Thai woman - flounced up to the tranquil pair and started shouting at Hannah, disrupting their obscure ambience, "I know! I know! He have power? Ha haaaaaa! He have power?"

Hannah answered quickly, in an attempt to divert attention, "Yes - he has power."

"Aaaaaah, he have *power*!" said the prostitute, flexing her muscles, "But does he have POWER?!"

"Yes, he has power," Hannah stated shortly, seeing no reason to be embarrassed of her shenanigans with the island's strongest Muay Thai man. At times like these she wore her Westernness, not seeing the use in adopting a Thai manner; lowering her fluttering eyelids and claiming, *'Oh no! We just friends! We just talking!'* The prostitute knew better anyway and, silenced by Hannah's forthright honesty, went back to boiling up a fish curry. The German girl continued working her magic and, though pleasant, Hannah had big, ungainly knots in her back from boxing that no holistic stroking could re-order. Still, they were even, and Hannah owed her nothing more as she bid her farewell in the late afternoon rays and walked away.

35. Wontons

Fight night felt strangely flat. As they were leaving, Squishy Nose looked over at Hannah with an eerie flash of warning. Still, she stayed close to Kit, and outside the stadium entrance he motioned her over to his motorbike. To Charlie Chang's they did not go; instead, with a small fleet of Thais from the gym, they rode to a soup shack on the side of the road.

The group sat in the blue-dark slurping on soup in near-silence as frogs gopped into the void. Hannah and Kit sat on their own table in the dark, him tucking into his bowl, her attempting an awkward smile. A sweet boy she had nicknamed 'Little Smiler', came to join them; choosing to eat his soup with Kit - his adopted father from the gym – who stole a dumpling from him, drawing it into his succulent brown lips, "You not eating?" he asked Hannah with concern. She shook her head, the inane grin still on her face as she pointed to her plastic bottle of leftover local grog. Kit sped up, finishing his bowl quickly as if he had business to attend to. A smirking girl hollered over at him in a high-pitched, crude tone, and though Hannah couldn't quite catch the words, she heard something like 'song…sahm…' – *two, three*? Kit didn't respond, just turning to Hannah signalling 'time to go', and without a by-your-leave, they left.

Zooming through the night on his high-speed motorbike he took no caution, and when they arrived at the yellow *bahn itsalam* they rushed in the front door and bounded up the stairs two and three at a time. Joyously they entered room 203 and demonstrated no niceties in getting naked and to bed.

Despite the sinister undertones of warning, tonight she had felt close to him; he was working so she had kept her distance and Tee had taken it upon himself to look after her. Afterwards it felt a simple thing to mount Kit's bike – despite the somewhat disapproving onlookers.

There in the room there was no-one to judge them, and their bodies knew each other now, their third consecutive night together. They slept till early morning when Kit arose, cracking his back muscles and kissing Hannah before departing for a long day's training. She rolled over and smiled as she watched him exit – she'd see him later at the gym.

At the shop Jeab was a little brighter now that her monthlies had eased, hooting and laughing at the mangy old men who wandered in for lunchtime beers.

Hannah reserved her energy for the afternoon's training session and didn't make the mistake of napping when she got home. Instead, she cleaned up her room, got herself ship-shape, showered and into her training gear and started the walk to the gym.

She could hear Kit's low, commanding voice as she approached. Obedient to routine she went straight to the rubber tyres to begin her bouncing and switching. Kit didn't turn to look at her nor did he approach; but he was a man at work, after all. When she was warm, she looked about for an instructor to hold pads for her, but everyone was busy. Tee shook his head, and Kit kept his distance.

But of course, lazily sitting on a step was old Squishy Nose, who nodded at her, and so resignedly she climbed through the lower ropes to train with him. She was strong – energised with positivity - and the three rounds flew by easily.

Now came the stomach-churning moment: Kit was sitting in the ring, facing outwards, deep in contemplative thought and exhausted. She smiled at him, "Okay?"

"Yes – same! Working, boxing, tired!"

"Okay," she said, and nothing more – she didn't want to *have* to ask him for a lift home, it was more of an unspoken arrangement between them. Still, she felt uneasy as she wandered outside - there had been a strange undercurrent to their interaction.

She sat on an upturned crate and pretended to check her phone. After an uncomfortable few minutes Squishy Nose wandered up to her, "You have motorbike?" he asked. She shook her head, "You?"

"Noooo, no." Somehow his conversation provided a small comfort, and though down-in-the-mouth, she reasoned that she could walk, and so painfully and deliberately she gathered her things should Kit suddenly notice at the eleventh hour and come running to save her. Couldn't he just pop out to reassure her that everything was fine? No. Instead, another ungainly form bounded out of the gym - Mel!

"Hiiii!!!!" she drooled, faux-concerned, "You need a lift?"

It was exactly what Hannah needed but from exactly the wrong person. Still, as beggars can't be choosers she accepted and they wobbled up the track, Mel forcing her voice into Hannah's ear as she drove, "I know you want space, so it's okay if you don't want me to come in."

Hannah had managed to keep a careful and deliberate distance from Mel since she'd flounced back from her visa run in Penang, whence upon she'd been demoted to a back room at the gym after the mess she'd made with Ake and his angry wife. Hannah had a feeling that Jen had been instrumental in the 'wanting space' concept, but Mel *had* driven her home, and Hannah had no other company, and she did feel a little lonely.

"It's okay - come in!" she found herself blurting with forced enthusiasm.

She had planned not to let Mel into her new place – it was out of bounds, only for her and a certain other - yet now Mel claimed her place, lounging like a lazy lion on Hannah's bed.

"So, what's going on with you and Kit then?" she blurted intrusively as Hannah showered and handwashed her gym clothes.

"Aaah, not much." replied Hannah, "He's been here a few times but-"

"HE'S BEEN HERE?!!" gasped Mel in shock.

"Yeah!" said Hannah - why was that such a surprise, and what the hell did it have to do with the leeching crustacean currently sprawled across their marital bed? She could almost hear Mel's gelatinous brain ticking as she turned the conversation to other things. They went to eat at Kanchana's Kitchen, and Hannah was relieved to have swept Mel out of room 203. Afterwards Mel went home, Hannah grateful for her absence, yet empty inside; numb and worn out from training, but still came the yearning - the never-ending yearning. She turned to words:

At night when I'm lost and lonely,
I won't text but you never phone me.
Wanna tell you you're my one and only,
You don't want me - I'm afraid you own me.

36. Lover, you Should have Come Over

Hannah's emotions were doing her no good, she wanted out from sorrow and confusion, and so the next day she made a plan: she would bite the bullet and call Kit - just a few touches of a button on an unassuming object - it couldn't be *that* hard. The best time would be at sunset – six or seven - when he'd finished training. She would just call, say '*hi,*' and possibly arrange to meet him.

At 5pm for distraction she found herself walking south, past the higgledy-piggledy Muslim eateries, with no particular destination in mind. Sunset approached and, just before the road turned left up into the hills, she turned right towards the ocean. Scrabbling for her phone, she held it in her hand - her pulse quickening as she searched for Kit's number. Gripping it tightly - but still awaiting the nerve to call - she walked closer to the water where the forest path met the sand and young Thai lovers sat nuzzling as the sun smiled its last.

She sat on a concrete bench - she had to do it! She couldn't bear another night holed up in her room, useless and lost. As the clouds turned to milk and the tropical pink seeped through the horizon, she gazed at a small cluster of silhouettes in the sea: a small group of four or five Thai girls frolicking and having fun, taking in the sleepy warmth of dusk.

Wading out from the water they swept towards her, and she continued to enjoy this moment of calm. When they reached just a few metres away there came an unexpected moment of simultaneous recognition: one of the beautiful mer-women gasping in delight as Hannah rose to meet them - Faa and her lovely ladies from the gym.

"What are *you* doing here?" Faa exclaimed.

"I'm not sure! I was just out walking and-"

"Where you going now?" asked Faa, as the group swarmed gracefully towards their motorbikes.

"I guess I come with you!" Hannah replied, climbing onto the back of Faa's motorbike like the old days and going with destiny's flow.

Quickly, she texted Mel: *'Coming to the gym – any chance of a tea?'*

The chance meeting with Faa and elusory cup of tea with Mel was by far a better prospect than some fumbled phone call.

They parked up at the gym and Hannah turned to see Kit's figure in the distance – he was still in the ring, training some students who were to fight on Sunday, so he couldn't have answered his phone anyway. *That* would have left her in a sorry state perpetual purgatory at twilight.

She trotted up to Bungalow Six, where Mel had re-installed herself - eventually forgiven after the faux pas with sleazy Ake. With the kettle on and biscuits produced they chatted aimlessly, Hannah treading water till a chance arose to pounce. In cahoots, Mel suggested that they meander down the hill to the entrance of the gym, where the boys now sat, under the pretence of needing an internet connection, and though Mel had appointed herself chaperone (to Hannah's repulsion), it was her only way in. The girls picked their way like cautious goats down the uneven verge, at the bottom of which two figures sat

234

motionless, silhouetted by the dimmed lights of the gym. Tee swigged absentmindedly from a bottle of *lao kao* while Kit sat - still and silent - his back turned towards them and his skin glowing in the half-light.

The girls approached them from the front, so as not to startle, and when Hannah's eyes met Kit's he smiled a melancholy smile of acknowledgement, then beckoned for her to sit cross-legged beside him on the ground, sniff-kissed her once then regained his poise. His shoulders were lightly dusted with cooling powder and his chest was bare, with just a simple pair of linen trousers covering his legs. He sat silently like a golden Buddha, and Hannah was relieved just to bathe in his presence for a while.

Mel tapped away on her computer whilst Tee swigged on his grog, and though they all attempted sparse conversation Kit was visibly troubled, and Hannah knew to sit and be quiet and patient. His phone rang several times in the duration and he engaged in involved discussions with the caller. Hannah smiled weakly in the hope of offering reassurance, and Kit explained, "My brother – Bangkok - have trouble."

Lek came out from the office and spoke with him in earnest. Hannah could make out something about sleeping arrangements – was someone coming to stay?

Meanwhile, Tee was drunk and being troublesome; poking Mel in her belly while singing a song about fuck buddies in Thai. At least it detracted from the tension of Kit's troubles that lay thick in the air around them. Squishy Nose wandered out from his room somewhere in the depths of the gym,

"Together?" he asked, "Darling? Sweethearts? You?" pointing in dark curiosity at the wistful pair on the platform.

"Nit noi," said Hannah softly.

"Nit noi," concurred Kit - *just a little*. Hannah stayed silent but hopeful - oh how she had fallen.

After Tee had given up jibing Mel, he wandered off to facetime his girlfriend in England, Mel also taking her leave; nodding at Hannah to come up and see her afterwards. Hannah's body overtook her mind, and she reached out to touch Kit, "Ow," she said: *I want you.*

"I know, I know," he replied, "Little, little," and gently pushed her arm away. As they sat, he lightened up a little, linking his leg over Hannah's and swinging them together.

"You stay with me tonight?" asked Hannah. Kit shook his head.

"Don't know – 50, 50." Hannah nodded in agreement - why force it?

"Can borrow Mel's motorbike?" she suggested. He nodded a maybe. They sat a while longer, staring into the void, still swinging.

"I sleep in the road!" he quipped, "You sleep in the sea!"

She smiled. It was dark and the night was over; it was time for bed.

"Okay, I walk you - where you stay? Mel?" Hannah nodded. So, the two of them got up from Buddha's seat of contemplation, and headed slowly up the hill, where Mel lay inside, the light off. They stood apart, facing each other, and in yearning for the past Hannah motioned to the porch on which they now stood.

"Remember?" she asked – referring to that first time they had lain as lovers together, under the moon.

"Yes, remember," said Kit, abashed by her romanticism, "Okay, you stay here - I go to my room," he said, hugging her tightly. His expression showed a want for explanation, but neither them nor their half-hearted dictionaries could translate this confusion. Though soothed to have seen him, an unmistakable sadness hung in the air and inside her very bones, as he left her.

Quietly, she knocked on Mel's door and, finding it already open, entered. Mel was tightly tucked up in bed, "Been snogging yer boyfriend have ya?!" she jibed.

Hannah clambered in beside the large heap to lay to sleep in silent sadness.

"No," she replied, quietly but curt.

37. Go on Now Go

In the morning the heat blasted in, as the nearby construction workers began their incessant drilling. Hannah abruptly left to scuttle home - remnants of last night scattered around her head. When she finally reached her room and had shut the door firmly behind her, she collapsed on the bed, her hand to her forehead. *What. Was. Going. On?* How could something that seemed so good now be something so confusing? Begrudgingly she washed and changed, then sat at her desk and poured her little heart out:

> *'Go on now go,*
> *Where I can't find you.*
> *It's easy, it's easy I know,*
> *I can't be near you.'*

At ten-past eleven she received a phone call from the shop – Jeab wanted to know where she was. Hannah had presumed that their casual working relationship was Thai-style, with no *real* timescale, but perhaps she had got it wrong. Either way, she hoped that Jeab was concerned rather than annoyed. And so it was that she snapped out of her melancholia and made it through the hot streets to the mart, where she set to work hard.

At lunchtime Jeab looked at her quizzically as they ate, and Hannah knew it was time to confide. Jeab was a true friend – not some information-sucker like the expats seemed to be. Hannah hadn't yet shared her story with Jeab in full – and certainly not the late-night visitations – but she had suggested that she liked someone. Hannah wasn't sure if Jeab would be shocked that she had slept with Kit, and that was her premise for not talking about the whole sorry mess with her before. She could only hope that the winks and grabs from the prostitutes saying, '*She like chocolate!*' had also gone unnoticed.

Somehow now she didn't care; she'd reached her limit and needed to share her feelings with someone kind and fair - and brutally honest.

She began, "I really like my Muay Thai guy, but last night when I saw him, he was in some kind of trouble - but I don't know what it is or if it's about me or something else."

Jeab couldn't see why on earth Hannah even liked Thai men – she didn't speak the same language and most of them were half her height and unfaithful, with no pennies to their name.

"Yes, I like *this* Thai man-"

"But why?"

"Not *all* Thai men. Just *this* one," she explained, "He's kind, honest, true, beautiful…"

Jeab was finding the whole thing very funny indeed – Hannah swooning over a mystery Thai man.

In the doorway she stopped, "Is your boy black?" she asked – pertaining to a hard-working Southern boy, not a bleach-skinned boy from Bangkok who stayed out of the sun.

"Yes, he is." Kit had previously boasted to Hannah with working-class pride that his daughter was also black.

"I like bad boys from the jungle!" Jeab suddenly blurted out, before disappearing to re-hang the postcards. Hannah yelped with surprise and glee - it

240

felt great to talk about boys with her true friend. She followed Jeab outside where there was a poster on a lamp post for Sunday's fight. She walked over to look who was on the card and...yes! There was Kit's picture: proud and brown, smooth and strong.

"Jeab! Jeab! Over here!" exalted Hannah, "Here! Here!" she pointed at Kit. Jeab had a good, long look, then they went back into the shop to sit behind the counter.

"Yes, I can see!" deduced Jeab, "He is a good man, yes! Traditional, he has a good heart, yes! I can see in his eyes."

Hannah was so pleased – approval from a woman who meant so much to her. Her heart was soothed by the companionship; and though she had no solution she would go to watch her sweetheart fight – only four days to go...

* * *

That night Hannah was restless and pre-menstrual to boot - these next four days were going to wrangle with her insides. She planned her outfit carefully: conservative with a sexy twist – the 'Thai wife' look. She had been doing squats at any opportunity to ensure she would fit into the heinous purple tights Mel had donated to her: *yes*, they were horrible, but they were tantalisingly tight and perfect for the occasion – with the right thighs Hannah could pull them off.

She had taken to drinking Hong Thong of an evening, and tonight was no exception. The sky was only just turning to sunset orange when she took her first swig – there, that took the edge off. Jen called her, bored out of her skull, and the pair agreed to go and eat soup.

"Mr Green's," said Jen, "It's the only place for soup." Jen should know - being an island veteran - but last time Hannah had gone there the toilet had fully known about it afterwards. She told Jen about this unfortunate incident, along with the news that the Grandpa of the Green family had found a wagon from somewhere and started making his own 'special' soup to sell from it – complete with gnarled old chicken bones. Still, Jen persisted so there they sat, Hannah ignoring her bowl of gruel as Jen tucked into hers - a fried egg floating on top. Hannah had brought her bottle of Hong Thong with her and was far more interested in tending to that. Jen wasn't drinking yet seemed oblivious to Hannah's slightly drunken swagger.

The straggly-haired jungle boy from New Year's Day all those moons ago - who'd sat in silence and shared his music - suddenly arrived at their table with vigour, inviting himself to sit down. Jen grabbed hold of the reins, leaving Hannah to sulk and drink, and gossiped with him in Thai. He'd just got back from Bangkok where he'd gone to pay off the police to avoid prison after hitting someone very hard with a large stick. Hannah grunted - she was disenchanted with sensationalism of glamourised violence, however slapstick.

Reggae Reggae Bar was next door and they decided to go there to try and have a good time.

The bar was quite empty and the girls weren't feeling it.

"Let's go back to yours," suggested Jen.

On the way they stopped off at the local shop. Though the woman there had a sweet concern for Hannah, she gave her a wide berth when she clocked the near-empty bottle of Hong Thong that Hannah clutched to her in deranged confusion. Hannah pointed at a 65-baht bottle of Similan whisky – the one that Jeab said the prostitutes drank every day but seemed fine – and they sloped back off to the *bahn itsalam.*

Back at Hannah's pit of gloom she grabbed the tarot cards from the side, finished up the current bottle of whisky and started on the next - she was drunk and she didn't care! The girls sat on the floor and began the tarot spread. At around the fourth card Hannah suddenly looked up and slurred, "Y'know...it's quite hard reading your cards, 'cos, like, you're really intuitive and intelligent, and...and...I don't think I *make it up* exactly when I do a stranger's, but...but I don't want to bullshit you..."

Jen suddenly noticed the empty bottle, "My God, how drunk are you?!! How did you drink that much whisky?!"

Hannah stopped proceedings for a moment and, ignoring her comment, informed Jen that they both had got carried away and that the cards were *actually* saying that she should start her own business, right away!

They sped up to the end of the reading – it was past 1am - and Jen zoomed back off to Mon and Hannah to bed: rancid and boozy. Exhausted, she collapsed into a fitful sleep.

38. The Photoshoot

Hannah roused, full of Similan confusion and vague recollections of hatching a plan last night, somewhere between the soup and tarot cards. A path to Kit, perhaps? After all, the plot needed to continue if she was ever to write this book. A photoshoot! Yes! Hannah and Jen would go to the gym this afternoon, Jen taking her snazzy camera to snap away at Hannah training.

Wretched, she pulled together whatever of herself she could, and got to the minimart. A woman in a pinny was cleaning the hot-water boiler.

"Jeab not here! Gone to Krabi!" she said - no work today.

On the way home she stopped in to see Mama and Papa at her old lodgings. Papa welcomed her with outstretched arms, shrieking, "Ma eeeengle!"

"Um?"

"Me aaaaangul," he attempted again. He flapped his arms - *My angel!*

Yes – a stinking, sweaty angel fallen from the clouds. Mama grinned briskly, as was her way, but refused to touch Hannah - declaring her 'wet'. Hannah ate fried eggs and tried to recover from the cycle of whisky abuse, the weather so hot she had no idea if she was hungover, hallucinating or, for all she knew, about to die. She got the eggs down her and retained them, struggled back to her room, and coerced herself into her training gear.

Sod it - a plan was a plan.

Striding towards the gym, Faa sped past, halted abruptly and beckoned for Hannah to climb up back, like in times gone by. Hannah obliged and Faa took her as far as the turn-off to the gym, then Hannah went back to collect Jen.

As usual, the door was open and Jen could be seen inside, busily making leather purses on the floor. Always a bit loose with time, Jen scuffled about for a bit, then got her camera and they mounted her powerful motorbike together. As they rode, Hannah barked out instructions, "I want LOTS of shots, but more videos than stills! Make sure you catch the funny things that happen!!" Jen nodded - Hannah was a hard taskmaster.

The gym was busy and Jen walked in naturally, gabbling in Thai at Tee - whom she regarded as the hottest thing since *tom yam* - while Hannah attempted nonchalance. She started warming up, keeping a beady eye on Jen to make sure her camera was at the ready. No one seemed to want to do padwork with her – she was no longer the new blonde on the block –old news, used goods.

So instead, sweaty and excited, Hannah punched and kicked bags for Jen, screaming at the camera, "No one wants to train me! Look! A camera at last, and no one wants to train me!"

The gym boys caught on to her frustrations and looked about them awkwardly, wondering who would take the baton. There was always Squishy Nose: Hannah strode up and propositioned him, but he motioned to his foot - he'd slipped whilst mopping the gym mats under Mel's strict supervision and twisted his foot, so now he couldn't train.

Hannah was raring to go. She stared at the trainers in the ring – Man, Tee, and Kit. Tee was busy in combat with his new fuck buddy, the horse-faced Susan, who was getting rather angry with him as he taunted and tutted at her every move. Man was busy too, but Kit, well Kit seemed to be free.

"Oh COME OOOON!" whinged Hannah, ballsy in front of the camera, "Na beua!" – *boring*!

Defeated, Kit agreed apprehensively, and Hannah climbed straight into the ring. This was exactly the point at which she forgot the presence of the camera - of Jen - of everyone.

"Mow kang!" she grinned at Kit between rounds – *hungover* - and he grinned back, "Gooood!"

As she supped on water, Jen ran up excitedly, "Look at him! You can see he likes you! It's so sweet - the way he's smiling!"

Hannah smiled too; she hadn't given up, she could feel the live wire of electricity sparking between them, knowing for certain that their fire had not burnt out.

Pleased with the successful accomplishment of the photo session, Hannah exited the ring and instructed Jen to get going. As she did, there was a thudding explosion from the back office – Mel, with a face like drained thunder, "Oh hi guys! I didn't know you were coming! Jen, you *never* take pictures of *me*!!"

Jen placated her with moronic chatter and they escaped back to Hannah's place, where Jen had a 'top 'n' tails' wash - the water was off at her shack and she had a wedding to attend in Nakhon Si Thammarat, leaving tonight.

"You sure you don't wanna come?" she drooled.

"It sounds interesting, but it's best you go and do your thing without me."

It turned out someone else *was* keen, her interest transmitted by sterile email, '*Why didn't you shower at mine?*' The message from Mel gasped, '*Why did you go to Hannah's?*' Mel had been angling for an invite to the wedding – woe betide should she miss out - but would she *really* enjoy sleeping on the floor on mats, with no one speaking English, and no-one waiting on her? Mel needed comforts, Mel needed attending to, and so it was that Jen went on her way alone, down to the restaurant where Mon worked to wait for a late-night, squashed-in lift to the wedding in the jungle, and Hannah was left to shower and relax.

39. Messy Sheets

After another night on her lonesome, Hannah caved into Mel's probing and accepted an invitation to dinner. Jen was away in the jungle somewhere and Hannah felt weak and somewhat vulnerable - Mel's favourite time to strike. Before Mel arrived, wobbling on her moped, Hannah hatched one final ploy to reach out to her man: she would send him a good-luck gift for his fight tomorrow. Jeab stocked an impressive array of overpriced farang products and traditional Thai wares, and Hannah had discovered an ancient-recipe Chinese ginger soap. She had already bought some to take back to England, but she had one spare for Kit. She added a packet of green SMS cigarettes and wrapped them in a tarot flyer as a surprise. Mel was texting constantly, Hannah's phone bleeping away, but she must get to the fitness centre to deliver the package to Faa before it closed, *and* before Mel encroached.

'Just going to the shop! I'll meet you at Lung-Lung's!' texted Hannah.

'Which shop?' retaliated Mel, her urgency creating the parallel narrative of a stalker-film. Speeding up, and discarding her phone, Hannah hoofed it up the dark road to the bright, sterile lights of the fitness centre, where Faa was alone – the perfect scene. She strode in.

"Wow...you look so happy!" said Faa by way of greeting.

"Really?!" remarked Hannah, flushed and excited, "I'm just in a hurry!"

She presented the package to Faa and asked her to deliver it safely to Kit. Though the go-between was a traditional role in Thai culture, Faa didn't look too pleased. She came around the desk and stood close to Hannah's face, speaking calmly yet firmly, "Okay - I will give it to him, but I think he have girlfriend already."

Hannah nodded, delirious with the plot but aware that there was a hefty Mel nearby, most likely driving up and down the road at this very moment searching for her.

"He has a wife, yes, but no girlfriend I think?" speculated Hannah.

"And he have two children!" said Faa.

"I thought he had one – a daughter?"

"Yes, a woman. But he had a girlfriend, but I think three years ago, but she mad!"

Trying briefly to digest this nonsensical message, Hannah firmly checked that Faa would deliver the package and, still grinning, her heart quickening with the playing out of this artificial drama, rushed back to Lung-Lung's in the dark to meet Mel.

She could see that the lights of the chicken shack were already out. With a commotion from the bushes, he appeared from the dark - packing up, tired and ready for bed with Aunty. Hannah smiled and waved at him, as a clumsy figure lurched up to him in the darkness, squeaking, "Excuse me! Excuse me! Are you still open?"

Hannah got to them and laughed, "Mel, he's closed. Come on."

"But where can we go?"

They looked up and down the road. Hannah was avoiding Kanchana's Kitchen after waiting over an hour for a bowl of soup last time. The lights were still on at the Muslim place across from Hannah's room.

"Come on, the food's quite good there - and cheap," she instructed, so the pair took a seat outside on the quiet road. Hannah knew the family a bit – they spoke no English, but with the aid of a menu and Hannah's sparse Thai she managed to *nearly* get what she ordered. Water was brought to their table, and Hannah ordered a spicy squid salad - Mel, as usual, two or three dishes: not for sharing.

They ate, Hannah's heart thumping from the earlier drama, knowing Faa would be at the gym by now, and the special package delivered. She took a healthy dash of relish in the fact that Mel was none the wiser. Mel began, "So, Kit - have you seen him?"

"Not recently, no."

Mel reached over, and with bear-like paws, pounced on Hannah's salad, drawing it into her gob then near-choking on its spiciness. She continued, "Oh that must be hard – well, he *is* training twice a day now for his fight on Sunday."

"Yeah," said Hannah, nodding slowly but starting to hasten her eating.

"Are you going to go and watch him?"

"Definitely, I wouldn't miss it for the world!" Hannah stated with strength.

"I've been training with him for the past few mornings, actually!" said Mel.

Hannah nodded slowly with strong internal disdain – she was starting to feel hot and provoked but was determined not to spit out a reaction. She continued to chomp away – she was over half-way through now and could leave soon enough.

"Yeah, Kit's really good at training, isn't he?"

Hannah shrugged. Was Mel intentionally trying to push her buttons? She put down her fork, and though she tried to bite her tongue, it set itself loose.

"Have you ever tried to talk to him about me?" asked Hannah.

"What do you mean?" said dumb-ass Mel.

"Well, have you ever tried to tell him that I say hi, or ask him anything about me?"

Mel paused long and deliberately, her eyes darting left, "No, I haven't actually!" she replied cheerily, continuing to shovel food into her greedy mouth.

"Has he ever mentioned me?" Hannah probed further.

Mel's eyes moved to the left again, "No, he hasn't actually!" she quipped light-heartedly, shovelling in more. Hannah was starting to lose her cool, snorts of breath expelling from her nostrils like a bull raring.

Mel continued, "Goodness me! You're really tucking into that food, aren't you! It's good - it's the first time I've ever seen you really eat!"

Yet it wasn't through enjoyment that she took the food down, it was logistics; when that plate was clear, and the sixty baht had been laid on the table, Hannah would be free to run from the churning monster before her. *Jealous! Jealous!* Hannah *was* – all that time around her man and training with him too - surely not *his* choice? Was Mel making a move on him?

"Ooooo, the other day we all went to the beach at sunset!" announced Mel.

"Who?" grunted Hannah.

"Oh, Faa, Pla, a few of the other girls, some of the new trainers, and, actually, Kit came, yes, Kit!"

So, she had been herding up the troops like a sheepdog, had she? Forced Kit to join in her silly games? An image flickered through her mind from Mel's Facebook - a failed 'free-spirit' sunset scene. Hannah couldn't bear to draw her eyes up to meet Mel's faux-innocent gaze, so she left the money on the table, mumbling something about having to go and do some writing. She scarpered across the road to her room and banged the door shut. She sat down at her computer and released the vitriolic rant she had managed to suppress at the dinner of spiritual demolition.

How dare Mel meddle around with her head and heart? Well, no more; no more enquiries, and no more tepid comments on her Facebook as if she was friend number-one. She logged into Facebook and typed away, '*If you are a sociopath you may no longer be able to comment on this post.*'

Immediately and deliberately with stoic satisfaction, she changed her settings so Mel could no longer defecate upon her wall. People commented to check they were still okay, but there could be no word from Mel. *Ha! Get off my wall! Stay away! I will block you!* She seethed with relish. A sudden pain to her lower stomach sent Hannah to the toilet - and there it was - the blob, the red messenger, the *fai deng* – oh! As she continued to bask in the temporary satisfaction that blocking Mel had brought, a greater anxiety overcame her: Oh no! Mel knew where she lived now! What if this wasn't child's play and she really *was* a psychopath?

It was twenty minutes or so since the blocking - in which time her fallopian tubes had started to expel their monthly glory. Perhaps it was time to calm down a bit and let Mel back in...She went back to the privacy settings, but suddenly the internet cut out. *Bollocks! What now? What if Mel's ignition had finally been sparked – her cold, cold heart turned into rage? What if Mel would come and break into Hannah's room tonight? What if?* She bled, the connection came back, she tinkered and adjusted and-

Suddenly, the door flew open and in marched Kit, with no '*Solly, solly*' this time; she had sent for him by way of soap and cigarettes. He stank of booze and stared at her, panting, beginning a short, frantic speech, "You! No!" shaking his head, "Soap - yes! Cigarette - no! I take care me and daughter, you take care you!!" He pointed to the crumpled pack of green SMS smokes that he had chucked onto the side; next to the decomposing *juicy fruit* gum he had brought on his first ever visit to her room. Hannah had left it lying there like a body of evidence.

He seemed quite serious and Hannah had no idea how to respond. She borrowed from observations in Thai-ness and laughed, trying to pass it off as a joke, then in resignation she retired to the bed - the conspicuous presence of her period making her even more awkward. He had finished his speech, it seemed, and before she could try to explain that it was probably 'best not to go down there', he was on her. She managed a protest, indicating a 'no entry' to her lower regions, and he looked hurt and confused.

He rolled off her stroppily, and she grabbed her translation dictionary.

"Aaaaah!" he said, "No problem!"

Quickly, Hannah ran to the bathroom to sort herself out, and they got down to it, but she resented his strong insistence. Why had he come here? To tell her he didn't want to look after her or for a quick bunk-up? It certainly didn't feel like make-up sex, and she hadn't got much out of it – just freshly stained sheets. And yet, she *had* sent for him, and he *had* delivered himself. They showered and got ready for bed: the bit which Hannah liked the most - when he draped himself over her in close comfort. Inside she was wrecked and ruined and in turmoil still - wasn't this what she wanted?

In the morning he left, leaving her bleeding in uncertainty. The dream was turning sour. Could anything be salvaged, a new spark ignited? Could she ever come close to playing partner to him?

40. Thai Wife

Though no perfect reconciliation, she was satiated enough, and so laid patiently in wait for Sunday's big fight. Laying lackadaisically while purging out last month's ova, she would occasionally burst into 20 squats – she *must* fit into the purple polyester pants!

Sunday came, and she was as ready as she could ever be, but she needed backup. She called Jen and begged her to come along.

"Oh, I'm *definitely* up for coming," said Jen, "But not in this freakin' rain!!"

"What rain?" Hannah replied in surprise.

"Have you looked out the window?" Jen asked, "It's friggin' pissing it down! I can't come out in this rain; if it stops or when it calms down, I'll get on my bike - I'll call you," and in true Thai-style, Jen hung up.

Hannah hitched up her now slightly sagging polyester tights and wobbled to the window, drawing back the curtains to reveal a rain-soaked, blackened Koh Talay night. As she opened the flimsy back door, a gale blew in and the smell of wet earth and clay greeted her. Maybe tonight would be called off - that would be right – *'Thailand is what happens when you're making other plans!'* she thought.

And somehow in her tired, wretched, emaciated state, it didn't seem to matter. She crouched down feebly to the fridge – she knew there was nothing in it, but –yes! A rescued sachet of raspberry jam from Kanchana's Kitchen's bizarre yet satisfying 'English breakfast', in other nutrients – sugar! She shakily peeled back the welded-on foil and dipped in a miserly finger. The thin, pink jelly felt good even nearing her teeth, and zoomed straight into her bloodstream, giving her the shot of energy she needed to check the crater on her nose: it was passable - now she just had to keep herself alive until Jen turned up.

A sudden wave of self-critical mortification swept over her – what the hell did she look like in these hand-me-down trousers?

She rifled through her wardrobe and changed into a denim skirt and vest – safer, conventional - and the call came: Jen was on her way. The subsequent sugar crash sent her hurtling into internal turmoil: the man that she loved was about to step into the ring, and she was to watch! *'Calm down!'* she lectured herself, *'Jen is coming - two is better than one! You only have to sit, watch and attempt to smile – you can run off straight after if you want to!'* Why was she always so nervous and cowardly in matters of the heart? Why so ready to lose? Why wasn't *she* a fighter?

In actual fact, she *could* fight and *had* fought back at home in England – and she did have a brave heart, just not the winner's hunger. She would smile as her hungry opponent smashed her in the head, and she could demonstrate great technique and stamina, but the drive to win just wasn't in her. She felt no primal need to beat anyone, unlike those who'd faced great struggle in their lives and she'd been lucky enough to not have to fight to survive. So, was that why she wasn't fighting now, caught up in this confusing Muay Thai love affair? She had ventured way too far into this mystical forest to turn back now, and though there were trees and branches obstructing her view, they whispered all: *'Come a little bit closer…'.*

There was a knock on the door, and Jen entered, scuffing her feet lazily and jangling her motorbike keys. She slung her hand-made leather bag onto the bed – for her it was just a normal day –nothing out of the ordinary in her hare-brained life.

"Why aren't you wearing those pants? Oh, *go on*! You look so cute in them!"

"Mm... not sure," replied Hannah flatly.

"Put 'em ooooon!" Jen jibed in a low tone.

"Okay, okay!" Hannah concurred, her speech and breath becoming fast and high-pitched, "Did you bring any jewellery?"

Jen lazily jangled through her trinkets, found a simple chain with a set gemstone, and fastened it around Hannah's neck.

"It's still early," she remarked as they mounted her motorbike, "We shouldn't go in yet - have you eaten?"

"No, I don't want to go in bloated." Yet she couldn't enter in this wretched state either, so they went to Mr Green's to order soup and stir-fried morning glory – Jen's usual. Hannah loosened up as she drank a beer, went to the toilet to adjust her peculiar pants and, with no further excuses nor need for delay, walked the final few meters to the sludgy stadium entrance.

Everything seemed very quiet – there was a queer, sinister edge to the air – perhaps the rain had kept the spectators away. Hannah's heart jumped into her throat – Kit could appear at any moment. Lek sat at the front desk, and tired from the rain, shook her head first at Hannah and then at Jen, then nodded them through without paying. It was quiet ringside, too, making Hannah jabber nervously. From the bar, she could make out a few people in the warm-up area. Firstly, and unmistakably, Kit, who stood stealthily and motionless like a bronze figurine. Next to him, propped neatly on a chair, a painfully pretty, young Thai woman. On the table between them, a shared bag, out of which Kit retrieved something. Hannah switched back to look at Jen, who had also noticed the intriguing scene.

Jen stated clearly, "You know, a man doesn't share a bag with a woman in Thailand - unless it's his wife."

They moved away slightly and stood as inconspicuously as they could in the near-empty arena, their drinks balanced on an uneven wooden ledge. Though in shock, Hannah couldn't afford to show it, so concentrated on suppressing her emotions – on the outside, at least. *Why did things never turn out as expected?* Always little let-downs - saddenings against the warm glow of her malfunctioning heart, and now this!

Little Smiler appeared at Hannah's side. He nodded and smiled at her, sent over to act as a buffer between Hannah and Kit: as if Hannah would waltz over and sling her arms around him now! Yet with only two choices – get out or go with it - she reached for the Similan, grabbed her best friend, and took a seat to watch the fights. She never would have predicted the *real* Thai wife showing up – poo-pooing all over her polyester drainpipes - as sure as she wouldn't have predicted falling in love with a Thai boxer.

The zany pipe-music struck-up its beguiling wail, but instead of its usual exciting effect, it took on an eerie tone, as Hannah attempted to focus on the action and block out her flailing thoughts. Trapped in a prison she had freely walked into. She slurped on her whisky as the *Ram Muay* dance started: one knee bent leaning forwards, the drawing down of the arms then up to the sky, thighs pulsing. After the first fight a figure neared Hannah, stopping in close proximity. A hand slipped onto her left buttock – the skin-tight pants hadn't gone unnoticed it seemed - and Tee leaned in close to her, "Okay - you talk with your friend, you watch fighting, you go home!" Hannah's face remained neutral, and he left.

"Oh my God, he was coming onto you!" Jen enthused – she had a bit of a 'thing' for Tee and his effortlessly carved physique. Hannah just shrugged and, ignoring his warning, they repositioned themselves closer to the ring. Hannah instructed Jen that at no time was she to look over at Kit's wife, who was sat motionless and pale on the other side, then went to the bar, seizing the opportunity to stand with Tee.

"Who is she?" she demanded. Tee replied with a blank bemused look.

"Who IS SHE?!" Hannah repeated. Tee just shrugged.

"I know - I KNOW!" retorted Hannah, staring at him with truth and accusation in her eyes.

"You come party with me afterwards!" said Tee, "You take me home!"

Meanwhile, a young Scottish fighter - Cameron - had entered the ring, so Hannah scuttled back to her

261

seat to watch the fight. She could vaguely recall seeing him at the gym – a strapping lad leaning against the ropes, watching her as she trained with Kit. He was an interesting fighter – strong, tattooed and determined, with excellent technique. His opponent, on the flipside, was nothing of the sort – a short, plump man, fighting for dough. Cameron knocked him out in Round Two - the fight was over - Kit's fight was imminent. In the near-silent stadium, the competitors climbed into their corners and began their walk around the ring, blessing each side. Mesmerised, Hannah quietly took every moment in.

The *Ram Muay* dance began: a demonstration of artistry and intention, and an omen of what was to come. Kit's young bride sat on the other side, still and scared like a little bird. Hannah's expectations mounted - she knew how good he was; to him, Muay Thai was life. His opponent was also no joke. In round one they tested each other's reach and judged their opponent's fighting style, slowly and carefully landing a few punches, but mostly displaying deliberate and calculated defence. The bell signalling the end of the round sounded – so far so good. Everything was quiet and efficient in the corner break.

Round Two burst into life, as the fighters started to put on a show. Kit landed a strike with a flying knee, sending his opponent reeling against the ropes. His body triumphantly shone under the stadium lights, and he must surely be leading now for points. Suddenly, Round Three arrived - time for the action to accelerate. Punches flew, an agonising low-kick from Kit knocked his opponent completely off-guard, as red marks appeared around his kidneys from ferocious round-kicks and knees. Surely it couldn't be long, and…DOWN! The other guy crumpled to the floor – TKOOOOOOO!! Kit's signature bass-music signalled victory, and it was a Bangkok bounce with his arms in the air, before exiting without ego nor aplomb. Hannah turned to Jen, her face a picture of admiration and awe, "How do you say 'excellent' – 'really good' – 'the best', in Thai?"

Jen had to think for a few moments, before choosing the most appropriate term, "Sud yod!"

Hannah practised the phrase several times, then slipped away from the bench, making her way through the small crowd to the back room, where the boxers got oiled and hyped up, ready for their fights. She stood several metres away from him, feeling Thai eyes on her from every direction. But she knew to be quick, and standing in the doorway looked to Kit strongly and with conviction, then delivered her words, keeping quite still, "Sud yod!"

"Thank you," he murmured back in his gruff British accent. She exited quickly. Jen caught up with her at the bar.

"Let's go!" said Hannah.

"Where?" asked Jen.

"Home!" exclaimed Hannah. But Jen, as usual, had other ideas; *she* was in charge of the motorbike and *she* wanted to party. So it was that they did *not* stop at the looming *bahn itsalam* on the corner, but instead continued on into the night, curving around bends with their cool gum breeze, to Charlie Chang's – a concrete dive of ill-repute.

"There's a prostitute I know!" said Jen, pointing to the bar, as they dismounted in the makeshift gravel car park, "Come on, she's with an old guy - he can buy us drinks!"

Hannah nodded, following her like a lost lamb into the hideous cave. At the bar Jen chatted animatedly to her green-eyed friend, as Hannah stared wistfully into space. They drank vodka - hitting Hannah hard - then joined the Thai bargirls for dancing. At first the girls took delight in Hannah's over-zealous display, but quickly sensed an unleashed wildness in her step, and pushed her away from their money-making display. Hannah attempted to explain her rash behaviour by shouting over the appalling music, "Jai noi!" – *little heart*.

"No!! NO!!!" insisted green-eyes aggressively, "You not sad, you HAPPY...Must be happy! Never miiiiind!!"

As she turned away from the scene, she caught the outline of a dark man whizzing past on his motorbike with a beautiful girl behind him, her long hair tailing in the wind. It could only be Kit.

The club was starting to fill up, and some people she knew were sat at tables outside drinking cheerily. She went to join Tee and the young Scottish fighter, to whom she raised a glass. Tee picked up his phone, "Kit - he come. Ten minutes."

"But I saw him go back to the gym!" Hannah insisted.

"He coming now!" Tee insisted. He didn't explicitly order her to go home, but Hannah understood the instruction. Jen came and sat strongly by her side – they weren't going anywhere – and the

264

night dissolved into a haze of drunken abandon. Hannah sat tight as Kit indeed did appear, his wife in tow, grinning after probable reconciliative sex. Hannah nodded cordially as half-introductions were made. Kit grinned like a foolish baboon – what fun for the hero of the hour!

Hannah wanted a cigarette. She smiled politely at Kit's wife, who sat demurely to her left, and asked if perchance she might have a cigarette in her purse to lend? The wife obliged, courteously reaching into the faux-Gucci bag, pulling out a single L&M green – a survivor from Hannah's unwelcome gift.

Funny though it was, Hannah was in no mood for clowning. She visited the bathroom, debating whether or not to get a drink, and spotted Cameron, the Scottish fighter, propping up the bar. She strode up to him in her special polyester pants and introduced herself, cheekily suggesting he buy her a drink from the fight purse he clutched tightly in his hand, "You're jokin' man!" he exclaimed, "This is ma food money!"

So instead, she bought him a beer and they went to sit down. A stony silence engulfed the table. Jen was looking decidedly flushed - Tee was crying!

"That's why I left," Cameron muttered, "It all went serious and weird - that girl was really laying into Tee!" What had Jen done now? But as Hannah and Cameron continued to banter, things gradually became less tense around the table. What a breath of fresh air having someone new to talk to, someone who seemed charmed by her sharp wit.

"You got a boyfriend then?" he enquired with bravado.

"Well, I *was* seeing a Thai guy," she stopped and counted, "The one three to your left? Until his wife showed up!" Cameron clutched his sides in hysterical laughter, near falling off his chair, enjoying the absurdity of the situation.

He shook his head, "Thai guys, eh? He is good lookin' though – quite Western!"

Hannah continued to wryly swig, adopting a look of fierce bemusement, fired by the booze.

Soon enough, the concrete den was shutting down for the night. Kit and his missus left without further incident, leaving Cameron, Tee, Jen and Hannah in the darkness. Jen was still spitting out words in Thai at Tee, as he shook his head violently, crying again.

"What's going on?" asked Hannah.

Jen let out a flow of snappy garbled American twang, "I'm saying that *he* was the one caught knocking on Mel's door the other night, and *that's* why he got into trouble at the gym, and that it's his own fault!"

Tee sat looking wounded, "No! No!" he pleaded. Hannah went over to him - it was time to go. She stood behind him, sliding her arms around his neck to comfort him, but he didn't move – his heart was cold and empty inside. Jen stood up and marched over to the motorbike, yelling at Hannah to remove herself promptly. Hannah ignored her, instead saying an overlong goodbye to Cameron and planting a playful, lingering kiss on his mouth – the booze had made her loose in the lips, and she had nothing to lose it would seem. Jen hollered at her one final time, and they rode home.

"What was all that about?" asked Hannah, referring to the incident with Tee.

"Ah nothing. Hey - I asked Kit about his wife, and *apparently,* he didn't know she was coming, and she rode all the way here on her own on a motorbike in the dark and rain just to see him! I feel a bit sorry for her actually - *apparently*, they're just friends."

Hannah didn't reply; it was all a bit much to compute, and her brain needed to unravel the evening in more solitary surrounds, so she sniff-kissed Jen on the cheek warmly and said goodbye.

41. Within or Without You

She awoke, heavily laden with the after-effects of alcohol, which handily provided an effective barrier against neurosis, but not paranoia. Her brain was like a barnyard, its hay blowing about in the wind. She was still too intoxicated to piece together the events of last night; or to make any sense of them. Jen came to save her from herself. She entered the room to find Hannah honking out *Real Love* on the guitar, all forlorn. Unshowered, the girls went together to the beach where Hannah took a rejuvenating swim, but by the time they got to the coffee shop she had begun to feel seasick.

"I can't believe you're not a hot mess!" bleated Jen, "I would be!"

"Hnnnn," replied Hannah, grouchily, "What's the point? I'm very business-like in my affairs." Thank goodness she was writing a book that she could plough all of her emotions into. Jen was busy on her laptop, completing a questionnaire for an online MA she was about to start, *'What are your goals? What are your priorities in everyday life?'* asked the online questionnaire.

"Fucking my Thai boyfriend and making leather!" Hannah quipped. Jen smiled – she wasn't a typical MA student.

After porridge, which hadn't thickened at all, they bade each other farewell and Hannah staggered home, passing Uncle Lung-Lung who hollered out that she was *especially* beautiful today – something about her salty sea-hair, traumatised heart and hangover giving off a certain air.

269

Back at her room, she finally began to feel a little better and the hangover gave way to a heaving tiredness. As the day gave way into night, she became more melancholy, and allowed herself to lament her love, still with some hope that he *might* come tonight, while giving herself excuses why he might not. All this overthinking didn't help, so before she could cause herself any more damage, she dragged herself to bed - Dr. Flameheart nestled by her side: *I listen for your footsteps, but they don't arrive…*

* * *

She slept heavily, and when the new day came a fresh excitement arose within her – a new scheme, a new opportunity to further her story. At work she kept her emotions steady in anticipation of the judgement call – later she would know once and for all if Kit would be hers or not. Tender and vulnerable, strong and determined; it was time.

Her heart beat out a heavy battle-cry on the march to the gym, *'Come on Hannah, you can do it!'*

On arrival at the gym, she went on automatic, striding to the tyre to start a gentle bouncing and switching. And there he was - her love.

"Sawadee ka!" she said as neutrally as possible.

"Sawadee kap!" came his even-toned reply.

She continued on auto, numb with nerves - he seemed to be ignoring her. She could deal with it - *it wouldn't exactly be the first time* - and with no-one else coming forward to train this old-news farang, she accepted a few rounds with Squishy Nose.

Afterwards, she hung about on the rickety platform just outside the gym's entrance - the place where Kit had sat like a shining Buddha all those days ago -

which now creaked apologetically under her heavy bones. On that day her heart still had a song; now it hummed a muter tune. Squishy Nose came out to see what was going on, "You have motorbike?"

She shook her head. She allowed five more minutes' wait, taking her rucksack off her sweat-drenched back. Still nothing. Most of the students had now left the training area, soon the mosquitoes would come to suck upon her sweaty calves. Now was the time. She stood up and steadily moved towards the ring where Kit and Tee were energetically doing pads - one lanky Swedish girl each. She stood, her face neutral, at a little distance away, yet near enough to be noticed. To be heard. In the break she seized the moment to speak. She beckoned him over firmly. Kit flinched, not wanting to comply, but after beckoning for the second time, he moved to the edge of the ring hesitantly.

"Kit...you no come?" commanding his attention - though he looked nothing short of terrified, "I...I training!" he said, "Solly, solly, working...solly!"

"I know," she said, curtly and straight-faced, "Busy?" she started again. Kit shrugged his shoulders, his mouth ajar, his hands motioning to the training ring in absence of words, "Working...solly...working!" He started to move away.

"You - you not come?" she implored, louder. Kit stood, emotion and worry crossing his brow.

He stammered, "I – I... no motorbike!" He started to back off.

"You don't like me?" she blurted out - desperate for more closure.

"Me…I…me…wife! Wife come back!" he said, miming a whirring head whilst shaking it all the while.

"Kow jai," she said – *I understand.* She reached into her soggy rucksack and pulled out a dictionary she had bought for him that day in the port – not much point trying to communicate now - but all the same, it was for him. Smiling mildly, she handed it to him through the ropes. Taking it from her, he thanked her, sweetly and gruffly. She put her right hand on top of his boxing glove, and he smiled back at her.

"Jut jop," she said in quiet surrender, sadness leaking through her smile, "Kit wah peuan dee gwah." *Finished, I think just friends is better.*

Kit's tempo changed, and he looked about himself desperately in an attempt to express himself, but with no discernible words and no ability to translate his exasperation – to turn shock into sound - he could only stand there, clutching his dictionary.

As the Swedes returned from their break, Hannah exited. Turning on her heel, she calmly and evenly began the difficult walk up the hill; her rucksack heavy, wearing a sad smile. She adorned her sunglasses and held back a torrent of tears. The two gym dogs appeared either side of her, comforting her plight with dignity and care. Still composed, but with a glassy sheen coating the lenses of her eyes, she continued, and only when she reached a safe distance did her mouth begin to quiver, her sunglasses still shielding her tears, as she moved steadily out of sight. Stepping into the reclining sunset, she felt an enormous gravity, and let the salt-water flow fully. The dogs left her and she trod the rest of the path alone, the sun descending into the land and sinking with it too, her heart.

* * *

With a 65-baht bottle of Similan by her side, she attempted to nurse out her bruises. Late into the night, the cup of tea that should have been sitting there had become a cup of coffee, gone cold, laced with slugs of whisky. Playing her self-penned track *Love Hold Me in Your Arms*, recorded all that time back in icy Sussex – a million moons away now - she drank and punched out her emotions onto her enslaved keyboard, '*As I dumped him he kept stammering "me...me...me," and each time he did, my mind mouthed the word 'beautiful.'*

Only when her tired and drunken eyes could stare at the blurry screen no more, she crashed onto her bedraggled bed – her guitar by her side.

KNOCK!

Huh?!!!

KNOCK-KNOCK-KNOCK!

She stirred, drool drying at the sides of her mouth. Squinting at the guitar and laptop next to her, she scrambled to get up and nearly tripped over herself, still wrapped tightly in Kit's blue blanky as she was.

She let him in then flumped back down on the chaotic bed, not bothering to attempt any pidgined language.

He stood over her, staring and out-of-breath, "Peuan...PEUAN?" he jeered, panting: *Friend*? She looked up at him as he deliberated his next move. He snarled, sniggered, then made his way gruffly to 'his' side of the bed, slung off his clothes and emptied his pockets. He reeked strongly of booze and was still

273

panting. Hannah had seen him breathless before: but then he had been nervous or exasperated, never enraged.

"Peuan!" he looked at her sideways – Hannah wasn't sure whether to offer a reaction, but with no more time to ponder, he was on her, forcefully pulling off her clothes then roughly pulling her to the end of the bed. He unbuckled himself and helped himself to her body, grabbing painfully at her breasts, pulling them as he grinded - hiccupping and slipping out of her, as he feigned a stallion-esque prowess.

When he came, he planted a single kiss on her lips which stung from the heat of chillies. Her lips used to burn for days when his love had lit her into the twilight, yet she suffered no such delusions of romance tonight.

He shouted for aircon, "ACTIVATE!"

She felt blank – why had he really come? Was it the booze or the pride or the plain, simple horn? She would never know – for now he breathed deeply in sleep next to her.

   * * *

He woke up with the sun, said "Peuan?" one more time with a snigger, and left.

'That's what friends do, is it?' she thought, as she closed the door behind him.

42. Into Your Arms

She didn't tell anyone about his late-night visit, and instead attempted to continue with 'normal life'. She and Jeab decided now that high season was over there wasn't much need for her to continue her shifts in the shop; but instead Jeab asked her if she would tutor her son in English, who was back for the Songkran holidays. Hannah hadn't much idea of what to do, but Jeab reassured her, "Anything is fine! Just make him speak English!"

So, she trundled to Salee Mart 2 every few days, and they marched around the shop pointing at items that she knew were the same in Thai and English, and encouraged him to say, "I love my dog!" The dog, unfortunately, was another matter. Yappy and overweight, it sat on the shop counter glaring at Hannah, before revealing its lipstick.

At night she dined alone, then went straight home to catch up on writing. She was behind, what with the drama and turmoil of recent events. In truth, she probably couldn't handle many more real-life episodes.

One night she was sitting at Kanchana's Kitchen with her laptop, happily tap-tapping away, when little Smiler from the gym came to hand her a flyer.

"Me fight, Sunday night!" she nodded, "You come?" The mother in her leapt out and before she knew it, she had already agreed to go.

Behind them in the background sat the ugly form of Don and his perverse cronies, hunched over a plastic table feasting on deep-fried pork and whisky.

With mischief, she instructed little Smiler to fetch her a glass, and in obedience he brought one back. She raised it at Don then wickedly drank it back, as she punched out further absurdities on her keyboard. It dawned on her that she didn't want to go to fight night at all - she was tired of it and didn't want any more drama, and yet...she couldn't let the little boy down.

Sunday approached with menace. She got dressed as she would for any night out and remained sober and good-willing. Continuing nearer the stadium she stopped at Kanchana's Kitchen for a glass of cheap red, and received a text from Mel, *'Kit at stadium. Wife and child also there.'*

What a message, but good to know all the same. Hannah was curious to see Kit's little girl of whom he spoke so often, and the wife's presence would be nothing new; in fact, his wife had quite warmed to Hannah that time she had pranced around in her purple pantaloons. At the entrance to the stadium sat Lek, shaking her head at Hannah once again, saying, "I'm not sure about you!"

She charged Hannah 200 baht, and she went into the stadium; bright, busy and buzzing. She took a seat on the far side away from the boxers and their trainers. Across the ring, Faa and Pla were dancing to Beyoncé behind the bar. To the right of them stood Kit, and just a little further away sat his lovely wife – their child upon her knee. The scene presented itself as a picture of happiness, rousing no negative emotion in Hannah – in fact, it felt easy to see such a picture-perfect scene, if a little morally dubious. Kit stood, handsome and radiant, shining with pride and joyfulness. His wife was also happy and the little girl cute and loving: so it was. Suddenly, the wife caught Hannah's eye, and before she had a chance to turn away, started waving excitedly at her like a little Asian dolly! Hannah half-grimaced, but finally managed to force out a smile: *Oh wife, oh wife, if you only knew! I'm not just the funny girl from the bar; I've been fornicating with your lovely husband!*

A moment later, the family of three retired to the back of the stadium - Kit taking his little girl's hand as she looked up adoringly at him. A truly warming scene, Hannah felt no bitterness - just a misplaced longing for belonging such as theirs.

She stayed where she was and watched the fights, but little Smiler whom she'd come to see didn't materialise. It must have been cancelled - a sore throat or some such – who knew the *real* reason behind who got to go on and get their bones crushed and who stayed behind to clear up the beer bottles.

Kit reappeared and marched around the imposing ring to man the corner for a fighter. He strode up to Hannah and warmly put his arms around her. She smiled lovingly into his eyes – she couldn't help herself. Still, she was surprised and couldn't understand his actions, especially so publicly - but that was nothing new.

"Everything OK?" he asked. Before she knew it, she had followed him and his gang to the corner where she stood hollering and straining on her tiptoes to see the action, waving her hands and shouting encouragement. It was hot under the lights, and her heart pummelled from the adrenalin of the fight.

At the end of the evening everyone filed off to Charlie Chang's. Kit's wife and child had disappeared - probably gone home. Faa offered Hannah a lift and, contrary to good judgement, she accepted. Once at the hideous bar, they sat around a big table - boxers from the gym and some students who were training there. She didn't recognise them - she was a stranger now. To her left she spotted the two leggy Swedish blondes who had been training with Tee and Kit as she had told him it was over that day. They were shamelessly drunk, and one of them draped herself over Kit, sitting on his knee. Smiling – perhaps out of politeness - he accepted her advances, but whatever the reason, Hannah was horrified. Now was the time for bitterness, and she sat like a spurned widow, glowering in the shadows.

As the booze kicked in, she couldn't let the hussies defeat her any longer, and in reaction started doing the rounds herself – flirting with Cameron at the bar, singing TV theme tunes with a giant Swede, and dancing with the bargirls. Yet eventually it was time to return to the table, and resignedly she plonked herself down next to Kit on a spare chair like a spare wife, as he continued to accept the brazen blonde's advances. When she caught a moment, she turned to him, "You like her?" she interrogated.

"No! No! Cannot speak English!"

"She likes you!"

Over in the corner, the promoter from the mainland and a few old, *nak muays* sat jeering and speculating about Kit and his many girlfriends. He turned to them, and suddenly his demeanour changed. He freed himself from the persistent Swede and spoke, slowly and sternly, "She was my girlfriend before," nodding at Hannah. Suddenly, there was a stop, and Kit became calm. He put the Swede firmly back in her place and turned to Hannah, who started on a last, desperate clamour, "I waited for two months – no men!"

"I know." They sat in silence for a while.

"Your daughter - she loves you."

"You see my daughter?" said Kit, swollen with pride and fatherly love. She looked to him for further protection, "I have no motorbike, can...can you take me home?"

Immediately, he showed a kindness, "Yes, of course – now?" she nodded. They got up, and on their way to his bike the rich promoter from the mainland smiled, saying something leery to his mates, aimed in their direction.

"You go with him!" said Kit, "He take care of you!"

Hannah shook her head, "I don't like him. I only like you."

They mounted his bike, and as soon as they zoomed around the misty corner Kit drew Hannah's arms into him, "Solly, solly," he spoke soft and low. She held onto his strong body - but only for a moment before letting go - the fight had already left her. The smell of wild gum from the forest flew by her, as did the feeling that if she were to live for just this moment, it would be worth it - the thrill of the dark night in the jungle with this man on the speed-defying motorbike.

Alas, the thrill ended as soon as it had begun - for here was her *bahn*. Kit parked expertly and looked to

279

her uneasily. She could feel what it meant: he kissed her - his tongue in her mouth, but without feeling.

"Cannot come in – wife, child," she nodded, smiled finally and took another kiss, then ran off to her room. With the door closed behind her she knew that it was the last one - and she had stolen it from him.

43. Marionette

She awoke to a mild, broken hangover. At around lunchtime she went to look for something to eat - maybe she would go to the man who made cooked breakfasts with freshly squeezed orange juice. As she passed Uncle Lung-Lung's, a gruff voice called out to her from one of the bamboo booths - it was Tee, sitting, swaggering in his way, smiling with his scars and his Chinese eyes: drunk.

He called her over to sit with him and so she did. He pushed some whisky at her.

"Have to teach!" she exclaimed, before taking a tiny dram out of courtesy, "Teacher cannot smell of whisky!" She looked at him – wasn't he a teacher too?

"Why you not come train?" he asked.

"I don't learn anything – one, two months - no one trains me. I don't learn anything, so why should I come?"

Tee considered this information, "Marionette," he said. Hannah attempted to decipher his peculiar language.

"Marionette?" he asked again.

"You!" he demanded, indicating her ring-finger, "Married or not?"

She laughed at the linguistic farcicality and shook her head, "No, it's not the same in England!"

"I go Bangkok soon. See wife, baby."

"You okay?" she asked.

"Scared," said Tee, drinking the remains of the bottle, "Little, little. I not meet baby before! I not know about future!" He drank, "We same!" he said,

281

grasping the whisky bottle in his hand, firmly, "Have trouble - drinking, drinking. Understand each other."

They nodded together thoughtfully. She was having a good time. It struck her that this felt like the most genuine experience she'd shared with anyone since coming to the island, and more like a date than any of the bizarre love-offs she'd invented with Kit: in the day, here at the chicken shack, with Tee, Uncle Lung-Lung and a bottle of whisky.

As they slurped on rare-beef soup - prepared especially by Aunty for Tee, as if to mark an occasion, Hannah told him simply in Thai that she loved him.

"Same," he said, in a bold, brash yet respectful way, slurping in a satisfied and tender silence.

"You? How are you?"

She looked into his eyes, and she knew that he could feel the pain that she felt. She took her right hand and made a snaking motion in the air – a rollercoaster of existence – and he understood. She had to go.

"Where you go?"

"My room, I have to teach – you want to come?" she joked. He smiled, the whisky had done its work, and shook his head coyly, whilst grinning like a banshee, his muscles melting into the bamboo.

When she re-emerged ten minutes later to teach the 14-year-old who wouldn't say 'boo' to anyone, Tee was still sitting at the table. He got up and moved towards the roadside in the burning heat, "Where you go?!" he cried at her, swaying on his feet in the sun. Smiling, she flicked her hip at him, "Going to teach!" and that was the last she saw of him.

That night, sitting quietly at the café across the street from her room, listening to 70's funk and piano-bar versions of 'Speak Softly Love', she picked up a book, *Sand and Stone*, by Khalil Gibran, with Thai and English translations. She hadn't seen many 'real' books in Thailand – just Mills & Boon style trash or motorcycle manuals, and Jeab was always complaining about the lack of decent reads. She became transfixed on one page, 'On Love'.

She read aloud, the music fitting the relaxed mood around her in the dark night, as she sat around the little fishpond on seats carved from tree-trunks.

Later, back at home, she lay pontificating on the bed. Her mind scoured over the lunch with Tee, and she considered him with admiration and a tender sentimentality. He used to be a tattoo artist – that was right! The words from 'On Love' came to her - they stung and touched her in equal measure. She resolved: let the man who made her feel true love etch the word into the very life of her, let love be created between bamboo, needle and flesh!

44. The House of Bamboo

She woke up and as was oft the case, attempted to gather her thoughts from before sleep had found her.

The tattoo.

She left for Salee Mart 2 bright and early to be greeted by two new students; smiling, happy little tots, a chubby serious one and a cutesy, useless one, plus a three-year-old who sat on the counter-top, putting beer in plastic bags and repeating everything any foreigner said. *She* was the best student, of course - a true island baby, destined to grow up with a market-wagon, a heavy dose of common-sense and a cunning way with money. The little girls remembered everything Hannah had taught them the day before and whizzed among the mini-mart aisles shouting out colours and milk and talcum powder, before sitting on the floor to play alphabet games.

Afterwards, she wandered home via a stretch of open land, which had on it a thrift shop – vast and empty. She trotted amongst the aisles, flicking her hands through rows of retro nylon tops and cheap, see-through flared skirts; chiffons, yellows, polka-dots and bows. All the while, hiding from eye-shot, the owner - an ancient lady in a cotton gown - hung things up and mended things with patches and safety pins. Hannah's path led her towards the lady, and just before she reached her, she noticed a low-slung hammock, rocking to-and-fro: what was inside, a baby? Yes, one of sorts - a cute and cautious cat, complete with a fresh litter of kittens, who clambered about with their eyes closed, hungry for mother's milk.

Hannah sat with the shopkeeper, adoring them. The lady's eyes shined, delving deep into Hannah with a certain curiosity - a Thai nosiness that escaped no-one.

"You on your own?" she asked, "How can you speak Thai?"

Hannah shrugged.

"You have boyfriend?" the old woman asked.

Hannah pretended not to understand; in honesty her Thai wasn't good enough to follow most of the conversation. Yet speak Thai she needed not, as the old woman twinkled at her then drew her index fingers together till they met.

"Maybe before, but a little trouble, so…no." Hannah confessed.

The woman spoke of her own family – a daughter in Phuket doing goodness-knows-what, another in Singapore, and her husband in a village some 200 kilometres away with gammy legs that hadn't worked for seven years and a drink problem – but still, hers.

A hideous tourist wobbled in, picking up a sequinned top. "Is it all one size?" she asked, providing a moment of hilarity amidst the heartfulness.

Hannah retained a degree of melancholy throughout the day, with thoughts of Tee and the tattoo interspersed with a loneliness which insisted itself upon her under the foreboding sky. After sundown it was time to eat, but she saw only a blank darkness, as she peered out onto the road after the Call to Prayer: no sign of Uncle Lung-Lung, nor the Muslim eatery being open; she would head towards Kanchana's Kitchen to see what she could find. Just after her place was a newly-built bamboo restaurant, run by a kind woman who used to cook at Kanchana's Kitchen before some rift sent them their separate ways. Smiling in the quiet dark, Hannah took a place in the end booth. As she passed the other seats in darkened silence, she noticed just one other figure - sitting hunched over like a Rodin statue. It was Cameron – the Scottish fighter, surrounded by a thick, moody fog. She fingered through the menu and ended up on the page of soups. Though she didn't want to disturb him, as the only customers it seemed strange not to at least mutter an acknowledgement. He sat, shuddering, his headphones on, and his eyes narrowed and dramatic, youthfully angst-ridden.

"Hi," she half-murmured. He continued to shudder.

"You okay?"

"No, I'm not!" he seethed through gritted teeth, pointing at his shins.

"Which leg?" she asked.

"Both."

His food arrived and he shovelled it in, turning away from Hannah. Though she had by no means followed him there, he still held her heavily under suspicion. She continued to wait for her seafood soup, and took out a pen and crumpled paper, staring into the void to reminisce and welcoming sentimentality in:

You drive me crazy,
You drive me wild.
Mama never said I shouldn't love a Muay Thai fighter,

287

So I'm happy just sitting on the road:
'You sleep in the sea,' he said,
'I sleep in the road.'

We've all got casualties to be looking after,
All getting older:
Ten years since high season,
Gently, hushedly getting older,
The sun swooping lower on us all.
The story has an ending-
Young boys' voices breaking, hair getting too long,
Less smiles for me now.

45. Back Again

Don's strange, pasty-white girlfriend lurked in the corner of the gym, as Mel buzzed away in the back office. Hannah made herself discreet, and when it was time for padwork she stood, available and un-manned, waiting to see to whom she would be allocated. Kit stood motionless and emotionless and strongly pointed at a new guy, "You train with him."

Obediently she went over to him, his face was twisted and scarred, angry and gormless at the same time. Like a gnarled old tiger, he ground his teeth incessantly – it was likely he had been sent here by a Bangkok gym, a form of rehab. Hannah looked at him, exhausted, and wondered if it would be worth it. He stared back at her with haunted eyes, *"Mai yahk som muay gap kon thai!"* she protested: *I don't want to learn with a Thai!*

The psychotic man before her nodded sharply, holding up his pads in challenge. She would try one round, and if he was no good or treated her as a joke she would give up.

His pad-holding turned out to be seamless, fast, focussed and tough; Hannah snapped kicks and drove in punches, blocked with her knees and threw elbows to the head. The other trainers stood around aghast, wondering how you trained girls to fight like this.

Still, she fired ahead, "Break?" she asked. He shrugged with an 'up to you', and they continued. Sliding in with side kicks, she tried out some kickboxing moves – hammer punches and hooks to the head.

The trainer jabbed her hard in the belly with a side kick, but she didn't care – it felt great to feel physical pain again, and her abs were strong. She jabbed him back, twisting her ankle slightly as she came in – the pride before a fall. Wincing and hobbling, she attempted a few more rounds, but it looked like that was all for today. She walked past Kit who was paired up with a flabby, white farang, "Good match!" she joked, elbowing him in the chest as she passed.

She warmed-down ringside, and watched as Kit demonstrated the *wai kru* for a girl who was fighting on Sunday: Susan – the one who'd been knobbing Tee before he left for Bangkok – with a face like a horse. Don's girlfriend came over to see Hannah.

"Is Susan ok now Tee's gone?" Hannah asked.

"Oh, yes, no problem there!" she replied, surprised at the suggestion. Hannah could hear Kit instructing Susan in Thai, "Eek tee!" - *one more* - as they counted out three steps before a knee circle. She finished warming down and went outside. She hung around for a bit - not expecting Kit to emerge - and he didn't. Instead, she waited around for a ride, and soon enough a tall Westerner appeared and got on his bike.

She grasped the opportunity, "Going to Yao Beach?"

"Yep! Hop on!" And off they rode, new friends united by wheels, chatting about the way things were.

"A bunch of us are going to this really cool little place for dinner tonight, you should come!"

"Oh thanks, but I don't really like groups, and I don't think some of the guys from the gym like me."

"C'mon, don't be stupid, come with me! What is it, man trouble?" he asked.

"Noooo, not *really,*" she covered up thinly.

"That's why I always end up leavin'!" he said.

They reached her *bahn itsalam*, she thanked him kindly, and left.

* * *

The next morning her body ached from training, and she had no cash, food or even coffee at home but she was starving, so she hobbled to a new shop that had opened on the path down towards the sea. The woman in there seemed cold, and the space had a bare, concrete feel to it, but they'd priced things up wrong and the chocolate toenail cereal she liked was cheap.

She took a few items to the till, and explained in her bravest Thai that she had no money but would be back to pay this afternoon 100%. The woman wasn't keen, but in the end agreed to the deal. Hannah didn't go home immediately, instead continuing on to the opening towards the sea, to catch a glimpse of the wild waves and remind herself why she was here and what it was she loved. To the right a smiling woman called out to her, surrounded by family. Hannah didn't recognise her, but she was so welcoming that she went over. The woman ran a tiny booth that exchanged money. In her dank and tatty purse Hannah had some rupees and ringgits from travelling days gone by, and she asked if she could exchange them – she didn't know or care about the rate. The woman totted up the notes and gave her a few hundred baht and so it was that Hannah could pay back her debt early.

Pleased with her haphazard productivity, but stinking, she scuttled back to her room, catching sight of Lung-Lung on the way. He was eating sticky rice from a bamboo cane in an attempt to placate a nasty hangover, and they laughed together in dishevelled spirits.

On her way to teach the children in the afternoon, seeing Faa, she stopped by the fitness centre. Faa was making arrangements for the following night.

"What's happening?" nosed Hannah, bored with her own, uneventful existence.

"Oh, it's a friend's birthday."

"Are you going out?"

"Yes!"

"Can I come?"

"OK," said Faa, not looking too pleased. Sod it, Hannah was B.O.R.E.D, and inviting herself along was desperate, but necessary. On the way to catch a lift with Yim to Klong Kung, a poster stared her in the face: 'Big Fight! Sunday 25 March, with the special headline: Lady fight!' There she was – Susan - the 'lady' with the horse-like face, who'd been training with Kit at the gym and cavorting with Tee. It put Hannah's nose out of joint for no good reason – pure green jealousy, Hannah no longer feeling part of the Muay Thai community.

She rode with Yim to Salee Mart 2, where the cheeky kiddies coughed and spluttered obediently on the floor; overturned plastic baskets for desks, chanting the alphabet then singing 'Heads, shoulders, knees and toes'.

Hannah dilly-dallied on the way home. With fresh banknotes from the ATM in her pocket, she splashed out on a bottle of 399-baht Peter Vella red and tucked into some well-earnt porky buns. But she didn't dally for long, as two Thai girls drew up, stopping for her on their bike. Riding three aloft Faa, Pla and Hannah whooped and laughed: Hannah's arse hanging off the back, Faa driving and Pla in the middle with her tiny, languid frame.

"It's your birthday tomorrow, isn't it?" Hannah asked Pla.

Faa replied from the front, "She can't speak English!"

Maybe that explained her shy quietness.

"Can you translate for us?" Hannah requested.

So Faa explained to Pla that Hannah knew it was her birthday, and Pla became a little excited, "You come!" she managed.

So now, with an official invite under her harem-pant belt, Hannah alighted, running back to her apartment full of mischief at the prospect of escaping her lonely room for some much-needed, hedonistic relief.

46. Almost Nothing

She had nothing to do the next day except wait until sundown to cause some mischief. At 11am she received a call from the shop – Jeab had stayed in the stock room last night because Yim had needed to take their son back to Nakhon Si Thammarat for the new school term. Just like Hannah, Jeab couldn't drive, so when the Mart turned out its modest bulbs at midnight, Jeab had tucked herself in between the coke cans and made herself a nest. She announced that they were to eat lunch together, and that Hannah was to choose the restaurant and order whatever she liked. Hannah got clean, and wandered up the road past the Muslim family, to Kanchana's Kitchen, to order their lunch.

At Salee Mart when the delivery arrived half an hour later, Jeab paid and they sat down to munch; Jeab tasting each dish with a downturned mouth and tilting her head from side-to-side in mediocre approval, "It's okay – not as good as Mr Green's!" That's what Jen always said, *despite* the time the old man had served them up rancid chicken legs that had seen the dark side of the toilet bowl shortly after. Hannah and Jeab ate, chatting about books. Jeab loved to read, but there was a lack of good fiction in Thailand – writing was usually reserved for formal situations and quite separate to spoken language, so it didn't translate well into tantalising tales. Hannah thought back to the love columnist she had met in the travel agency when writing her own love letter in Thai – *he* had a passion for writing but had given up due to the smoking and drinking that came with it – something Hannah could relate to right now.

She served a few customers, thanked Jeab, and left, wandering around the little village for a while saying hellos here and there. Back at home, in the absence of anything useful to do, she napped.

Six o'clock came, with the call to prayer and darkness falling - just the right time to finish the bottle of Peter Vella sitting on her dresser. She was slightly merry as she made-up her face, listening to sixties Motown with the odd dance move thrown in.

She popped across to the coffee shop and had another wine, which had been 'found' under the counter, and was most likely antique. Aeisha, the sweet little Muslim girl, came in from next door, demanding to play 'cake' on Hannah's laptop, which she was taking to the shop to leave with Jeab. A dodgy Thai crew had moved in opposite her, banging on doors at all hours and fiddling with their phones all night whilst peering through Hannah's keyhole, and she couldn't afford to lose all of her writing to petty thieves.

Back down the pitch-black track she tramped: Faa and Pla would collect her from the shop at midnight to party. Hannah invested in another bottle of Similan and was relieved that Jeab never passed judgement on her drinking. Jeab herself rarely drank; working so hard and being a traditional Buddhist from the jungle - who hadn't even had cow's milk growing up, let alone wine or Campari spritz. Just occasionally, at New Year's, she would have a drink: *Sometimes I drink the cocktail! I LIKE THE BLUE ONE!!*

Tonight, streams of young people sloped around the modest aisles, and Hannah silently lamented the days when she used to pop by for some booze to take back to *Clayzy house* to get her ankles bitten by sandflies. She allowed herself to seep into the alcoholic haze, relax, and flirt with two buff Canadian guys who were sitting outside on Jeab's stone table drinking Chang. Jeab laughed as Hannah peered out of the window at them. It was nearing midnight, and as Hannah fidgeted in anticipation of her hosts' arrival, an unexpected visitor burst through the entrance, shocked and dishevelled, "You need to help me! I don't know what to do, I'm scared," she started. Hannah and Jeab nodded at her to continue, "I'm staying over there," she pointed to the dark bungalows behind the shop, "And there was a man on my balcony! I made a loud noise to make him go away, but he's still out there. He's...he's peering through the window, and I don't know what to do!!"

The woman was shaken. She bought a beer, took a huge glug, and started to relax now she had found sanctuary. Jeab took the reins, and together they formed a plan.

Hannah, wobbly from the whisky, marched out to the Canadian hunks, "Boys, would you mind helping this lady out?"

"Sure!" they said, puffing out their pecs.

"Can you go to her bungalow with her –it's just over there - and check she's safe?"

"Yuh! Uh-huh! Sure!"

The boys left with the lady, and Jeab started to turn out the lights. Hannah drained her glass and looked outside, to see the birthday girl and her glamorous friend pulling up outside - right on time! Jeab glanced up momentarily, letting out a huge gasp – you had to see Faa's beauty to believe it. Hannah hopped on the back of their motorbike and the delighted trio made off into the night: to Chalerm Rock Pub they would go!

They parked up amidst a gaggle of badly organised, drunk-driven vehicles, and entered the club with swagger - only to find it far too bright, and empty too. They found a table, ordered a bottle of whisky with mixers, and began to drink affectedly – three people didn't feel like much of a party.

Hannah ran out of things to say in Thai while Pla looked around nervously for more friends. As they speedily hit their fourth glasses, the lights dimmed and the hip-hop beats began, as people from other tables started to join them randomly. Cake time! Mouthfuls of oversweet fluff were joyously spooned into Hannah's gob, despite her slightly horrified protests. 'Happy Birthday' was sung out-of-key with aplomb and inaccuracy. Hannah spotted a table full of boys – she was in that kind of sugary mood – and she hopped over to them, "Hi!"

A man with good English and a pleasing face replied, "Remember me?"

She kind of did, but he looked young and she had no idea where she knew him from. He informed her that they had met at the gin bar around Christmas – all those moons ago when she was fancy-free. She had declined his 21-year-old advances back then, but had chatted to him all night, propped up on a stool at the bar. It was coming back to her now: he was an orphaned boy from Nepal who sold clothes in the market by the port. Right now, he was very drunk *and* very good-looking, and he wanted to take Hannah home.

She returned to the party table – her clan, her tribe - where the girls jibed Hannah suggestively, telling her that he was the best-looking guy on the island and that she should go for it. In all honesty, Hannah wasn't bothered about him, and she was no stranger to the

'girls go to bar, girls have miniature identity and confidence crises, girls get rip-roaringly drunk, girls go home with random boys' formula.

An influx of ladyboys dragged everyone onto the dancefloor and the party took off –Hannah feeling slightly out-of-her-depth in this rip-roaring sea of effervescent hormones. Suddenly Pla and Faa left without announcement, and Hannah was alone. 'Baz', the 21-year-old, re-approached her, saying he'd take his brothers home then come back for her. She was drunk and giddy and felt almost *sad*, but the young boy was so keen, and ten minutes later he strolled back into the club where she had first kissed Kit - bare-footed and more innocent than now – and obediently she followed him outside. They rode to Hannah's in the night - the feeling of riding up behind a strong boy was comforting. When they reached her apartment, they did not leap up the stairs but climbed them in angular silence. They sat on the balcony, and it became apparent just how drunk he was. Suddenly he rushed to the bathroom – was he being sick? Eventually he emerged, gasping for water. He drained the dregs from her gargantuan water carrier, then demanded more, but Hannah had none and it was way too late to wake the family downstairs in her brazen state. She couldn't have been more numb or resigned when it was time to do the deed.

"You take a shower!" he instructed.

"Nah…" she slurred.

"But you've been dancing!"

Was he referring to her nether regions?! Whatever; she couldn't cope with all that water spraying over her, so instead she dragged him over to the bed and they started kissing, in a far more sensual style than she had become accustomed to - the stinging Thai lips which she so craved.

Then started a hopeless fumbling – he may have perfected the movie star kiss, but his other bedroom skills showed an extreme lack of experience. Hannah reached for a condom, and Baz moved over to the side of the bed, then entered her. It seemed nothing remarkable to Hannah, but he seemed to be reaping great joy from the occasion, gasping and yelping before climaxing in explosive release. Afterwards, he showered while she lay near-motionless on the bed, her mind blank.

He returned, "Are you going to take a shower?" he asked again. She rolled to face the wall and grunted - she couldn't wait for him to leave.

As he caressed her limp and unwanton body, he begged her, "Please, show me just one thing! I really don't have any experience – except for movies…" She grunted again then attempted to fall asleep as he continued to grope her breasts unconvincingly.

"I don't really like people touching them," she muttered under her breath as she started to pass out.

"I know," he said, "You have almost nothing! But it's okay – you have this!" he exalted, grabbing an ample handful of her rump.

'Almost nothing...I'll give you almost fucking nothing!' Her mind scorned in complete contempt.

When daylight finally came, he was still there, as the call to prayer bleated out its familiar cry.

"What time is it?" he panicked.

"Er…9:30."

"I have to go to work!"

He rushed out of the door, and as soon as she shut it, she prayed that he would never dare try to enter again. A few fluffy pubes marked his existence. She wiped them away. Now, all she had was a feeling of repulsion and a broken-ness; for in the throes and wails of their drunken copulation she could only think of one man – and it wasn't a market trader from Nepal.

Hungover and wretched, she escaped from her room and out into the street. She rummaged in her tattered bag and, finding 200 baht remaining, stopped at the nearest place to try to quench her terrible ache. The woman at the bamboo booths made her sausage and eggs, then she vaguely continued onwards with an absence of purpose. As she passed the fitness centre, she saw Faa and Pla behind the counter, larking about hungover. She threw open the glass door and strode up to them with swagger and nonchalance.

"Aroi mai?!" Faa asked cheekily – *was he delicious?*

"Hm, okay – normal!!" Hannah responded unabashedly.

301

"Good kisser?" Faa continued, as if butter wouldn't melt – two could play at that game.

"He was okay!" she replied.

The familiar silhouette of Don loomed in the background, his eyes glaring and calculating: So…the young farang had fallen last night at Chalerm Rock Pub, eh? Who might this get back to? Hannah didn't care.

"Do you want to be his girlfriend?" Faa asked, sweet and sly.

"Oh no!" said Hannah, "It's the first since-"

"I know," said Faa. She knew.

47. Lady Fight

Time rumbled on like a faulty exhaust. Her menses came, thank goodness: even though they'd used a condom, life could be cruel. Her periods were coming every 24 days, perhaps urged on by her overactive ovaries: *Spring forth an egg! Impregnate me!*

She had run out of cash again, so she hauled herself over to Klong Kung and the nearest ATM. She took out some cash, then treated herself to a delicious sandwich at Dieter's Deli, with sauerkraut, swiss cheese and pastrami. The strange little place was run by a frantic, terse woman who kept zipping about checking everything, but not actually doing anything. Hannah went in to order another bucket of coffee from a Thai member of staff, who was sat plumply on a high stool, picking her ears with a small metal scraper.

"You mustn't do that!" the strange woman reprimanded the Thai server, "It's not polite!"

In a saving of grace, they played Neil Young over the speakers, drowning out various Germans discussing the size of plasma screens, '*Because I'm still in love with you…*'

Hannah finished up, slid off her uncomfortable, upright chair, paid and waddled off. Seeing as she'd come all this way, she headed further towards the port, and found an opening leading to a small field, where a temporary market had been set up by the locals. Her clothes were all but threadbare, and with vigour she dived in. The stallholders sat messaging on their phones, or eating soup from polystyrene bowls, whilst their offspring charged about in spiderman pyjamas. Hannah was quite happy being left at will, trying on hippy pants under her skirt. She bought a pair of harem pants, blue with an apple print, then found another pair in grey on her way out – only 200 baht each! The day was looking up.

As she sauntered home with new purchases under her belt, she saw a face she knew and loved: Uncle Lung-Lung!

"Han!" he called out to her, beckoning her over, "Have something for you!" He produced a small piece of paper: *'William's Stadium, Lady Fight! Admits 2!'*

"You come with me?" he proposed. It seemed there was no escape from the inevitability of ending up at the fight night on Sunday, when horse-faced Susan would meet her match.

"Yes, I'd love to!" she answered – for although she had been avoiding drama like the plague, *of course* she would go anywhere with her dear, chicken-grilling Uncle.

* * *

Hannah met him outside the stadium, near the four-by-fours and motorbikes, and, linking arms, in they went together. Jen was there with Mel and her daft friend from back home. Lung-Lung found a space at the bar and started chatting to his gambling buddies, softly ushering Hannah to go off and hang with her friends.

Jen sat next to Hannah as they watched the fights, "I'm not being rude but I'm here with the girls, so if you don't wanna sit with them I'd better-"

Hannah nodded, transfixed on a small figure on the other side of the stadium.

304

"Are you okay about him?" asked Jen.

Hannah nodded, letting out a snort of air, "Fine," she turned and stared into Jen's eyes, "But I love him." Jen laughed at her typical nonsensical behaviour, then shifted over to the other side of the ring to sit with Mel and her friend, Hannah staying where she was.

The fights were unremarkable – high season was over, and the stadium half-full; soon it wouldn't be worth holding fight nights anymore. The traders would go back to their hometowns and wait for the rains to pass before coming back for the next high season on Koh Talay.

Right now it was Susan's turn to enter the ring, in the highly-anticipated lady-fight. Hannah didn't understand her appeal – she seemed braindead and gormless, yet had managed to tantalise Tee into the bedroom. Perhaps Hannah was an alpha-female who didn't like other bitches on her turf – or perhaps she was jealous that she hadn't made it into the ring herself, and was unlikely to now.

Susan's opponent was a short, out-of-shape girl from the mainland, who was probably paying off debts, or needed money to feed her kids. It didn't look a fair match. Susan held a few extra pounds around the waist, but she also had good power – and won the fight easily, even if unremarkable to watch. Victorious, she limped out of the ring, breathing heavily and sweating profusely. Hannah spotted Kit sitting at a table in the background and had the uncontrollable urge to talk to him, so she walked over, bumping straight into Susan on her way.

"Well done!! How do you feel?"

Susan, looking deranged, stood in front of Hannah seemingly dumbfounded, her hands on her hips, still panting and sweating. She didn't look directly at Hannah, keeping her head down and replying in thick monotone, "I'm just so pleased that I did it!"

Hannah continued to the table at the back. As she approached Kit he flinched – certainly no invitation to take a pew. She took one anyway.

"OK?" she asked, straight-lipped. He nodded, giggling a little in unease. Everyone on the table disbanded and they were left alone.

"Mee eek kon?" enquired Hannah, pre-rehearsed – *Do you have another girl?* More uneasy giggling from Kit, who would strictly never lose face - especially at work.

"Krai?" asked Hannah – *who*? Kit shrugged and looked down, she wasn't getting anything:

"KRAIIII?" she demanded. He started to mumble, as fury overtook her and adrenalin unexpectedly pumped into her legs, making her stand up and eject herself from the table, striding off in the direction of the door angrily. Security watched as she approached, reared up like a Queen Cobra, raising her hands to the sides of her head and shaking them in 'jazz-hands' before escorting herself off into the night. She was drunk and livid, but she needed something else. She walked into Reggae Reggae Bar, dark as usual, languid Rastas lolling about.

"You got whisky?" she asked. They shook their heads, stupendously stoned.

"Closing," said one.

"I want whisky!" she shrieked melodramatically – partly to entertain and partly to excuse her overt behaviour.

"Mee banha!" she said – *this girl's got trouble.*

She had a think: there wasn't another bar between here and home, but there *was* the shop across the street, that was open until midnight. She walked in and pointed at her usual bottle of Similan, the woman laughing at her as Hannah handed over the money.

"Mee banha!" said Hannah again. She needed to release her almost comical anger, and still she smiled, as always: this time with fire, delirium and whisky. She trampled past the whores, who sat around in rude nonchalance, and reached her room. Staggering around sloppily, she played Northern Soul classics and attempted to dance, swinging around the room as she poured whisky with aplomb down her neck.

Just as Hannah felt that she was the most alive she had ever been, and that nothing could stop her, an ominous warm feeling started to rise from her guts up into her throat, and the party for one disbanded as she raced to the bathroom - just in time to hurl the contents of the evening down her gurgling crapper.

Feeling purged, she sat at her desk, now less giddy, and brought her eyes into focus. She peered at her laptop to see what damage she'd done on social media: nothing too bad, mainly Northern Soul classics.

She switched everything off and collapsed. The party was over.

48. Invitations

The severe after-effects of last night hit Hannah instantly as she prised open her eyes, trudged to the toilet in her swamp pants, then collapsed on the bed to strum Dr. Flameheart. Before she had managed to shower, there came a knock at the door with a voice following immediately after – Jen's unmistakable southern drawl. She invited herself in, "I'm going to Burma tomorrow, so today we're swimming with elephants!" she announced.

"Burma?!"

"Wanna come?"

"You know I can't."

"But - swimming with elephants?"

"*You* are!" asserted Hannah, "Let me have a shower - I'll be quick." A day out would do her good, and she was leaving the island soon and didn't know when she'd see her good friend again.

Heading southwards into a storm over the old town, Jen pointed out a small brick structure surrounded by jungle, "That's the traditional school," she explained, "They offered me a job but were going to pay me 3000 baht a month without even school dinners!"

Hannah continued to enjoy the hard-hitting wind in her face, her hair whipping the back of her neck reminding her she was free.

"3000 baht!" Jen guffawed again, "Do you know how little that is?!"

They turned onto a dirt track where Hannah had never ventured before, and around the bend arose a grandiose, wooden ranch surrounded by brush.

"We're here."

They stepped off the bike and approached the lodge, whence upon a man greeted them cordially as Jen squeaked on in Thai about the elephants. The man went to fetch the mahout, and a waitress appeared. Hannah grabbed her, "Coffee!!"

Jen stripped off into a tiny bikini as Hannah gawped at the two large elephants who were heaving towards her. Behind them the sea chopped and swirled, dark and low foreboding thunder clouds signalling a warning – was this such a good idea? Hannah looked up at the slate-black sky.

"Are you ready to record me?" babbled Jen excitably.

With unease on her face, Hannah tripped onto the sand behind her, spilling her nescafé and stumbling over shingle. She kept away from the elephants who were trumping towards the ocean in front of her, still in their adolescence and not quite grown. With no medical insurance, and Thai 'hope for the best' safety protocols, she was taking no chances. Jen, on the other hand, was straight into the choppy sea, along with the mahout and the two pubescent elephants. The incredible creatures swam and frolicked in the waves, throwing Jen off their backs roughly as they did so. Hannah captured every ridiculous moment on Jen's phone, laughing nervously as the epic adventure turned ever more disastrous, the sky opening and a storm pouring down on Jen's elephantine adventure.

After drying off and one more coffee for the road, the girls set off for home - Hannah's arms wrapped around Jen, the dust track now deep mahogany from the rain. Before it was time for Jen to return to Mon's protective arms, they stopped at a fried chicken stall by the roadside where Hannah munched on fleshy delights - hungry from the rain. Now time for sweet goodbyes, Jen delivered Hannah before the sun had fully set.

That evening Jeab and Hannah stood side-by-side, staring into the dark dusty air of the mini-mart. A clang of a van crawling past alerted them, blaring out a pre-recorded message, 'ONE...NIGHT...ONLY!' shrieked the muffled megaphones strapped onto the four-by-four, 'KWAAAAAANG in concert!' On jangled their greatest hit on exuberant electric guitar, a tinny, reverberant rock-voice wailing over the top.

"You know Kwang?" asked Jeab excitedly.

"Yes – you showed me them on your computer!"

"They're coming to Koh Talay! Next Tuesday!"

"Yes - I heard!" joked Hannah.

"I book a table already! Six people - get one bottle of whisky free!" She shifted her hip, "My daughter, Salee! Yeeessssssss, back from university! And my friend from the ticket shop! Uhuh! Have my friend from there, and her husband. He young - he VERY, VERY young! Yim joining too! Want to come?"

She wanted to come.

49. Making Waves

Jen had fleed to Burma in the night, and the date of Hannah's departure started to creep towards her; there was no changing her flight, and her visa would run out soon along with her money. This was it, and every day with ascending poignancy she appreciated what she had come to know and cherished the moments she still had to experience – here on the Isle of Talay - before the countdown to departure, when she would fly back to a land that felt so foreign now.

Thai new year – the three-day Songkran water festival – was also speedily approaching.

The kids had a month off school, and the heat became unbearable, so families nationwide got together in their hometowns and prepared for the quieter time of the year ahead, when the rains would fall after the blasting, furnace-like heat of May, June, July. With time to spare now the tourists had thinned, Jeab had started crocheting, and all over the island locals grew lazy in their chairs, growing out their hair, or re-indulging in past vices that couldn't be sustained when working hard. You could feel it in the atmosphere, the weather, the mood, the waves.

Hannah tried to keep in shape following workout videos on her whirring laptop: 'Ashleigh's kickbutt workout', 'Build a better booty'! Her nose had morphed into a crater from too much MSG in the pot noodles, which lined-up on the top of her antiquated telly.

Jeab found this incredibly funny, "How is your nose?" she would chuckle.

This particular day, she had woken up with her period but was still determined to exercise, so she loaded up a particularly energetic dance workout. Outside, the winds were rising and the weather was unusually heavy – a good time to stay inside and sweat. In the middle of her routine the telephone rang – it was Mel – what did she want?

Hannah was compelled to pick up, "Have you heard the sirens?" she gasped on the other end of the phone.

"What sirens?"

"The sirens in the road! The tsunami warning!"

Hannah *had* heard a couple of off-key honks, but was used to obscure and random noises in the land of no-sense.

"Where ARE YOU?" she panted.

"At my 'ouse, doing exercise!" Hannah replied.

"We're up on the roof of the new condominium!" Mel announced dramatically, "Kit too – he's brought up a bowl of food for everyone! You could come here?"

How on earth would Hannah get there? With no solution and after a little more

superficial concern from Mel, Hannah hung up. She looked out of the window – there was just the road looking quiet - the sea was a good few hundred metres away and it didn't really look windy or anything. She turned on the TV and saw a mild warning; yet equally as important to her as death were pert buttocks and clean hair – she would not go out of this world flabby and rancid!

She finished her dance, washed her hair, then decided to make a vague effort to ward off her possible demise. She climbed the stairs to the top of the building and walked out onto the roof, where in all her time there she'd never been. Looking at the few ne'er-do-wellers sat idly, she reasoned that she would be better off in her room, even with its broken sliding doors.

Time passed, eventually people scantily started to reappear in the road, and Hannah was hungry and in need of tampons so she headed out. The island felt deserted, as if all the people had been washed away after all. Nowhere was open, save for the shop that sold the Similan: it was running on an emergency generator, and everything felt very much like an aftermath. The aisles teemed with local people needing a fix of this or a packet of that. The man from the tattoo shop stopped Hannah in the aisle – she knew his face well, but he had never spoken to her before.

"Where did you go?" he asked in Thai, as the shop-woman listened in with a caring smile.

"Nowhere!" she said, as the lights went out.

50. รัก

The false alarm had come like a mighty wind, blowing away the cobwebs from the past, creating a new sense of calm and direction. Hannah got up early to go for a fresh morning walk, stopping on the way at Uncle Lung-Lung's chicken shack.

"Where did you go - tsunami?!" he asked her politely in finest Lao.

"Nowhere!" she said with her baby-tongue, "Dancing in room!"

Down at the cheap choc-cereal shop she ran into Aeisha - Little A - from the Muslim eatery. The cheeky beanpole of a girl grinned at Hannah, still unwilling to even *try* to speak English. She and her older brother were choosing an ice-cream. Hannah bought one too – chocolate – then the three of them hazardously got on Daddy's pop-pop bike and zoomed up to the road shrieking. Muslim Daddy came out to greet them, and Hannah announced that she would be flying home just after Songkran.

Crossing back over the road to hers, Hannah glanced over at Tiger Tattoo – Tee had long left the island, but perhaps there was still a chance... She spotted the tattooist crouched down beside his shack, fixing something. Gingerly she crossed back over the road and enquired if he was working today, and if so, might he have time for a small tattoo? He said that he was – later – and that was as specific as it got. Back in her room, Hannah had a word with herself - did she really want a tattoo saying 'rak'? *Love?* What did it really mean?

It meant that love had flowed through her for these past few months, and she had felt something different than ever before – Thailand had breathed into her, and no-one could take away her secrets nor the lightness of joy in her heart as she wandered its paths.

Losing love was as meaningful as finding it – both awakenings. She looked out of her window to see if the tattoo shack's lights were on - they weren't - and she knew the only way forward was to go there. When she reached the door still she saw only darkness, but she could hear faint rustlings from the back, and could make out a leather chair, on it a man silently waiting. For her?

She walked in silently, the man smiled, telling her that his name was Tiger, and asked her what she wanted.

She pointed to the inside of her left wrist, "Rak! Just here!"

First, he sketched out the word in calligraphic Thai script, but she wanted it plain and simple – printed - like a boy at school had doodled it for all the world to see. He went back to his sketchpad, holding it up for approval: รัก.

She nodded and reclined on the chair and, just before the needle went in, unmistakable salt-water tracks seeped from her lower lids, telling a tale. Memories of other times she had been marked by a needle returned to her in ritualistic trance. These new marks, cleansing and purging her now, would too one day become old:

Mark me, etch my skin so that I can't forget - for I don't ever want to forget here: this time, these changes, these feelings, mark them forever on me.

When I write, or raise my glass, there shall remain three simple characters: r-a-k: รัก.

Tiger worked swiftly and with ease, and it only snagged and scratched enough to just feel.

When it was done, she went back home, with not much to be done now that the bulk of her book had been set. She went for dinner, as she was accustomed, at Kanchana's Kitchen, and after to the Similan shop for supplies. Walking back home, she passed the whorehouse, tonight only one or two shady customers sitting out front, but with an unusual jovial feel in the air - a birthday!

Usually the girls' tired smiles for Hannah seemed empty and forced, but now that the island had quietened, it was clear that she was a long-termer. The working girls wore party dresses, brandishing buckets of KFC that had been hauled all the way back from Krabi Town and nuked back on arrival: capitalism at its best. They yelled at Hannah to come over and join them, and with no choice she sat down, smiling politely and accepting a glass of Coke and some fluffy cake. She appointed herself party photographer, and as she snapped away her slightly tender wrist advertised that which any of them would ever need for a good night: a little love.

51.Salty Eggs

Tonight was the night – Kwang rock band were coming to Chalerm Rock Pub! Though woozy from the painfully humid weather - big, bruisy clouds swept in late afternoon from the mainland, crashing into Hannah's woozy head – tonight was the Kwang concert, and Hannah was going at all costs.

At six, she left for the shop where she would meet Jeab and they would subsequently make their way to the concert. Over the road at the Muslim eatery Little A was sitting in her pyjamas with a plump prostitute that Hannah recognised from last night. Little A saw Hannah and grinned, before smirking cheekily and continuing her drawing. The prostitute also smiled – more of a wince - and beckoned for Hannah to come over.

"*I think you miss your friend*!" she said, in a patronising tone.

"Friend? Which friend?" clipped Hannah brightly. The prostitute sipped her tea and motioned for Hannah to sit with her. Hannah budged Little A up on the wooden bench.

"Do you come from around here?" Hannah enquired politely.

"No, I come from the North, but my family live in Songkhla, do you know it?"

Hannah nodded: Songkhla – the dangerous province in the far South of Thailand known for ongoing conflicts and regular bombings.

"I come here to make money, but sometimes customer not kind to me!" she looked almost tearful, "I come here, chat with her," she said, pointing at

Little A who wrinkled up her nose. "She good to talk to. Drink tea with me! I buy for you!" She passed Hannah a cup of weak dishwater, which she politely accepted before guzzling down and departing. Jeab was sitting quietly pricing things up in her sweet, curly handwriting, and she smiled warmly and chuckled to herself as Hannah came in.

"Sooooo Hannah! Ready for Kwang?" she asked brightly.

"Yes!" replied Hannah. Jeab chuckled again, then they sat together, Hannah drinking a little but Jeab declining. This evening the mart was mellow: sleepy travellers strolling in and wandering around, before buying beer and giant bags of chips, each chatting to Jeab as new relationships unfolded before Hannah's eyes. Hannah was on her way out - out, but not over yet – the rock concert was waiting.

Yim turned up around 11.30pm and together they set about closing the shop. With the postcards inside, the ice-cream sign behind the counter and the last few pieces of stock on the shelves, the lights were off and with a last glance around, the door locked.

Hannah rode in the sidecar along with three gargantuan bin bags. Yim was up front and Jeab behind him, and as they pulled onto a random piece of turf, Hannah slung out the bin-bags with vigour – Jeab laughing at her enthusiasm.

Of course, they weren't going *straight* to the concert - no - first to the family home at the back of Salee Mart 2, where Jeab's sexy, hopeless daughter awaited in her latest jeans. The large lady from the ticket shop scuttled in, her young, feral husband behind her.

"You - go with him!" ordered Jeab.

So, Hannah rode up back the feral young thing, Jeab with the large lady, and Salee with Yim. Though only a few hundred metres away, Thai people always chose wheels over feet - there were dogs in the dark. After whizzing up to the club and parking willy-nilly, Jeab and the others marched in, but Hannah, being foreign, had to show her ticket to the doorman, then rush in and search for her crew.

Chalerm Rock Pub was busy, but the music hadn't yet started. Hannah couldn't see Jeab, nor anyone she knew for that matter, in the swarm of brown faces, but Jeab shortly appeared, collaring her and leading her to their table - right in front of the stage. Set on each table was a large bottle of whisky and mixers, which Hannah and the feral husband tucked into, whilst Yim took a beer and Salee sat giggling while Jeab disappeared for a long absence, eventually returning brandishing a bright blue cocktail. They sat drinking, and before too long the speakers boomed out, '*THE GREATEST ROCK BAND IN THE WORLD! HERE...KOH TALAY, FOR ONE NIGHT ONLY!*

PLEASE...WELCOME........KWAAANGGG!!'

Out they strutted in bandanas, their long, rock-hair flowing behind them, waving, grinning and cheering as they took their positions and struck up the first almighty power chords: the crowd went wild! Jeab and Hannah stood up to wave their hands in the air along with the throng, Jeab singing every word with glee and Hannah attempting to join in. The other members of the table, in contrast, were considerably less animated – in fact, Hannah had never seen such a

323

show of cold stoicism. Suddenly and without warning, the feral husband, who had been sitting not moving a whisker, cut loose; standing up and entering full throttle into Kwang elation!

There was still something missing for Hannah: this aging rock-band weren't *really* her cup of tea, though she could have been persuaded if a certain someone had come along. Her eyes darted around the room in search for him, and Jeab caught her - nodding all-knowingly, then laughing rather loudly at her friend's display of sentimental pathos.

The concert rocked on, and the group began to tire by the end, as was the way with extended sets, endless encores and relentless reprise, so just before the mad rush they nodded in agreement and made their way outside to the chaotic entanglement of aluminium and steel.

Hannah had certainly had her fill of whisky, and had snacked earlier in anticipation of it, so she was now full, drunk and ready to drop.

"Now, to Mr Green!" commanded Jeab.

With no room for argument, for a very late-night meal they went. Under the bare bulbs of the cowshed eatery, the motley crew crowded around a plastic table. The restaurant was buzzing after the concert - one of the few places still open in the early hours in this slow and sleepy month of April.

Jeab ordered - a woman who knew what she wanted - checking ingredients and cooking methods before approving what seemed an endless list with a frown. Hannah relaxed as well as she could under the glaring lights of the shack, as they feasted heartily on fiery-hot squid and sliced beef salad and slurped on soup with salty eggs. Salee sat picking at tiny bits to taste, while Jeab ate with deliberation; ordering more of the teeny, curious bowls of watery rice with which they mopped up the various sundries until all were contented and full.

As they munched, Jeab chattered excitedly about her plans for Songkran: everyone was to go to her little house behind Salee Mart 2 and help prepare for the day ahead. They would have to start early, because there would be a lot of cooking to do: green curry, kanom jeen, fried chicken and salad. When Jeab became impassioned, she drew her hands together with fervour, inviting Hannah along as one of the family. She would make an early morning start to Klong Kung to avoid the scorching sun before the water guns appeared. They'd eat together with enough for anybody who passed by to join: friend or stranger. Songkran was a three-day festival, with water fights only on the first day, the following two a more traditional holiday and a chance to relax after high season. Hannah's flight was booked for the day after.

"When do you leave?" asked Jeab.

"I   think   the   17th."
Jeab sat thinking for a moment.

"You know my son?" she said, "He go back to school next week! Have to go past airport! We can take you: ten of us - we can take the big truck!"

Voracious nods abounded as the group continued to chomp and chew, then without warning Jeab whipped out her giant purse, Salee efficiently counted out the notes, chairs were pulled out with a screech and people were directed as to whom should ride with whom.

Hannah's room was only a few hundred metres away, but of course she would be escorted home on wheels. The feral husband was again allocated to ride her home, and she enjoyed the experience – not having had so many late-night rides of late. With a courteous goodnight, she ran upstairs solo to her resting place, a full belly from a magical night, but another day closer to departure. Before bed she checked her computer: a certain someone had been bombarding her on messenger, '*Hi babe! It's my birthday on Monday! Yeah, that's right! The end of Songkran! We're going for a meal – can you come? Please?*'

Of course, the thought of Mel - never mind her troupe of farangs - made her shudder, but that was the night before she left, what did she have to lose? Not a big fan of goodbyes, it could act as an unofficial leaving party, she just wouldn't tell anybody, '*OK*,' she wrote back, '*Tell me where and when, and I'll be there.*'

52. Songkran

Sunlight rudely invaded Hannah's room and, though unaccustomed to early mornings, she rose. What should one wear on such a day? She started with a swimsuit to cover her modesty, then covered up with an old tee-shirt and shorts that she didn't mind being soiled. To be watertight she wrapped up a few notes and coins in a plastic bag and stuffed them in her pocket. That would do!

Cautiously, she started on her journey to Salee Mart 2. With a tense expectation of mayhem and water-shootings, instead she found only tranquillity and empty roads with not a soul to be seen. The sun had not yet unfurled its full fire, and she trotted contentedly past family resorts and the small row of karaoke houses; 7-11 glimmering in the far distance, and Salee Mart 2 a little way ahead.

Jeab was in the kitchen helping Grandma prepare the feast.

"Can she eat spicy?" Grandma enquired.

"Yes, she can!" chuckled Jeab.

With nods of approval all round, Hannah went outside the front the shop to hang with the kids and teenagers. Songkran was not just a party but a family time, and not unlike a Christmas morning, Hannah sat idly drinking powdered coffee and waiting for the festivities to begin. Just before midday, steaming pots of green curry and noodles appeared as Songkran sprang into action. Thai folk in oversized, sodden t-shirts stood on the back of four-by-fours bopping away to pop hits and slinging buckets of water over anyone in their paths, grinning from ear-to-ear.

When suitably soaked, Jeab and the gang returned to the shop-front to help themselves to ladles of delicious food from Grandma's kitchen. Revellers from the streets were invited too, to taste Granny's delights! Hannah's mind wandered around the corner – what was going on at her end of the beach, at the stadium, at Kanchana's Kitchen and Uncle Lung-Lung's, Little A's and the coffee shop?

After filling up on fried chicken, curry and spicy salad, Jeab and Hannah stood in the road for Jeab's favourite part of the festival. Holding a pot, Hannah and Jeab dipped their fingers into a mix of talcum powder and water, and gently dusted the cheeks and arms of passers-by for good luck. Faces smiled into faces; the celebrations continued.

It was time for Hannah to venture, so she announced her departure and with a pat on the bottom, Jeab nodded her off. With more smiles and waves Hannah exited, now walking through constant showers of water-spray delight. It wouldn't be long until she'd turn the corner, heading blindly through mayhem on her way back home.

First up was Don's stadium, everyone well-lubricated and partying. Hannah herself hadn't had a single sip to drink. Her favourite woman of all time, the glamorous and insatiable Faa, stood handing out free drinks. She handed Hannah a generous cup spilling over with beer and ice, and together they partied in the road, gyrating with buxom females Hannah had never met before. If only Kit was there to see her in all her glory – where was he? Little Smiler came at her with a bucket of whisky and a straw, and she took a gulp before issuing a tongue-in-cheek scolding.

Hannah was stood in the road, still jostling and gyrating, when Faa and Pla promptly jumped in their Songkran-wagon and hooned off to round up more troops – leaving her with no posse. And of course, it was now - from the distance and to imaginary fanfares - that Kit appeared on a borrowed bicycle in his Saturday best with a beam to match; the man of the moment! The horse-faced Susan and some other students from the gym were stood in the background lamely bopping to the DJ, and, though Kit noticed Hannah first, with a flinch he strode straight past her to greet Susan, robustly and warmly - who also flinched in awkwardness - then joined the young whippersnappers, who still giddily slurped from their whisky-buckets.

The booze started to settle in nicely, and she couldn't help but get closer to Kit. When she was within spitting distance, she tapped him on the buttocks with her foot.

"NOOOOOO!" he turned suddenly and fiercely, shaking his head.

"NOOOO!" then continued frolicking without her.

She was not welcome, and he was to be obeyed; but this time she wouldn't accept his rejection with resignation and stood her ground - wincing in the sunlight in her drenched clothes. Kit was behind her now, with Susan. He took a giant, fluorescent water pistol, filled it with water from the trough and shot at the partiers with vigour.

This could be Hannah's only chance to tell him of her leaving and so, simply and plainly, in the best

Thai she could muster from the depths of her disappointed soul, she spoke, "Kit," he edged away, "Kit!" more firmly this time, "I'm leaving."

That got his attention. "When?" came his sombre, motionless reply.

"Tuesday, early morning, after Mel's party."

He nodded - information received – and with no further reaction returned to sour-faced Susan and his water gun.

Hannah, relieved to have broken the news, departed immediately – into the huge crowd next door at Reggae Reggae Bar, which was spilling out into the road. Pale hippies in cotton trousers and old Thai Rastas alike attempted to reclaim their youth, bopping along to the deafening music. Hannah danced her way through but, finding no real friends there, continued on her jaunt.

Next door at the pool maintenance shop, voices called out for Hannah to join them. She didn't think they knew her but perhaps they had been silent observers, and now - whiskied up – they were singing karaoke in their cramped office on an old tinny microphone, a meagre buffet and empty glasses splattering the scene. Though she felt like a farang out of water, it *was* Songkran after all so she accepted a glass of whisky and soda and chewed on a stick of fishballs, grimacing mildly as the pool-people shrieked out of tune 80s pop hits on maximum reverb.

She moved onto find two magnificent trucks, full to the edges with dancing people. Hannah was offered hands which heaved her onto the gargantuan machine, forcing her to join in the dance. Thais young and old grooved on and the girls from the coffee shop grabbed her: stick-thin and bursting with happiness, they raved on all in white.

Yet Hannah's wet attire was now cold and clinging, so shivering but contented with her celebratory efforts, she scuttled off to her room, running into the shower to avoid the chills. As the storm clouds swept over the island in the late afternoon, she slumped down on her bed to snooze off the day. A different new year, four months on from the naïve fireworks of December, back when she hadn't known how far she would venture into the Thai heartland, now just three days to go before taking her leave: boarding the boat, watching Koh Talay disappear out of sight.

53. Truckin'

On the second day of Songkran the water festivities had subsided, just a few kids left, eking it out with their super soakers. Hannah took a wander down to the little backpackers' haven where her journey had begun: the minimart, Mama and Papa's, Noi, Nok and his remote-control cars, the Brothel Ma'am and the prostitutes. She ventured first to find Nok, but got there to find his row of bungalows empty, just his beautiful wife hanging out the washing between two huts in the sun. As she turned to collect more pegs, she saw Hannah.

"Hannah! I think you go already! Someone say you go!" she said – her English curiously better than that of early December. She flung her petite arms around Hannah with tears of joy in her almond eyes, and Hannah returned the embrace.

"Not yet - two more days!"

"No problem! Just happy to see you! I know you come back – Thailand is in your heart!"

Another familiar, impish face mischievously jumped out at them – her sister - the prostitute from Charlie Chang's who had jibed Hannah about 'liking chocolate'.

"Where you go? I not see you!" she squealed, "Where you go Songkran?"

"Just around here, everything in tung - plastic bags!" said Hannah, miming soggy possessions.

"Tung!" laughed the sister, "Ha haaaaaah! Everything in *tung yang*!!! Ha haaaaaaah!"

Hannah's face wrinkled up in confusion – what was she talking about?! The impish woman grinned, revealing her dimples, then opened her eyes wide as she mimed blowing up a balloon made out of a condom.

"Have to put everything in tung yang!"

Hannah smiled widely and gave the sisters warm hugs goodbye.

"See you next time!" they chirped in unison, as she waved and disappeared up the dirt track, glimpsing Mama and Papa in the distance, fussing about in the lobby of Grand Palace Hotel.

Sidewinding the pool of muddy brown water that had collected from both the rains and water fights of yesterday, she popped into the shop where Jeab was glowing brightly. She handed Hannah a slice of slightly stale Danish pastry, "What you think? I get from Krabi. Nice?"

Hannah chomped whilst wiggling her head from side-to-side in Indian fashion:

"*Quite* nice," she replied, not wanting to insult Jeab's taste. Jeab laughed – she could read Hannah like a book.

She changed tack, "Hey! Remember, I tell you about the family meal in the Old Town - once a year, every year? We go today - want to join?"

Hannah nodded enthusiastically.

"I work this morning, then my friend – the cleaner – she will look after the shop until evening."

Hannah would rendezvous with the gaggle of relatives back at the shop later, to truck it together to the south of the island. Swinging back through the village she waved gaily at all of the characters from her story.

Passing Noi's new organic farm, he called out to her, "Hannah!" he yelled, smiling, "Come and join us!"

In truth, he hadn't been her favourite person since the guitar incident way back when, but today he was in great spirits, and surely it was better to let bygones be just that. She walked past the vegetable plots to a grassy patch whereon a group of straggly gap yearers obediently looked at Noi for their every instruction. She settled on a wooden platform, next to an ancient lady who was preparing kebabs in the festering sun. After a failed attempt to exchange niceties, she turned to Noi, who was marauding his merry parade of unkempt backpackers in a game of pétanque. Laughing and smoking, he chastised their every fault – grinning and swaying as he slurred. Hannah sat with grandma and the flies on the wooden platform, watching from afar in good humour, granny still laboriously plunging chunks of rancid meat onto sticks.

Time was speeding, and she made a swift exit up to the road, past the Fitness Centre and Kanchana's Kitchen, to the ropey whorehouse.

"Han! Over here!" A prostitute - the one who knew Little A – called her over. She obliged.

"Donuts! You must take one!"

Krispy Kreme to boot, procured all the way from Krabi town. Hannah took one to be polite but protested as the prostitutes tried to push further dough on her, for there was a grand family banquet to attend and she needed to stay hungry.

At the bamboo shack, always half-open/half-shut, the kindly cook smiled at her. She was sitting with a

friend in a bamboo booth, and she too beckoned
Hannah over. Again, Hannah obliged, and sat
momentarily with the kindly lady and her friend as
they ate unripe mango dipped in chilli and salt. Time
really was moving on now, so she scurried off to
freshen up, receiving a stilted call from the shop
issuing an instruction to meet back at Salee Mart in
twenty minutes. So, with time only for a quick wipe
of her face, she grabbed a cotton scarf and legged it
back to the shop. Upon arrival she found Jeab's
slightly bereft son, sitting on a barrel with Tong the
oversexed dog, Grandma hobbling about in the
background, and Yim busy fetching things for the
pick-up.

"Hallo!" he smiled warmly, as bright as ever.
Jeab's daughter Salee poked her cheery little head out
of the store-room, giggling and covering up her train-
tracked teeth, before appearing in full colour and
jumping into the front with Yim.

"Do you want to sit inside too?" asked Jeab.
Hannah shook her head, and together they climbed
onto the open back, leaning against the cab of the car
and wrapping their heads in shawls, ready for the
dusty ride.

Up they bumped past Don's stadium and Hannah's
room, rocketing south past Muslim soup shops and
side shacks selling curry puffs. Zooming past the next
stretch of road before turning left sharply onto a
sloping track leading them through wild jungle, just a
smattering of small wooden houses and the scent of
gumtrees hitting them in exhilaration, scarves
whipping them in the face as they smiled and inhaled,
laughed and exhaled, bumping all the while. At the

end of the long woodland trail a sign: *To the Old Town*.

As they rode, Jeab shouted out stories of the ancient Isle of Talay through the wind, pointing out traditional wooden houses where ancient gypsies bathed in sarongs outside their front doors, staring back at them in untamed accusation.

Arriving at their final destination, they parked the wagon and clambered off, re-grouping and stretching, then meandered the short distance to the restaurant, which was built on wooden stilts over the water.

"We go to this one!" explained Jeab, "Used to go to over there but this one is cheaper - better food, good taste!"

They wound their way through tables of Thai families feasting and found their table. Hannah looked down between the wooden floorboards to see an aqua-green sea gently lapping beneath her. Jeab loosely organised people around the table - gently strict and officious. When they were all settled - the dog run off, Salee and her brother giggling constantly - out came the menus and the group started scrutinising the dishes. Hannah managed to make out one word in Thai – ปลา – *bpla* – 'fish', to great surprise and applause from her compatriots.

As usual, Jeab wore the trousers, and she ordered on behalf of the entire ensemble an impressive list of plates and delicacies, adding on special requests from the family. Now all there was to do was relax and wait for the food to appear, whilst dreamily admiring the view. The fodder arrived by the trayful, and whilst the Thais picked politely, Hannah couldn't help but get stuck into the spicy eggs and basil chicken, chilli

337

prawns and salt and pepper squid. The feasting continued, with chit-chatting, the yapping dog, and the beautiful surrounds. From time-to-time a furrowed expression crossed Jeab's brow.

She tasted the food and shook her head, "Good, but not same last year!!"

When they were well and truly full, Jeab unzipped the oversized pencil-case and Salee counted out the crisp notes accurately with her delicate hands.

"Yes!" declared Jeab in conclusion, and they dawdled off out into the afternoon sun.

Salee, though painfully shy and petrified of speaking English, stopped by a lamp post declaring, "Girl photo!"

She grinned, her blue train-tracks flashing in the light. Hannah stood next to her, awkwardly perspiring, and Salee directed a zillion snaps to show off her foreign friend to the girls back at Uni.

In groups of twos and threes the troupe wandered, idly glancing in closed shop windows at bric-a-brac and souvenirs, popping in the corner shop for water. The day was done and the sun had started to descend, so they climbed back onto the truck - this time Salee and her brother, Jeab and Hannah in the open air together. As Yim expertly wound around the twists and turns of Koh Talay, the folk in the back sighed and smiled, as the sky faded to black.

54. The Last Supper

Hannah rifled through her ancient moo-moos and monkey-bitten sarongs, to decide if they'd last another adventure, or were best off left by the wayside. From time-to-time she glanced nervously at Dr. Flameheart, her beloved guitar: should she chance him as a carry-on? Would he make it?

She popped downstairs to the odds-and-sods store to politely remind her begowned landladies that she would be leaving early the next morning, and that she'd leave her key tucked behind the front desk.

The woman from the beauty parlour came out to say hi, mock-begging in Thai, "You don't *have* to go! You don't *have* to go," her many cats quizzically eyeing Hannah before darting back to their mistress. Hannah returned to her room to continue to fold and pack her belongings. Evening was still a way off, and she cautiously took stock of her emotions; should she suddenly break down. Slate-grey clouds from the mainland loomed over the island, everything becoming momentarily mute, before a frenetic burst of thunder broke the silence and the rain poured down. Hannah rested, but was soon interrupted by a message, *'Hey babe, party still on, meet at Kanchana's Kitchen at 7.'*

It was already five, so she reached for her near-empty bottle of Similan, took a hit and screwed the cap back on. She went to the bathroom and lazily sloshed herself with water, changing into a comfortable yet provocative outfit – a frilly vest and Muslim pants from the market in Klong Kung. She felt strangely calm, save for the spitting rain and moody skies: she felt almost...*ready*. Silently she sat on the edge of her bed, ready to go, then out of nowhere a sudden wave unleashed: tears and sadness - a broken heart! How could she leave this place? How could she even go outside? She was able to hold her small heart together here in her room, but what would happen out there in the darkness when she was surrounded by false friends at a party that was, for her, a wake?

She turned to the internet and screamed out a cry for help on Facebook, and the messages that came back jolted her from the depths, *'Go on Han, you've made it this far!' 'All will be alright after a G and T!' 'Sad you're leaving, but great you're coming home'*.

She stood up, pulled her Muslim pants out of her crack, checked her shiny face for tracks of tears and grabbed her bag. She stared around the room for the last time ever after sunset, took a breath, then turned to face the door, stepping out and closing it behind her. She trotted down the stairs that were never swept - covered in storm-bugs - and exited through the silent swing doorway. Seeing nothing but bushes and darkness ahead she started up the road, then settled into a pace, feeling better; nearly everything had closed down already on this little island – perhaps it *was* time to go. She picked her way through the post-rain sludge to Kanchana's Kitchen and its bright lights – the only lights anywhere, save for a dim glow transmitting from the whorehouse. On her left came a rustling – someone was in the bushes, and it wasn't Aunty clearing down the chicken stall – no - it was Uncle Lung-Lung, alone in the dark with a bottle of whisky! If ever there were angels...

Tired, but with kindness, he insisted Hannah sit opposite him on his handcrafted bamboo stall, and with very little language, he poured a large measure of whisky over rocks of ice and added soda, then pushed it over the table to Hannah. He himself didn't take a drink – it was as if he knew she needed saving, and this was the only remedy he could offer.

Over sparse but heartfelt murmurings, Hannah drank until her eyes blurred and the bottle chinked with emptiness. In the fear that she wouldn't make it if she sat down any longer, Hannah stood up unsteadily, and with a 'See you next time', was off.

She could really feel the whisky now, and it wasn't even seven, as she stumbled up the path to Kanchana's Kitchen. It seemed to be speeding towards her, and with her defences down she marched in, the mise-en-scène bouncing in the naked lightbulbs around her, to find Mel and her dull cronies sat at a long table.

"Hannah! Where have you been?!" she squealed.

Not normally one to confess to inebriation, she explained, "Uncle Lung-Lung made me drink a bottle of whisky."

"We've ordered already, we're having burgers!"

The best Thai eatery on the island, and they were having burgers. Hannah ignored the vague birthday pleasantries and trotted up to the small, open kitchen where the chefs and Madame Kanchana worked in full view.

"Chicken, vegetable," she said in Thai: "Big plate, no rice, fried egg."

She returned sloppily to her seat, which was allocated on Mel's right hand, falling into her chair.

"Surprise!" Mel announced through the whisky haze, "Look who I found!!"

A wicked grin flashed across her ordinarily blank face. Hannah looked up to find Kit's beautiful face grinning at her opposite.

"Hello," he managed in his dry voice.

"I leave tomorrow!" Hannah replied.

"I know," he said, holding onto both of her hands comfortingly.

Though she ordered last, Hannah's food came first - loyalty and manners went a long way in this land - so Kit moved back to join Don and his cronies at the other end of the table. She picked her way through some of her plate then passed it to Mel. The burgers arrived in various states of inaccuracy, and as white-noise kerfuffle abounded, Hannah ventured to join Don's crew. Kit budged up on his plastic stool for her to share with him. His fixated gaze was too much for her to handle, and she couldn't help but turn away.

"Still beautiful," he said. Hannah was silent.

"You – still beautiful!" he repeated.

After a while, Hannah managed to piece together a sentence, "Why now?"

Kit looked confused.

"WHY NOW?!" she demanded fiercely. Don's portly body shook with scornful laughter as Kit's expression grew ever more bewildered.

"She said, 'why now?'" explained Don.

The group had finished eating and people were starting to make a move.

"Can you come to Reggae Reggae Bar with us?" asked Hannah, somehow the pleading in her heart making its way to her tongue.

342

"Not sure, have to train - 5am!"

"Just for a short time?"

"OK…one hour…OK?"

"Yes, me one hour too!" said Hannah, a bit too enthusiastically. She went to pay, as Mel pushed past her – plump with burger.

"You coming next door, yeah?"

"For a bit, yes."

Action in the restaurant revved up now the group had moved on; Madame Kanchana and her staff folding down tables and turning out the lights. In the dark outside, Hannah stood with Don and his crew.

Little Smiler jumped into the transit van, squeaking, "Come to gym! Come to gym!"

Hannah shook her head – she wasn't in the mood for a late-night juvenile disco. As Don fired up the engine, Hannah looked around her and, not recognising anyone, picked her way through the mud alone to Reggae Reggae Bar to finish the night. A live band churned out tourist reggae classics, the party from the restaurant scattered around, nodding along obediently.

Mel ushered Hannah over to the bar, "Hi babe - how *are* you?! How are you feeling about leaving?"

This casual chit-chat felt far from natural.

"Okay. I'd better go soon, I've got an early start. Do you know where Kit went?"

Hannah glanced around like a panicked meercat, scouring for her lost love. The truck was coming to collect her at six tomorrow morning. There was more silence as they drank.

"I haven't seen him…would you sleep with him again if he were here?" Mel asked.

"Yes," came Hannah's reply, too quickly, "Why wouldn't I - what do I have to lose?"

"I'll call him!" proffered Mel, her sudden, uncharacteristic eagerness to help a little unnerving – was she stirring?

Mel dialed his number and waited, "No answer," she said.

Hannah slipped away and, sweeping her eyes one final time around the bar, walked into the pitch black alone, hastily reaching the relative safety of her room. Observing her packed away things, her towel ready for a last shower in the morning and her rucksack waiting for the final fastening, exhausted, she laid to rest as best she could.

55. The Long and Winding Road

In the semi-darkness, before the alarm, she lay awake resting: a stringent headache announcing itself loudly. Wearily, she sat up to check the time. Using the bathroom and stuffing what seemed like never-ending last-minute things into her rucksack willy-nilly, she was still in time.

At ten to six she heaved her uneven, wobbly bag onto one shoulder and Dr. Flameheart onto the other, then frantically hobbled down the stairs in the already harsh heat of day. She push-kicked the front door into blinding daylight and hobbled a few more steps to the vacant bamboo stand, the shutters of the landladies three-quarters down in the pre-morning. She leant her heavy load against the sturdier beams then sat down, squinting in the light.

After a few moments alone, Grandma appeared. She walked quietly over to Hannah and together in silence they smiled in the golden light, the odd vehicle dawdling past.

Her mind starting to rouse, she popped into the store for yoghurt drink and stale wafers, then continued to squint as she munched. Granny sat demurely waiting on the platform - for what she knew not – a self-appointed guardian.

Soon, the sound of an overloaded wagon growled from behind them and Jeab and her rabble drew up to the side of the dusty road - *almost* on time. Jeab and Yim came round to the roadside to help Hannah load up, tying her bedraggled belongings onto the truck, tucking in a bag here and there, and covering everything in plastic should it be blown away on the hurtling ride to Krabi.

Hannah clambered in next to Jeab and Aunty on the back of the pickup, and Yim, Salee, the strange son, Grandma and Tong the unappealing dog, sat inside the cab. Hannah reached for her shawl, wrapping it over her head, mouth and nose to protect her from the dust and wind, and they set off. She looked out onto the open road reaching back to the shores of Koh Talay, strong twinges of emotion spiking her heart. Instead of tears, she searched for meaning, putting nostalgia back in its place. She rode, now gazing into the dusty track before her which stretched into the horizon in the crystalline morning light, speeding towards the new unknown:

'Cos I love you, and it's not a passing thing:
'I sleep in the road,' he said,
'You sleep in the sea.'

How did you lose your Thai smile?
Through floodgates of joy, tears also flow.

It's hard to leave. I can see us out there -
Stars like angels, night years apart:
'I sleep in the road,' he said,
'You sleep in the sea.'